LOVE ALWAYS BOOK THREE

Ciao Bella

BELINDA MARY

Cover Illustrations by Lorissa Padilla Designs

1st edition 2023

ISBN: 978-0-6456942-5-3

www.belindamary.com

For readers who need some colour back in their lives.

This one is for you.

CONTENTS

PROLOGUE

Bella

Florence, ITALY

I'M CRAMMED IN THE BACK seat of my brother Lucas's hired Mini Cooper as we zoom the forty minutes from our small village towards the city of Florence. Lucas has insisted I join him and his girlfriend Amy today, to act as a decoy in case Amy becomes suspicious of the true nature of our excursion, and also to play the role of photographer to capture their perfect proposal moment.

From my vantage point in the back of the car, I watch as my brother picks up Amy's hand and places a soft kiss on it. I sigh. I'm so happy for the two of them, and I love Amy, having become fast friends with her since their arrival from Melbourne four days ago, but I'm also bursting with envy.

Amy is twenty-five, the same age as me, and here she is travelling the world with the man she loves, about to get engaged in one of the most romantic cities in the world, while I spend my time sitting at home watching Netflix with my parents every night. Don't get me wrong, I love my parents and am happy to live near them and help them run their deli, especially since Papa got sick last year, but there's a part of me, a part that's getting bigger every day, that yearns for something more.

Since Lucas moved to Melbourne over two years ago, I've been fascinated with the place. I follow his sporadic posts on Instagram with an unhealthy obsession, which has only increased since he got together with Amy and her social media presence has doubled his. I obsess over their nights out in funky bars, at the theatre and live music, even at a game of something they call "footy," which looks nothing like our football because the players, bizarrely, can use their hands. Every time I get notified of one of their posts, I'm filled with a longing to get on a plane and see it all for myself, but I'm not even brave enough to broach the subject of me leaving with my parents, let alone actually fly all the way to the other side of the world to have my own adventures.

"Bella? We're here." Lucas's voice brings me back from my inner musings. "I'm just going to take Amy up to the lookout to show her the view. You can wander around and meet us back here, *bene?*" he says, slipping into Italian and giving me a meaningful look, making sure I understand the plan. The plan is for me to follow close behind them and hide in the bushes, ready to take a photo of Lucas down on one knee. *Let's hope she says yes,* I think with a smile.

"Bella?" Lucas repeats my name, sounding nervous.

"*Si,*" I reply quickly. "Yes. You go, I'll meet you later. Have fun, Amy." I hug her before they walk away.

I follow behind them at a careful distance and position myself in the perfect spot. And with my camera furiously clicking, I watch as my brother proposes to the love of his life. With tears of happiness running down my face, I watch as Amy says an emphatic "Yes!" and reflect on my role here today—that of the observer, the recorder—with a sense of melancholy. And finally, something snaps in me. I have to take control of my life. It's time I stop watching it go by from the sidelines. It's time for me to have adventures of my own. It's in this moment, standing in the city I have lived my entire life, that I decide I am going to Melbourne.

Three Months Later

The ground and all its buildings grow smaller, my homeland fading into the distance as I watch through tears. This is it; this is the moment I've been waiting and planning for since I made the big decision. It's taken a lot of soul searching, long conversations with my parents and saving every cent I have, and now I'm finally on the first of what will be a three-leg journey to get me from Florence, the only home I've ever known, to Melbourne, the place I feel I'm meant to be.

As the seatbelt sign turns off and the passengers around me all start settling into their seats, I keep an eye out of the small window next to me, unsure of when I'll be seeing this landscape again. If things go well, I hope to make a life in Australia with my brother Lucas there to support me. It's been a quiet dream of mine to spread my wings and learn to fly away from the small-town life I'd been living in *Valle delle Stelle*, a place that I love but feel stifled by in equal measure.

"Would you like something to drink?"

The QANTAS flight attendant is looking at me expectantly, her Australian accent already music to my ears. It's happening. I'm on my way!

"Just some juice, please," I say, testing out my English, excited that it's coming out as planned. In addition to everything else I'd had to do in preparation, learning to be fluent in another language has been on top of the list and I'm keen to try it out as often as possible.

When the view outside turns white and we are flying through the clouds, I pick up my well-worn copy of *Pride and Prejudice*, my ultimate comfort read, and prepare to get lost in the world of the inhabitants of Longbourn estate and their love interests. As Elizabeth Bennett meets the devastatingly handsome Mr. Darcy, I can't help the sigh that escapes me. It's so romantic. I wonder if I will ever experience a love like these two, one that can overcome all obstacles and will stand the test of time.

"First time to Melbourne?" the middle-aged lady next to me asks as our dinner is served. It's an ordinary-looking pasta dish, ketchup poured over some half-cooked penne. Very unappetising.

"*Si*, yes," I tell her, happy to practice my English again. "My brother lives there and I've always wanted to go."

She nods and smiles while we both attempt to eat the almost inedible food in front of us.

"I've lived there all my life. There's no better place in the world," she says with a look of pride on her face. It's one thing I've learnt from my time spent with Amy, my brother's fiancée and a proud Melbournian. They love their city with all their hearts.

"It seems like an amazing place to live." I can tell her this sincerely because for some reason I've been obsessed with the place for so long now. It's like it has some sort of magical pull on me.

"Are you planning on staying?" she asks, continuing the conversation and voicing the question that has played in my mind ever since I bought my one-way ticket.

I pause before answering.

"I'm not sure," I say eventually. "I'm not sure where I'm meant to be. But there's something in me that is telling me I need to have some adventures, to live my life to the fullest and I can't do that in my small village back home..."

She tilts her head and smiles for me to continue.

"I guess I'm just looking for a place to belong. A place to call home..."

And as I watch the map on the small screen on the back of the seat in front of me, the dotted line tracing my journey ahead, I wonder if that's what I'll find when I get to my destination.

Melbourne.

Home?

NOVEMBER

CHAPTER 1

Bella

Melbourne, AUSTRALIA

"**T**HERE'S NO TURNING BACK NOW."

This thought bounces around my mind as I stare out the window of the taxi. I feel equal parts exhilarated and terrified as I am driven away from the airport. The traffic in Melbourne is busier than I had expected, and while we are zooming along the freeway on the left side of the road (AKA, the wrong side), I'm delighted to see skyscrapers dotting the city skyline, interspersed with parks and ovals and patches of greenery. When we reach the city, the taxi driver dodges around trams and thousands of people on bicycles, and I hold my breath as he does some tricky right-hand turn. This manoeuvrer, he tells me, is a 'hook turn', and it's specifically a Melbourne thing. It looks like we are doing a right-hand turn across traffic from the left-hand lane. Madness! After we survive this, we drive past laneways filled with graffiti art and everything looks alive and colourful. It's a Saturday morning, and the place is already filled with people bustling around, sitting in outdoor cafes, walking their dogs and generally looking busy. I can't wait to get to Lucas's place and dump my stuff so I can get out and start exploring.

Lucas. I hope he'll be OK with me just turning up on his doorstep. When I bought my one-way ticket to Melbourne, I begged my parents not to tell him about my imminent arrival, hoping for it to be a happy surprise when I show up. In truth, I was a little nervous that he would try to talk me out of it. I know that having his little sister around, in his space, may cramp his style, so I thought it best to not tell him at all. Harder for him to say 'no' when I flew from the other side of the world to be here, right?

"This is you, Miss," the friendly Indian taxi driver tells me, pulling into the driveway of a cute, contemporary-style house, complete with a timber fence and a small yard out the front. I love it already.

"Thanks so much," I say, unbuckling my seatbelt and letting myself out of the car. The taxi driver has my overstuffed suitcase already waiting for me.

"Are you going to be OK getting that to the door?" he asks me.

So helpful. So unlike the taxi drivers where I'm from.

"I'll be fine, thanks," I say, paying him and slinging my bag over my shoulder. "And thanks for being my tour guide on the way here. I love Melbourne already!"

With a big smile and a wave, my first Australian friend leaves and I am alone. I take in a big breath and wheel my suitcase to the front door, hoping that Lucas is home, not sure what I'll do if he's out for the day. Maybe a contingency plan would have been a good idea for this situation, but I'm trying to be more spontaneous, and planning for the worst-case scenario seems a bad way to start along this path.

I knock and wait. And then wait some more. With a sinking feeling in my stomach, I wonder if perhaps Lucas is out and I may be stuck waiting on his front step for a while. I knock again, louder this time. *Perhaps he's out the back and hasn't heard me yet?* I think, trying for optimism. As I'm about to knock for a fourth and final time, the door is wrenched open and there in front of me is Mr. Sidney Parker, from my favourite TV show *Sanditon* (Theo James—sigh). Tall, dark brown hair, deep brown eyes, olive skin, chiselled jawline with what looks like day-old stubble. And he doesn't have a shirt on. Six-pack for days. Gulp.

The angry-looking, but also gorgeous-looking man is staring at me. His eyes are wide and his hands are running through his hair, back and forth, messing it up in the process. *Wow, that's some magnificent hair.* As we stare at each other, his mouth opening and closing as if to speak, but then forgetting what he is going to say, I search my mind for some English words. Any English words would work right about now. When stressed or flustered, like I am now, I forget all the work I did to learn fluent English and right now, if I were to speak, it would be in my native language and that isn't a good first impression.

Just as we pass the point of being able to stare at each other as strangers, without it being weird, Sidney Parker sweeps his gaze up and down my body. His nostrils flare and he closes his eyes for a brief moment. When they open again, they are narrowed.

"Whatever you're selling, I don't want it!" he says, his deep voice making my stomach do flip-flops. And with a final scowl at me (also hot!), he slams the door shut.

I blow out a deep breath. That had not gone well. I double-check the address Mamma had given me on my almost dead phone, then walk to the mailbox. *127 Harburn Street.* I have the correct place, which means the grumpy-looking man who had just slammed the door on me must be Daniel, Lucas's roommate. Lucas has told me a bit about him during our weekly FaceTime calls, but

I've never seen a photo of him. That has been a little secret Lucas has been keeping to himself; that his roommate looks like a leading man from a Jane Austen novel.

Now that I've confirmed that I am in fact at the right place, I drag myself back to the front door, my legs feeling heavy, the effects of the last 24 hours of travel catching up to me. I knock again, this time a little softer, not wanting to irritate Daniel any further.

"What?" he asks, as the door opens mid-knock. I see he has put a t-shirt on (shame) but is still wearing a frown.

"Umm, is Lucas home?" I get out, stammering only a bit.

Daniel looks me up and down again, slower this time, with his eyebrows raised.

"You want to see Lucas?" he asks, one eyebrow raised.

"*Si*, I mean yes," I reply, noting his head tilt at my little slip-up. "I-I'm his *sorella*. I mean sister!"

"His sister?" he repeats, sounding shocked. "Aren't you supposed to be in Italy? Does Lucas know you're coming?"

"Um, no?" I say, feeling nervous, but not knowing why. It's none of this man's business how I communicate with my brother.

"Well, that was a mistake. If you'd told him of your visit, he wouldn't have taken off on a holiday with Amy for the next week."

The next week! Like seven days? The words reverberate in my mind as I sway on my feet. I have been awake for over twenty hours, having only managed a few hours of sporadic sleep during the fourteen-hour flight from Dubai.

Daniel must notice this because he curses under his breath and grabs my arms, pulling me inside the house before going back out to get my suitcase.

"You-you don't have to do that," I stammer, stressed and not able to form my sentences. "I can do it myself."

He gives me a look that tells me he doubts that I can and wheels my bag to a stop next to me.

"So, what's the plan?" he asks, running his hand through his hair again. His eyes keep skating over my face, before finally settling on a point just past my shoulder.

"P-plan?"

"Well, given that Lucas isn't here to greet you, what are you planning to do next?"

Ah yes, that sort of plan. The sort of plan I'd been avoiding making in my bid to be more impulsive, and less anxious. Looks like that's not turning out so well for me.

"Ummm," I say, the only English word that comes out easily when I'm this stressed. "I don't have one?"

He curses again, looking more annoyed by the minute. "You mean to tell me you flew across the world to see Lucas and you didn't check that he would be home when you got here?"

When he puts it that way, it sounds irresponsible.

"Uh, yes?" is my lame response.

"So, no hotel booked? Nowhere to stay tonight?"

I look around the room we are standing in, which has a nice-looking couch, and all I can think of is my need to be lying down. Right now. He follows my gaze and then stands up taller.

"You can't stay here!" he says, his tone sharp and direct.

"O-of course not," I stammer, disappointed, but resigned. He shouldn't have to deal with me. I'm no one to him. "It will be fine. I'll find something."

I attempt to gather my wits and my bags at the same time, thinking maybe I can call my taxi driver friend to come and get me and take me to a cheap hotel. As I'm backing away, thoughts now on what to do next, Daniel puts his hand on my arm to stop me, pulling it back almost immediately.

"Wait, do you have somewhere to go? A working phone? Anything?"

I pull my iPhone back out of my bag and unlock it, seeing that there is only three per cent battery life left and no reception. My international roaming doesn't appear to be working. This isn't looking good.

"C-can I b-borrow your phone?" I ask, hating to annoy him more than I already have.

More curse words fly out of his mouth, causing me to flinch a little. Boy, have I made him angry.

Finally, after a long, awkward pause, he shocks me by saying, "You can stay here." His tone is filled with reluctance. "In Lucas's room. You can stay until he gets back at the end of the week."

Hope fills me as I try to catch his eye. He really does not want to look directly at me. "A-are you sure? I don't want to bother you."

"Lucas would kill me if I let his little sister wander around, clearly lost," he adds with a pointed look at me and my useless phone. "Just try to stay out of my way until he gets back and can deal with you."

It is not the most welcoming of speeches, but I'm grateful nonetheless. I give him a big smile, happy to have overcome the first hurdle.

"*Grazia*! Thank you!" I say, stepping forwards to hug him. What can I say, I'm a hugger.

Daniel takes a corresponding step back, perhaps not a hugger, and more awkward silence descends on us.

"I'll take you to see Lucas's room," he says, still sounding reluctant, and with my suitcase in hand, he wheels it down the hall, obviously expecting me to follow.

With a small skip in my step, feeling more revived than I was five minutes ago, I walk behind him, taking note again of his broad shoulders as I do. Lost in thoughts of his delightful manly frame, I don't notice him coming to a stop and slam right into the back of him.

"Oh! Sorry!" I squeal, feeling my face flush as he peers over his shoulder to look down at me. And by down, I mean way down. Daniel is at least six foot three and in my comfortable sneakers, I barely reach the top of his chest.

"Are you OK?" he asks, impatience coating his every word.

"*Si*, yes. Fine!" I say in my most cheerful tone, trying to mask how not OK I am. He's the most handsome man I have ever seen in real life. And even though he's snarly and angry, just being this close to him is making my heart beat triple time.

"You can stay in here," he says, opening a door to a bedroom. "Bathroom is just over there; kitchen is at the end of the house through that way." I watch as he points in various directions and then see him back away from me. Now that his job is done, he can't get away from me fast enough. "This is my room, but I can't foresee a situation where you would need to find me. Right?" he asks, his lips a flat line of disapproval.

What a grump!

"O-of course not. You don't worry about me. Once I've settled in, you won't even know I'm around."

He gives me another one of his long glances up and down my body, stopping at my lips and then up to that point beyond my shoulder again.

With a sigh, he opens his bedroom door and before he walks in, I think I hear him mutter, "I highly doubt that."

CHAPTER 2

Bella

Aᴛᴇʀ I ᴀᴄQᴜᴀɪɴᴛ ᴍʏsᴇʟꜰ ᴡɪᴛʜ Lucas's bedroom, which isn't much more than a bed and a desk, I decide it is time for a shower. It has been almost thirty-six hours since I left my parent's house in our small village in Florence, and that means it's been even longer than that since I've showered and changed my clothes.

A glance in the mirror confirms I'm not looking my best. My long brown hair is limp and mattered, hanging around my face. My blue eyes are red-rimmed from the lack of sleep, and I have dark bags under my eyes, pointing to the results of travelling halfway across the world. I take a long, hot shower, trying to wash off the effects of jetlag, and once dried, I dress again in jeans and a white t-shirt befitting the delightful weather outside, putting my wet hair up in a messy bun, not having the will or the energy to blow dry it right now. Although I'm feeling dead on my feet and my body clock is telling me to sleep—it's 1 a.m. at home—I'm determined not to give in. I didn't travel all this way to spend my first day in bed napping! I want to go out and explore.

But first, food is what my stomach is telling me. I have eaten nothing since the sad omelette and green beans they served on the plane (What is it with aeroplane food? Are they paid to make it bad?) and I'm desperate to get some food something in my belly. With quiet steps, I creep past Daniel's room—unsure if he's still at home, but not wanting to disturb him if he is—and make my way to the kitchen. Where it soon becomes very apparent that two men and no women live here. The fridge contains only beer, half a block of cheese and a jar of pickles. That's it. If our mamma saw that this is how Lucas is living, she would fly here and drag him back to Italy by his ears. Though to be fair, I think Lucas spends most of his time with his fiancée Amy, so maybe this sad fridge display is courtesy of my new roommate, Daniel?

Whatever the case, it is clear that I need to go out to find some sustenance. With my handbag packed, I'm about to leave when I notice a house key on the kitchen table, with a note attached. How thoughtful. Daniel has been kind enough to think ahead for me. I pick up the key and read the Post-it note out loud:

FOR TEMPORARY USE ONLY. UNTIL LUCAS RETURNS HOME.

OK, maybe not the sweet sentiment I thought it was, nevertheless, he had the foresight to leave it for me. So that has to mean something, doesn't it?

Filled with optimism—*I'm finally here!*—I leave the house, locking the door behind me. Without a working phone with internet access, I have no Google Maps to guide me and decide to just follow my nose. My knowledge of all things Melbourne tells me that a café selling good food and coffee shouldn't be too far away.

As I wander away from my 'temporary' accommodation, I try to note where I'm turning, knowing that I will eventually have to navigate my way back, but am distracted by all the sights around me. Lucas and Daniel live in a leafy suburb called Richmond, that runs along a river and is surrounded by parkland on one side, and funky, industrial buildings on the other. I love it! After about fifteen minutes of walking, I spy a café in the middle of a residential street. It is small and eclectic looking, squashed in between two Victorian-style houses on either side of it.

"A Thousand Blessings," I say, reading the name of the cafe out loud. It is perfect.

Inside the café, I manage to order myself a café latte and a ham and cheese focaccia without stammering once, and then take a seat outside while I wait for my order. The café is across the road from what looks like a sports oval and I watch, amused, as a group of young men play the sport they call 'football' over here. From what I can see, the sport has either a thousand rules or none at all. It makes zero sense.

"Here you go, love," an older waitress says as she delivers my food with a smile. "Can I get you anything else?"

I look down at my food, my mouth salivating, and shake my head. "No, thank you. This looks amazing!"

The waitress gives me another friendly grin and leaves me to eat and drink in peace.

I take my first sip of coffee and oh boy! TripAdvisor was correct; this really *is* the best coffee outside of Italy. I actually think it could be better! As I bite into my focaccia, which should be plain and boring, a small groan leaves me. There is some sort of relish in here and it is making my taste buds come alive. With what I know is a big smile on my face, I attack my sandwich. Once full, I sit back with my coffee and do some people-watching. The place is full of people, many lining up for takeaway food, while the outdoor area is filled with couples and families out for lunch. I watch as two young men around my age walk past me. One of them does a double take when he sees me, nudging his friend, and both of them stare at me as they walk by. Feeling self-conscious, I wipe around my mouth, sure that I have a milk moustache or something worse to attract that kind of attention. How mortifying.

With my belly full, I take off for a bit more exploring. I head towards the main street, which is lined with boutique clothes stores and cool trinket shops.

"I must come back here when I have a job and some money," I mutter to myself as I stop in front of a small art gallery. From what I can see from the outside, it looks like a dream to me. There are paintings on the walls, and sculptures and art installations scattered around the floor area. It is amazing! I'm so enthralled with this little find that I don't notice the few drops of rain until they have turned into a downpour. The people around me all seem to sigh simultaneously and open the umbrellas that they all magically possess. *What is that about?* I shiver in my thin t-shirt and try to decide whether I should stay here and wait it out or attempt to make it home.

A glance at the grey sky decides for me. If I'm to wait it out, I may be waiting all afternoon, and my jetlagged legs are protesting the job of keeping me upright. With a sigh, cursing my useless phone again, I take off in the direction I think I came from. It took me only twenty minutes to get here. How wet can I possibly get in that amount of time?

Ninety minutes later, I've found out just how wet a person can get—very—as I finally stumble upon the street where I now live. What should have been a simple trip home got derailed by the fact that I have no sense of direction at the best of times. Add in the sheets of rain and the foggy effects of jetlag, and I'm surprised I found my way home at all. I'm just about to pull out the key that

Daniel had left for me to use when the door is wrenched open in front of me.

"Where have you been?" Daniel asks angrily.

"O-out?" I reply, through chattering teeth. I'm so cold.

"Get in here. You're soaking wet!" he yells at me like he's telling me something I don't already know.

"Yes, that's what happens when you get lost in the rain," I attempt to reply with sarcasm, but then ruin it with a giant, full-body shudder.

"So much for being able to look after yourself," he says, his voice dripping with sarcasm.

"I can!" I protest. "This storm was unexpected. It was bright sunshine when I left."

"First lesson to learn about living in Melbourne: We have four seasons in a day. Always pack a cardigan and an umbrella, even if it looks like a sunny day."

Huh. Well, that would explain the sudden appearance of all the umbrellas earlier this afternoon. What a wonderful bit of local knowledge! I'm about to thank Daniel for sharing when I notice he is staring at me. At my sopping wet t-shirt, to be specific. My completely transparent t-shirt, my white bra clearly visible through the paper-thin fabric.

I cover my chest with my arms, causing Daniel's eyes to snap to mine. I watch, fascinated, as his cheeks heat up and see that he is back to looking at the spot just above my shoulder again.

"I'm sorry to have worried you," I say, to break the weird tension that has settled between us.

"Lucas would kill me if I let anything happen to you," he mumbles, repeating his earlier sentiment as he shrugs out of his sweatshirt and hands it to me. "Here, wear this. You're shivering. I don't want you to get sick and have to look after you for the next few days."

I take his offered shirt and pull it over my head, choosing to focus again on the sweet gesture and not the snarky commentary that comes with it. With a subtle breath in, I smell the collar of his shirt. *Yum.* His shirt smells like expensive men's cologne, and what Daniel doesn't realise right now is that he's never getting this back.

"Thank you," I say. "I feel warmer already."

Daniel's eyes travel over me wearing his shirt and without another word, he turns and walks out of the room. And slams the door to his bedroom when he gets there.

"What a grump," I mutter to myself as I make my way to Lucas's room, desperate now to get out of my heavy, wet jeans and into some pyjama pants. I think it's time to give in to this jetlag and lie down for a bit. I take my time, working the knots out of my bedraggled hair. Once I have changed—keeping Daniel's sweatshirt on because it's warmer and more comfortable than any of the clothes, I had packed for myself—I walk to the kitchen to make myself a cup of tea.

When I go to turn the kettle on, I notice a cup of what looks like hot chocolate on the table. Has Daniel prepared a hot drink for me? Picking up the mug, which smells like chocolate heaven, I see two big pink marshmallows floating on the top. With a delighted laugh, I take a small sip and then see a Post-it note attached to the bottom:

TRY NOT TO DIE BEFORE LUCAS GETS HOME.

I smile as I read this. He is trying to hide his sweetness behind his snark. And it makes me curious. Which one is the real Daniel? And why am I dying to find out?

CHAPTER 3

Bella

A<small>FTER ALLOWING MYSELF A LITTLE</small> five-hour nap at 3 p.m., I find myself wide awake in the middle of the night. It's 4 p.m. yesterday afternoon at home—confusing, hey?—and this jetlag is officially kicking my butt. I punch my pillow and try to get comfortable, hoping for sleep to find me, so I'm not a zombie tomorrow. As I'm tossing and turning, my thoughts drift to the man sleeping down the hall. Lucas had mentioned his roommate to me during several of our calls over the last few months, but I can't remember getting any specific details.

I wrack my brain, trying to recall any information that would help me understand the angry man who made me hot chocolate and gave me his sweatshirt when I was cold. I know he is roughly the same age as me, and that this is his place that I am now living in. *How can someone so young afford something this nice?* With these thoughts tumbling through my mind, I also have the additional anxiety of wondering what I'll do when Lucas comes home. He might 1) not be happy at my sudden appearance and 2) want to get me on the fastest flight home. I have to be ready for that. I better look for a job tomorrow, a place that requires someone cheap and flexible and available to start now. With these worries at the forefront of my mind, I close my eyes and pray for sleep to come.

It turns out my prayers must have been answered at some point during the night because when I next open my eyes, bright sunshine is streaming in through the window. What time is it?

"11 a.m.?!" I yell, having glanced at the alarm clock on Lucas's bedside table. I have wasted almost half the day sleeping!

I jump out of bed and race to get ready—as quietly as possible, because I don't want to give grumpy-pants Daniel any further reason to be annoyed at me. Once showered and dressed, I open Lucas's laptop. I need to get my phone up and running. With a lucky guess at his password—Amy's birthday, how cute—I manage to buy a SIM card that will allow me to use my phone here and access data. Yay, now I can use Google Maps and not have a repeat performance of yesterday's debacle.

With this sorted, I decide that the first thing I want to do today is to find the Love, Lilly café that I have heard so much about. Stalking Lucas and Amy's social media accounts over the years, I have seen them post so much about the place. Apparently, it's owned and run by Lilly, Amy's best friend, and it serves the most delicious treats and pastries. I've seen many Instagram posts about the cookies and cupcakes, and I am dying to try them for myself. So, this will be my first stop. Sustenance, then the serious stuff of finding a job. With this plan in place, I'm ready to leave with a cardigan just in case—see? I'm learning—and set off on another adventure.

Turns out that the café in question is only a 20-minute walk from Lucas's place, and I take the time getting there to admire the surrounding atmosphere once again. The area is bustling with people out walking their dogs, parks are filled with people having picnics and the temperature is getting just hot enough to make me sweat a bit. Surely, I won't need a cardigan today? By the time I arrive at the Love, Lilly café, I'm ready for a cold drink and something to eat.

A little bell trills as I enter the place and I take a deep breath in, appreciating the sugary smell that is permeating the air.

"Can I help you?"

I look up to see Lilly herself standing behind the counter, ready to serve me.

"Lilly?" I say, like we're old friends. Which is stupid because this person doesn't know me at all. She doesn't know that I've been obsessively following her life from the other side of the world.

"Uh, yes?" Lilly replies, her head tilted in question. "I know you!" she follows on, with a big smile across her face. Before I can form another sentence, she is out from behind the counter and I am enveloped in a big hug.

"I've seen you in photos. You look just like Lucas," she gushes, leaning back to peer at me. "Isabella, isn't it? You're gorgeous! Those are some good genes you have in your family."

"Uh, thank you," I stammer back, overwhelmed by her friendliness.

"What are you doing here? Does Lucas know you're here? You know that he's away at the moment, right?" She fires the questions at me, as she leads me towards a table at the window of her café.

"*Si*, I-I mean, yes," I say, feeling my face heat up as I stumble on my words. I'm so shocked that Lilly knows who I am. "I c-came to surprise him, but the surprise was on me."

"Oh," she responds, her mouth also forming a perfect O shape. "So, where are you staying? Do you need help?"

"No, no. I'm OK. Daniel is letting me stay in Lucas's room until he gets back," I reassure her. "But reluctantly, I may add."

She gives me an inquisitive look at this bit of information but gets distracted by a customer before she can reply.

"Sit, sit. I'll serve this customer and then we can get you some food. And we can catch up. I've heard so much about you from your brother!" she says as she bustles away, a ball of energy.

I do as Lilly tells me to, taking a seat and watching as she serves the line of customers that had formed while we were chatting. Lilly is run off her feet. I look around to see if she has any help. Apart from what looks like the chef out the back, it seems she is alone out here to take orders and wait the tables. Without a second thought, I jump up and start clearing the tables so that customers can take a seat if they want. I walk around the back of the counter and begin putting together orders that Lilly has written, all of this second nature to me after working for years in my parent's deli.

"You don't need to do that," Lilly protests between orders.

"I'm happy to help. Unless you don't want me to be back here," I say, feeling silly for overstepping her boundaries.

"No! Please stay and keep helping me," she says, her eyes wide and pleading. "I need to get some help here but haven't had the time to hire anyone. On days like this, I'm reminded that I can't do this alone."

I smile at this, and together we get through the lunchtime rush. The café is very popular, both with people wanting to sit and eat, and those who want to take away, and by 2 p.m. I'm dead on my feet and absolutely starving. I have eaten nothing in a very long time. Lilly must notice this as she forces me to take a seat at one of the tables and presents me with a plate filled with food. Croissants, straight from the oven, brownies and even a giant vanilla cupcake. I'm in food heaven.

"You sit and eat while I get you something to drink. An iced coffee, perhaps?" she asks, like the angel that she is. That sounds amazing!

"If you are sure you have the time?" I ask, not wanting to add to her workload.

"I think the rush is over now," she says, going behind the counter and assembling my drink order. "So, Bella," she says, casually using my nickname. "What are your plans now that you're here?" she asks, as she sits across from me.

I groan as I take a bite of the perfectly made warm croissant. "I'm hoping to stay for a bit. I have a working visa, so if I can find a job, maybe I can make this my home for a while?"

"Wow! That sounds amazing. You're so brave to pick up and move across the world," Lilly says, smiling at my obvious enjoyment of her food.

Brave? That word has never been used to describe me before. But I guess it does suit me now, moving to a new country on a wing and a prayer.

"What type of work are you looking for?" she asks, helping herself to one of her own cookies.

"Anything. I'm happy to work anywhere that will have me. Until I can figure out what it is, I want to do."

Her face lights up. "Why don't you work here?"

"Here?" I echo.

"Why not? You've just done half a shift with me, so I know you can do it."

I look at Lilly to see if she is serious. What kind of person just offers a stranger a job?

"You're Lucas's sister," she continues. "So, I know you're a trustworthy person. And you helped me today, without me needing to even ask. You know your way around a cash register as well," she says, pointing out that with no training, I had figured hers out. It's the same model we use at our family store.

"Really?" I ask, excitement bubbling in my stomach. "You'd let me work here?"

"Of course! It would be perfect. Then I wouldn't have to bother trying to hire someone. That sounded like a boring task," she adds with a visible shudder. "It can just be until you find your feet and figure stuff out. And we'll have heaps of fun together."

I let out the deep breath that I didn't know I was holding and smile at Lilly. "Yes, please! I will do it. I would love to work with you!"

She claps and rounds the table to give me another hug. "Fantastic news! Why don't you take a couple of days to get over your jetlag and then start here on Wednesday? Does that work for you?"

I squeeze her back, so grateful for her easy acceptance of me into her life. "Yes, of course. Whatever works for you!"

"OK. And we can work out all the boring details then. Paperwork and that sort of stuff. I'll get Oliver to sort it out tomorrow." Oliver is Lilly's husband and Amy's older brother. I've seen so many posts about him on Instagram that I feel like he's a friend already.

"Sounds good, Lilly. And thank you. You don't know how much this has saved me."

"Well, then, we have saved each other," she says, getting up to serve a customer. "Why don't you head home? You look dead on your feet. Give me your number and we can chat tomorrow."

I take the phone she has offered me and program in my details. When I go to pay for my lunch, Lilly waves away my money.

"You worked for over two hours today, Bella. *I* should give *you* money."

As I go to protest, she shoos me out of the door. "Enjoy your last few days off. I'll be seeing you here bright and early on Wednesday."

With one last smile, I turn and leave the café. Now my new place of employment. What a productive day it's been so far.

I make my way back to Lucas's slowly, trying to avoid yesterday's trap of falling asleep at 3 p.m. When I get there, I let myself into the house and am greeted by the most delightful sight I have ever seen. Daniel. In a fireman's uniform.

"Hi!" I squeak, after standing and staring at him for too long.

Daniel looks up at me, his gaze running over me, before he glances back down again.

"Hey," he offers, with little enthusiasm.

"You're a firefighter?" I ask the obvious question, to try to get a conversation going. What's his problem with me, anyway?

"No," he answers, shocking me. "I'm a stripper. This is my costume for tonight's party."

I feel my jaw drop open as I let my eyes scan him up and down. A stripper? I can't believe Lucas left out that piece of information. I mean, he's good-looking enough to make a lot of money doing that, and I can tell he has muscles upon muscles under that t-shirt, so yeah, that fits. Wow, lucky girls who get to watch him strip.

"Oh, um. Great," I say, as I watch him watching me with an amused smile.

"You should see your expression right now," he says with a quiet chuckle. "I'm just kidding."

I feel myself blush as I continue to stare at him, a little bummed that I have to delete the mental image I had of him dancing around a stripper's pole.

"My job isn't that exciting. I'm just a boring, actual firefighter," he tells me now, breaking our eye contact to look over my shoulder again.

"Nothing boring about that," I whisper, thinking of him running into burning buildings to save people and swooning inside.

"Where have you been today?" he asks, changing the subject, and going back to packing the bag at his feet.

"I got a job!" I tell him, feeling my chest puff with pride. Look at me standing on my own two feet and making things happen.

"A job, hey?"

"Yes," I reply, my smile so big it's hurting my cheeks. "I'm going to be working at Lilly's café!"

Daniel stops what he is doing to look up at me. He takes in my flushed cheeks and gleeful grin and a muscle twitches in his jaw.

"So, I guess this means you're planning to stay? Here in Melbourne?" he asks, his voice a little gruff.

"I guess it does!" I reply, excitement coating my voice.

He looks back down and grunts a little at this. "Well, at least with a job you'll be able to afford a place of your own," he says, picking up his bag and heading to the front door.

"Sure, thing!" I say, saluting his back.

With one last look at me over his shoulder, he heaves a big sigh and walks out the door.

"Thanks for your congratulations," I yell to his departed form.

What a jerk. *No matter*, I think. Today is a good day, and I will not let Daniel-the-grump ruin it for me. This is the first time that I truly believe I can make it here on my own. And despite having to live here with Mr. Snarky for a few more days, everything feels amazing.

CHAPTER 4

Bella

A FTER ANOTHER NIGHT OF WAKING at 2 a.m. and falling back asleep a few hours later, I force myself out of bed at a reasonable hour, determined to make the most of the two free days I have left before starting work on Wednesday. With a grimace, I stretch my tired body and trudge down to the bathroom, hoping a shower will wake me up enough to at least get me to coffee.

"Isabella," a deep voice has my head bolting up, my bleary eyes quickly coming into focus. "I think we need to set some ground rules around the appropriate dress code."

I look down at my perfectly modest pyjamas, a pink t-shirt and matching pair of shorties, and back at Daniel, trying to decipher what's caused so much offence.

"Umm, OK." I let my eyes travel over his outfit, a pair of running shorts and a tight black t-shirt that showcases his muscles to perfection, and think to myself, no problem with the current dress code from where I'm standing. "What does this dress code entail?"

"More material." His voice is flat, his focus back on the spot next to my shoulder. "Definitely more material."

I let my eyes wander deliberately over the expanse of his uncovered thighs and raise my eyebrow at him. "Does this go both ways?"

He has the decency to flush at this but then collects himself. "You can't be roaming around wearing next to nothing. I'm sure your brother wouldn't appreciate it."

"My brother isn't my keeper," I tell him with a bit of bite in my tone, because he's pissing me off. "But if my skin is so offensive to you, I'll make sure to cover it up in the future."

With that I walk past him, now thoroughly annoyed, and am surprised when he grabs my elbow as I go, his gentle touch causing a flurry of tingles up and down my arm.

"Nothing about you is offensive, Isabella."

And with that, he stalks off down the hallway, leaving me again to make sense of the puzzle he keeps presenting to me.

I sigh and decide to not let this brief encounter bother me. Yet as I let myself into the bathroom and turn the shower on, I can't help the flush that takes over my entire body as I replay his gruffly spoken words in my mind. *Daniel, I find nothing about you offensive either. And that may end up being a big problem.*

After a long shower and a strong talking to—must not fawn over grumpy roommate, no matter how cute he may be—I'm ready for another day of exploring. Having looked up the best places to go to experience what Melbourne has to offer, I navigate the public transport system and get myself to the fashion district of Toorak in one piece. Pleased that my day has taken a turn for the better, I treat myself to a coffee and a doughnut and indulge in some people-watching. As I'm admiring the well-dressed people buzzing about, I receive a text message from Lilly.

LILLY: Come by tonight for dinner? I want you to meet Oliver. Bring Daniel.

I feel myself flush with happiness. I've only been here a few days and I've made friends and even gotten an invitation to a dinner party!

BELLA: Thanks! I'll be there. Should I bring anything? Not sure Daniel will come, pretty sure he hates me.

Lilly takes a few minutes to reply.

LILLY: Hate you? That's impossible. It's like hating a puppy. No one hates a puppy. Give him a chance, he's a great guy.

That's what I'm afraid of, I think as I reply.

BELLA: OK, I'll ask him. Thanks for the invitation. I can't wait to meet Oliver!

With my plans for the evening now firmly locked in place, I take off at a leisurely pace down the main street, window shopping and marvelling at all the wonderful fashion on offer. I mean, I come from the fashion capital of the world, but some of the boutique stores here are really beautiful.

As I'm gazing longingly at the expensive shoes in the shop window in front of me, I take a moment to focus on my reflection looking back at me. The girl I've always been is there, but there is now a sparkle in my eye, a confidence in the way I hold my head. As I contemplate the changes in the way I feel about myself, I make a split-second decision that my outside needs to match my new inside. And so, I walk with purpose towards my next destination. A hair salon.

"Can I help you?"

I look up to see a striking young woman in front of me. She has long, platinum blonde hair, dead straight, worn down her back, well past her waist. With her warm brown eyes and her tiny pixie-like frame, she's a delight to look at.

"I know this is probably a long shot, but do you have any available appointments today?" I ask, feeling intimidated to be even talking to this beautiful creature.

"Today?" she repeats, giving me a long look up and down. "What did you have in mind?"

I pick up a piece of my long, thick brown hair and smile. "I need a change."

The pixie lady in front of me gives me an equally big smile in return. "Well, then you're in luck. Because change is what I do, and my next appointment just cancelled on me. My name is Amelia, and we can start now, if you're ready?"

I take a deep breath and step closer to her. "More ready than you'll ever know."

On shaky legs, because I may look confident but I also love my hair, I take the seat offered to me and sit quietly while Amelia stands and stares at me for several minutes. Just as I start to fidget, uncomfortable under her professional gaze, she picks up a strand of my hair.

"There is no way I'm doing anything with the colour," she states. "You have the perfect rich shade of brown that works with your complexion. But I think we should take off a lot of the length. To frame your beautiful face."

My cheeks heat up at her compliment. "How short are you thinking?"

She puts her hand up to my chin. "Here, with bangs."

I gulp. My hair has been long—almost waist length—since I was five years old. Am I brave enough to cut it all off?

"Let's do it," I say through a deep breath before I can change my mind.

Amelia grins at me. "Trust me. You're going to feel like a new person when I'm finished with you."

"That was my plan when I decided to move here, so let's get to it."

My new friend gets to work, turning me away from the mirror and straightening up her scissors.

"So, where are you from?" she asks as she snips away at the back of my head. Unable to see what she's up to anyway, I close my eyes and distract myself by answering her question.

"I just moved here from Italy," I tell her, wincing as I start to feel my hair falling from around my face and shoulders.

"Did you move here for work or love?"

"Neither. I moved here for me."

I go on to detail what my life was like back at home, how sheltered my world was in my small village surrounded by people who have known me my whole life. I find myself smiling as I detail how my aunties have a gossip network so robust that not a single life event in our village could go by undocumented. How, growing up, my friends and I had to find ways to evade their ever-knowing gazes whenever we had mischief to get up to. And how there wasn't a minute of my life that hadn't been witnessed or shared with at least three relatives nearby.

"It was both comforting and suffocating," I say as she takes me to the sink and begins the blissful part of washing my hair, complete with a soothing head massage.

"That sounds nice," she says. "Sometimes I feel lonely in a city surrounded by people."

I pause and let that sink in, wondering what it would feel like to be alone in a crowded place.

"I've never experienced that. There's always been a family member or friend within arm's reach, so being here on my own for the first time...well, it's liberating."

"I bet. And your English is amazing. Did you learn that at school?"

My cheeks heat up and I laugh with embarrassment. "We learned a little at school. But actually, I did most of the work by teaching myself," I admit as she gets to work blow-drying my hair.

"How?" she yells over the noise of the hair dryer.

"I watched a lot of English-speaking TV shows. Over and over again."

I peek up through the hair that is hanging in front of my face to see Amelia giving me a look of astonishment. "That's how you learnt to speak English? But you're so good at it!"

"Thanks," I say, feeling a sense of pride blossom in my belly. "Once I got started, I enrolled in an English-speaking course online to make sure I could speak fluently and I forced myself to watch these shows without subtitles."

She gives me a big smile and so I continue.

"There was one particular show I got hooked on and I watched all six seasons at least half a dozen times."

"Well, now I'm dying to know which show it is."

I pause, feeling foolish. "It's an old show. I found it on Netflix one day and couldn't stop watching. I watched hours and hours of it every day, with my Google Translate at hand for when I got confused. It was a way of immersing myself in the language."

"Come on, I need to know the show."

"OK," I mumble, as she styles the back of my hair. "It's *Dawson's Creek.*"

Amelia stops what she's doing and gapes at me. "I love that show. I mean, I love, *love* that show."

"Really? You do?"

"Yes. It's a bit silly and unrealistic, filled with teenagers talking like adults, which is probably why your English is so good, but I just love it. And I love Joey and Pacey together. They are so endgame."

I feel myself grin and nod vigorously. "I love Pacey and I love Joey and I love them together."

Happy to have found a fellow fan, I launch into a discussion with Amelia about which season is best and why Dawson is the most annoying character ever, and before I know it, she has finished.

"There," she says, turning me around to face the mirror with a flourish. "What do you think?"

I pause and move closer to the image reflected at me. Although the cut is simple, Amelia has weaved some sort of magic and made me both chic and elegant. Gone is the girl from a small Italian village, and in her place is a woman.

"Amelia," I breathe, playing with the sweeping bangs she has cut for me. "You've done an amazing job. *Molto bene.*"

She beams back at me, pleased with the compliment. "It was easy working with someone so gorgeous," she says, smoothing a few strands back into place. "See how the shorter style makes your eyes look bigger? You have such symmetrical features that this long bob really suits your face."

I nod because what she's saying is true. Somehow, with my hair curling in just above my shoulders, all my best features seem to pop where before they may have blended in. *Wow, the power of a good haircut!*

"Thank you, thank you, thank you," I say, getting up and giving my new friend an impromptu hug. "This is better than I could have imagined."

"You're welcome," she replies, squeezing me back. "I'm so glad to have met you. Let's keep in touch. I can show you around if you want?"

I smile and nod again with enthusiasm. "That would be amazing. Here's my number. Please reach out whenever you're free. I'd love for you to show me around."

With a firm commitment to see each other again, I pay for what was the world's best salon experience and float out the door. *Melbourne, so far you are as incredible as I'd dreamed you'd be!*

A few more hours of exploring later, I decide to head home and fit in a nap before the dinner party later tonight. With the effects of jet lag still lingering, I knew not to push myself too far and ruin what is hopefully a fun evening with Lilly and Oliver.

"You're back," a deep voice states the obvious as I let myself into the house.

"Yes, sorry to disappoint," I say with a touch of sarcasm, because it's pretty clear Daniel would be happier if I stayed away.

I look up, expecting an equally snarky response, and am struck by his expression as he stares at me. Feeling self-conscious, I touch my new bangs, moving them from where they now sit just on my brow line and bite my lip. Does he hate the new me? And why do I care so much about what he thinks?

"You cut your hair," he says with a hard swallow, his eyes roaming over my face.

"You are Captain Obvious today," I laugh at him somewhat nervously. *What's wrong with him? Why is he staring so intensely?*

"It-it looks...nice," he mutters finally, his gaze moving back to the spot next to my head. Not quite looking at me, more like in my general direction.

"T-thanks," I stammer back, feeling the tension between us but not knowing how or why it's there. "Oh, by the way, Lilly and Oliver have invited us over for dinner tonight."

"Us?" he asks, his eyes returning to mine.

"Yes, she sent a text asking for us both to come."

There's a moment of silence that follows this benign dinner invitation and just as I'm about to break it with a joke or a snort or any sort of noise to make this better, he finally speaks.

"Nope."

Nope? What's wrong with this guy?

"What do you mean, 'Nope'?"

"I can translate it for you if you need. Nope means no. I don't want to come with you to Lilly's place tonight."

Huh? Well, that hurts.

"OK, that's fine," I tell him, trying to keep my voice even so he wouldn't hear the wobble of hurt in my tone. "No big deal."

Daniel looks at me then, our gazes locked, and I feel the air rush out of my lungs at what I see in his expression. He looks so sad; it makes me want to comfort him. Which is strange given he was the one being rude to me in the first place.

"I just mean, I'm busy tonight," he finally says in a gruff voice.

"Busy?" I ask out loud because although I've only been here three days, I already know that he doesn't have the busiest of social lives.

"Yes," he snaps back. "Busy. You don't have to entertain me."

"Done. No more inviting you out for dinner with *your* friends," I say with sarcasm because this guy is being a jerk.

Daniel doesn't reply; instead, he just gives me another long look. His focus back on my hair that is now resting on my shoulders, before he mutters something under his breath and stalks out of the room.

"Good riddance," I say in a low voice to his disappearing back. "The night will be more fun without you." And yet, as soon as the words have left my mouth, I know that isn't true. Because despite his snarky attitude and his dismissive tone, I feel myself drawn to my new roommate, and I don't know what I'm going to do about it.

CHAPTER 5

Daniel

I close my bedroom door and lean back against it, lightly banging my head in an outward display of my inner frustration.

"Lucas, you need to get back as soon as possible," I mutter to myself out loud through a groan.

Since the minute I opened the front door and saw that gorgeous woman standing there, I've been cycling between two extremes of emotion, pure elation at having found her—the one who could be 'the one'—and abject terror at her arrival at this the most awful of times. And the worst part? She has no idea that she affects me at all. She just floats through the day, looking and smelling divine, without a clue how strongly I'm already drawn to her.

PING.

I look down at my phone and frown when I see a text message from Lilly. After Lucas finally got his girl and proposed, their small friendship group has been attempting to adopt me as one of them, whether or not I want to be. And even though I'm the surly grump at every social occasion they drag me to, they all seem determined to have me in their lives. To make sure I'm not alone. Lonely.

LILLY: Why are you being a jerk to Bella?

Great. Now Lilly is involved. I'm not getting out of dinner tonight.

DANIEL: Don't know what you're talking about.

LILLY: Bella said you flatly refused to come tonight.

LILLY: RUDE.

DANIEL: I'm busy.

LILLY: I can guarantee you're not.

LILLY: I'll just keep texting you until you give in.

I sigh as I read this last message because Lilly can be very determined when she puts her mind to something. Annoyingly so.

DANIEL: Fine. I'll come. But don't expect me to be happy about it.

LILLY: Great. See you soon.

LILLY: And be nice to Bella. What's wrong with you?

What's wrong with me? That's a very loaded question.

I put my phone down and with a sigh, I pick up the picture frame sitting in prime position on the table next to my bed. It contains a photo of me and my mum and just looking at it makes my heart wrench, not only because it's a painful reminder of happier times, but also because I know the person, I am now is so completely different from the man in this picture. This person, with bright eyes and a careless smile, is the man I was in my previous life. That's how I now think of my life. Before my mum's death and after. The man I was before she was taken from me was happy and light. Quick to laugh; some would say the life of the party. And then everything changed. Everything fell apart.

I sigh again as I lie back down on my bed and try not to think about that time in my life almost two years ago. It had been just another ordinary day. Mum had left for work and had been involved in a 'minor vehicle accident.' That's what the paramedics had said when I received the call on my way home from the night shift at the fire station. I'd rushed to the hospital expecting the worst. I remember feeling so relieved to see Mum sitting up in her hospital bed, chatting with nurses, seeming no worse for wear. We'd waited for the doctor to examine her and were both eager to leave once they completed the routine scans. And that was when our worlds came crashing down.

Because the routine scans had identified tumours in my mum's body, everywhere. She had been admitted for a check-up after a car accident and then had been given the worst possible news a person could receive. Cancer. Stage four. Metastatic. Terminal.

What followed were urgent appointments with oncologists and surgeons, which turned into discussions about palliative care and end-of-life instructions. And through it all, I was by her side. The woman who had given me everything in life. The single mother who had sacrificed it all to ensure I had everything that I'd ever wanted and needed was now being told that her life had an end date and that date was going to be soon.

I'd tried to be strong for her and I know she tried to be strong for me. But the cancer was more powerful than us both. And it wasn't long after that initial diagnosis that I was saying goodbye to the most important person to me. The woman who brought me into the world was taken tragically and far too early from it.

And what made everything so much worse was that once Mum had passed, I found myself alone in the world. The man who had contributed his sperm but nothing else had left me and my mum just after I was born, resulting in zero relationship with my father. And my mum's parents both died before I entered primary school, so I have little to no memories of them. It had been just me and my mum, a team, the two of us against the world. Until the cancer diagnosis and everything that followed. Until there was just me.

Both Lucas and Amy had tried to be there for me through it all. From that first day, they'd been by my side whenever they could, along with all the wonderful doctors and nurses who had tried to walk us through this tragedy. Lucas and Amy had tried to be my friend and were the only support network I'd let close to me, so wrapped up in my grief that I pushed everyone else away. And for that, I'll be forever grateful to them, to Lucas and Amy and then Lilly and Oliver, who all attempted to hold me together when all I'd wanted to do was fall apart.

I wipe the tear that had escaped from my eye and force myself to sit up and put these memories to the back of my mind. It's the only way I can get through most days, by focusing on the here and now, not the past and definitely not the future. Admittedly, it's not a great way to exist, living only half a life, unable and unwilling to allow anyone to get close to me, but it's a way of protecting my sanity and my heart. Because I know I'll never be able to get over losing another person I love again. That saying, 'It's better to have loved and lost, than to never have loved at all'? Well, it's wrong.

I let out a bitter chuckle as I think about this and mentally shake my fist at fate or destiny, or whichever deity is playing with me at the moment, by dropping Isabella—literally—on my front doorstep.

The lovely Isabella who stole my breath from the minute I laid eyes on her. She looked somewhat dishevelled, but so achingly beautiful that I'd had to take a moment to just look at her. And at that time, I knew I wanted her to be mine. She bewitched me instantly, and this feeling hasn't stopped since then. Her sunny disposition, her enthusiasm for all things, her zest for life—

I just want to be near her all the time and that has all the alarm bells ringing in my head. Because I can't want her, I can't let her get too close. Not only because she will inevitably leave at some point, this time in Melbourne is just a brief pit-stop in her life, but also because I know I'm too broken, and she deserves so much more than a man who is living in the equivalent of an emotional coma.

"Daniel?" I hear her voice through the door, her accent giving my name a melodic quality. With a quiet groan, I steel myself to open the door, because I know what will happen when I see her—my heart will race, the blood will depart my brain and I'll end up saying something stupid or off-putting, and sweet Isabella shouldn't have to deal with either.

"What?" I say as I open the door and am once again struck dumb at the sight of her. She was beautiful before her trip to the salon, her hair long and luscious down her back, but when she returned today, she looked simply stunning. With her short hair now framing her face, her bright blue eyes somehow look bigger, her cheekbones more prominent, and I can see with this transformation that she has gone from pretty to a legitimate walk down the street, head turner. A thought that makes my stomach clench.

"Lilly called and said you changed your mind," she says in her quiet and oh-so-soothing tone. "For dinner tonight?" she continues somewhat uncertainly when I stand here saying nothing.

"I didn't have a choice. Apparently, I need to be nicer to you."

She winces and I feel like the giant jerk that I am. I know that I'm being rude to her, but what she doesn't realise is that I'm doing it for *her*.

"Sorry about that. I didn't call her to get you to come with me. More of out of courtesy, to let her know."

"Well, whatever happened, it looks like you'll have a date for the evening."

She looks startled by my choice of words but isn't more shocked than I am. *Why did I say that? We aren't going on a date. Not now. Not ever.*

"W-what?" she stammers, something I notice happens when she's flustered.

"Nothing. Just an expression. You're probably not familiar with that turn of phrase." I cover for myself with an emphatic shake of my head, noting the blush that is heating up her face. Her beautiful face.

"Turn of phrase?" she repeats, her brow furrowing in that adorable way.

"Never mind," I say, wanting to move us away from the mess I've made of this conversation. "Are you ready to go?"

Isabella looks down at the outfit she's wearing, a simple summer dress that clings to all the curves I shouldn't be noticing, paired with sandals, and then back at me.

"I-is this OK for dinner?" she asks, her voice tinged with uncertainty.

"You look fine," I tell her while shepherding her out of my room. She looks more than fine and that is why I need to get her out of this small, enclosed space. Where the bed is tantalisingly close.

"Shall we go?" she asks after we've exited my room and I've taken two unsubtle steps away from her.

"Sure, may as well get it over and done with."

Isabella gives me a curious look but seems undeterred by my surly attitude.

"I can't wait to meet Oliver," she gushes, her sunny approach to everything in life bubbling over.

"You know Oliver?" I ask as we make my way to my car in the driveway. Without thought, I open the passenger side door for her and am rewarded with her blinding smile. If I'm not careful, I'll find myself wanting to do things for her just to get another glimpse of it.

"I don't know him at all," she says once we've settled into the car and are making the ten-minute drive to where Lilly and Oliver live. "I've just been following you guys on Instagram. Well, not you. You've come as quite the shock."

She clamps a hand over her mouth and looks at me, her blue eyes wide in dismay.

Shock, hey? I think, unsure whether this is a good thing or not.

"Shock?" I ask, my need to know her first impression of me outweighing my need to keep up the façade of the silent type. Though these days, it's not that much of a façade anymore.

"Lucas told me about you," she starts, making me wonder exactly what he'd said about me. "But I didn't know you'd look like..." she trails off and I glance over to see her cheeks are flushed a delightful shade of pink.

Does this mean that Isabella likes the look of me as much as I like the look of her? Damn if that doesn't get my blood pumping.

"Like?"

"Um, nothing. I can't think of the English word," she backtracks while winding down the window and letting the evening air cool her cheeks.

I decide to not probe any further, though I'm certain she knows the correct English word to describe me. It's probably best left unsaid. The last thing I want is to know that Isabella has any interest in me because that would make staying away from her next to impossible.

"That meal was...um," Isabella says an hour later, after Lilly had served up what looked like it was supposed to be lasagne but turned out to be a mushy sauce with slightly raw pasta sheets in the middle. I'm not sure how she bakes as well as she does because this dish was a mess.

"I don't know what happened," Lilly says in response to this unfinished sentence. "The recipe looked simple, and I followed it for the most part, or at least I tried to. I may have gotten distracted in the middle and perhaps missed a few steps."

Oliver leans over to pull her close, kissing her cheek and soothing her as he does.

"I thought it was delicious," he lies, kicking me under the table and spurring me into action.

"Yes, it was great," I say before taking a sip of wine to wash away the burnt flavour. *How did she manage to both burn and undercook this dish?*

"Absolutely," Isabella chimes in with that smile of hers. The one I want directed at me all day, every day. The one I must avoid at all costs. "It tastes just like the way Nonna made it back home."

Lilly gives us all a doubtful look before laughing.

"You guys are nice, but even I can admit when I've failed. And this," she motions to the half-eaten food left on all our plates, "is an utter failure. Luckily, I've made dessert. Another Italian classic, and I know this one won't disappoint."

I watch as the two women leave the room to prepare what Lilly is claiming to be her 'world-famous tiramisu' and my eyes follow Isabella until I can't see her anymore. When I turn back around, I'm confronted by Oliver smiling knowingly.

"What?" I ask with a heap of attitude in my voice.

"She's gorgeous," he says, motioning towards where Isabella just exited the room.

I feel a sensation close to jealousy gnaw at my stomach at the thought of another man looking at her in that way, and this pisses me off. So what if Oliver notices how beautiful she is? A man would have to be blind to not see it.

"So?"

"So, nothing," he says with that stupid smug smirk on his face. "Just making conversation."

"Don't you have a wife to be looking at?" I all but growl at him, knowing I'm acting unhinged but unable to stop myself.

"Hey, you know I love Lilly. I've always loved Lilly. But I can still objectively point out a beautiful woman. "

I wonder if Lucas would be OK with me punching his soon-to-be brother-in-law.

"Yeah, she's fine to look at. If you're into that sort of thing, which I'm not."

"Sure, OK buddy. You keep telling yourself that."

Before I can come up with a witty retort to shut him the hell up, both Lilly and Isabella return from the kitchen, loaded with treats for dessert.

"What are you guys talking about?" Lilly asks as they settle back at the table, Isabella's scent wafting over to me, distracting me from whatever it is I was thinking. She smells like citrus and something more. Something uniquely her.

I edge my chair away from her and clear my throat. "Nothing," I say, shooting a look at Oliver. "Just talking sport."

"Boring," Lilly says as she dishes out what looks like properly cooked and very delicious tiramisu. "I think we should say a toast, to welcome our beautiful Bella here to our city."

I watch Isabella as her cheeks pink up again, noting the sparkle in her eyes. Her smile causes slight grooves in her cheeks, a hint of dimples that I want to place my fingers in.

"Dan, do you want to make the toast?" Oliver asks with a silent chuckle.

When did this guy get so annoying?

"I'll pass," I mutter, feeling my heart stumble when I see my response cause the light to dim in Isabella's eyes.

"I'll do it," Lilly says, throwing a puzzled look in my direction. She raises her wine glass and motions for us to follow suit. "To Bella, may you enjoy your time here with us so much that you decide to stay forever."

I watch the three of them clink glasses and I reluctantly raise my own with a sinking feeling in my stomach. Because as much as I'm trying to fight it, I know I already want Isabella to stay here forever. With me.

CHAPTER 6

Bella

I T HAS BEEN RAINING FOR three days straight and as I lie in bed listening to the pitter-patter on the roof, I wonder what happened to spring. My thoughts of Melbourne at this time of year had always included summer dresses and trips to the beach; I didn't sign up for days trudging to work in wet weather, dodging puddles and displeased-looking locals. Though, crappy weather aside, I have no reason to be complaining. The last few days working at the Love, Lilly café have been wonderful. Lilly is the perfect boss because she doesn't act like a boss at all. My own parents had a more hands-on managerial style than her. Spending eight hours a day serving happy customers delicious coffees and treats has been a fulfilling experience, one so different from the days spent wishing the hours away at my parents' deli back home.

"What in the hell?"

A loud, angry voice from somewhere nearby has me shrieking and falling out of bed in one swift motion. I look up to see a tall silhouette in the doorway and I let out a scream. Looking around,

I grab the closest weapon I can see—a lamp—and charge at my would-be assailant, determined to save myself.

"Bella?" the voice has me halting before I can crash the small and ineffectual lamp down on the stranger's head. "Is that you?"

"Luca?" I say at the same time as Daniel, who has rushed to my room, holding a cricket bat and looking determined.

"What's going on here?"

We all look to see Amy arrive just in the nick of time, turning on the light and exposing all the players. Me (with my lamp), Daniel (with his bat) and Lucas looking bewildered.

"Hi, guys. Surprise!" I say in a meek tone, thinking that this reunion is not going the way I wanted.

"Surprise?" he repeats, running his hand through his hair and looking between me and Daniel, a questioning look on his face. "What on earth is going on here?"

I look at Amy with pleading eyes, needing Lucas to be in a calm state of mind before I dump all my unplanned plans on him.

"Babe," she says to her fiancé, taking his hand and instantly soothing him. "Why don't we give Bella—and Daniel—a chance to get dressed before you start the interrogation?"

This seems to draw his attention to the fact that Daniel is wearing only pyjama pants—*oh, yum*—and I'm in my small shortie set. A fact that doesn't please him.

"Fine," he sighs as Amy tugs on his hand. "We'll be in the kitchen making coffee. You two have some explaining to do."

We watch as the two lovebirds head back down the hallway and I send Daniel a nervous smile.

"That went well," I joke.

Daniel snorts. "I don't know why he's angry at me. All I did was take in his lost little sister."

Ouch. I try not to let his honest yet harsh words hurt me and instead turn and re-enter my room, hoping to get this next part out of the way. If I can't get Lucas on board with my plan to stay here, then everything else falls over. He is like the table that is holding my precariously stacked deck of cards.

In a rush, I put on my most comfortable yoga leggings and my new favourite sweatshirt—Daniel's—and hurry to get to the kitchen. Because even though he's confused and somewhat angry that I'm here, Lucas is my brother and I love him more than anything. Having him here with me makes Melbourne seem even more like my home.

"Start talking," he says the minute I've taken my coffee cup and sat down at the small kitchen table. "And you'd better make this good."

I swallow hard and take a deep breath. "I'm here to stay."

He gives me an incredulous look and motions with his hands for me to continue.

"I've moved to be here with you in Melbourne," I elaborate, taking a big sip of coffee for courage.

"Do Mamma and Papa know you're here?"

I roll my eyes at this. "No, I snuck out in the middle of the night," I say in a dry tone, because honestly, what a ridiculous question. "Of course they know! They gave me their blessing to come out here, to have an adventure. You know I wouldn't just up and leave them, especially with the deli and all the extra work that involves."

Lucas dips his chin in acknowledgement. "OK, you're going to need to walk me through this. Obviously, this wasn't a spur-of-the-moment decision."

"No," I agree. "It's something I've wanted to do for a long time, ever since you moved here, really. But I made the decision the day that you two got engaged." I motion between Amy and Lucas. "It just took a while to get everything organised so I could be here with everyone's blessing."

"Well, your English has improved so much since we left you," Amy chimes in with an encouraging smile. "You must have worked hard and really wanted to do this to get so fluent in such a short amount of time." She says this with a meaningful look at my brother, who is still looking at me like he can't believe that I'm here.

"I did," I say, grateful to my almost sister-in-law for her support. "This is something I really want."

"But for how long?" comes the question from the dark-haired man who had been watching this all unfold from his standing position beside the fridge. "It's not like you can stay here indefinitely."

I give Daniel an annoyed look, not happy about his contribution to this conversation, and then ignore him and turn back to my brother.

"Please don't be mad, Luca. This is something I want. I was so tired of being in that village, knowing that there was a whole exciting world out here just waiting to be explored. And what better way to do it than in a place where my big brother will be around to look out for me?"

He tilts his head, acknowledging the thick layer of flattery I'm spreading in his direction, and then lets out a small smile.

"Are you sure Mamma and Papa are OK with you being here?"

I nod, holding my breath for what is coming next.

"Then I guess I have just one thing to say…welcome home, Bella."

Amy lets out a little cheer as she gives me a bear hug, one I return with gusto as tears fill my eyes. Lucas is happy to have me here. That's the last piece in this messy puzzle I've been trying to put together.

"Ahem." The grump in the corner clears his throat, silencing our girly celebration. "While I'm thrilled for this little family reunion, no one here seems to be focused on any practicalities. Like, I don't know? Where is Isabella going to live?"

Lucas gives Daniel a strange look while I send him a frown of my own. *Who invited him to this family meeting, anyway?*

"Why doesn't Bella just stay here?" Amy asks while I squeeze her hand in gratitude.

"Here?" both men repeat in unison, one with confusion, the other in pure horror.

"Sure, why not? She can take your room, babe. You're never here, anyway, so why not let Bella stay here and you can stay with me?"

I watch as Lucas muddles this through in his mind, indecision etched on his face.

"It would mean you're with me every night...in my bed," Amy adds, sweetening the deal and effectively making his mind up.

"OK, that works for me," Lucas says, flashing his heart-shaped eyes at his fiancée.

"Excuse me," comes the voice of doom again. "Do I not get a say in this?"

The three of us turn to look at Daniel, who is not happy about this turn of events.

"Sorry Dan," Lucas says. "We didn't mean to cut you out of the decision. It's just that I'm almost always at Amy's house now anyway and was planning on leaving soon. Now you won't need to look for another roommate..."

I watch Daniel's frown deepen with a sinking feeling. He doesn't want me here, and it's his place. No one should be forced to live with someone they clearly don't like.

"It's OK, Luca," I say, putting my hand on his arm and drawing his attention back to me. "I'll find somewhere else to stay. This is his house; he should decide who he lives with."

My brother gives me a puzzled look before glancing back at his friend.

"But you're my sister. Why wouldn't he want you here?"

Again, all eyes are on Daniel, who is now looking like he wants to be anywhere but here.

"It's nothing personal," he says. "Maybe it's time for me to live alone."

Amy lets out a snort before smothering her smile with her hands. "Dan, I love you, but the one thing you don't need is more 'alone time.' I think having a woman's touch around here will brighten things up."

"And besides," Lucas chimes in. "Bella is easy to live with. You'll barely notice she's here."

Daniel gives me a once over, pausing on his sweatshirt that I'm wearing with a pained expression. His eyes lock on mine, which I know are shamelessly pleading with him to let me stay, and he gives a reluctant nod.

"How about Isabella stays for a trial period," he says, rushing to continue when Lucas looks like he's going to argue. "To see if we're *both* happy with the living arrangement."

"That seems fair," Amy says, sending me a beaming smile.

"I'm OK with that," Lucas adds.

Everyone turns to me. "Of course, I'm OK with that!"

"Good, it's settled. I'll feel better knowing Bella is staying somewhere safe, with someone I trust watching over her."

"Luca," I protest. "I'm not a little girl. I don't need your friend looking out for me."

"Nevertheless, Dan, you're one of my best friends. I know you'll keep an eye on her."

I watch as my brother's said friend gives me another long look, causing the now customary goosebumps to take up residence all over my body, and I sigh. I wish he would keep his eyes on me…and not just his eyes. His hands too…

"Bella? Are you listening to me?"

I snap out of my lust-filled thoughts to see Lucas staring at me with raised eyebrows.

"Sorry? My mind wandered off," I tell him, feeling my cheeks flush as Amy gives me a knowing smile. How obvious had my thoughts been?

"I said that I'll come back later today with some boxes and move my stuff out of my room."

Butterflies take off in my stomach. I'm so excited, I offer to pack up his stuff. When Amy jumps in to say she'll help me, it officially cemented the decision for me to move in.

"Don't worry," I say to Daniel as I pass him to head to my new room. "I'll be the best roommate a person could ask for. So good, in fact, that you'll never want me to leave."

I hear a muted sigh as I leave the room. "That's what I'm afraid of."

"Tell me everything."

Amy and I have been working ineffectively for the past hour, chatting and putting together piles of clothes in the most inefficient packing attempt known to man. Lucas is going to kill us when he gets back with the boxes and sees the mess we've created under the guise of helping. Really, we should've just gone out for brunch instead.

"I have told you everything. You know about all the studying I did to improve my English, how I got here and found you guys were away, how Lilly generously gave me a job. What else is there to tell?"

She shoots me a look. "Tell me everything about what's going on with you and that handsome man you now live with."

My cheeks flame as I avoid making eye contact with her. *Is my little crush so obvious to the outside world?*

"What do you mean?" I stall for time.

"Well, the Daniel I know is quiet and reserved, but never rude. The sense I got from him is that he wants you anywhere but here."

My heart sinks at this description. "He just hasn't seemed to like me, from the minute I got here. He actively avoids being around me, no matter how nice and pleasant I try to be."

"Hmmm," Amy says, smiling. "That is strange."

"I know! I'm lovely. Why doesn't he like me?"

She looks at me, taking in the sweatshirt with raised eyebrows, before shaking her head a little. "He's been through a lot," she says somewhat cryptically. "And he's slow to let people close. Be patient with him. He's a great guy once you get to know him."

"I don't doubt that," I say, perhaps a bit too eagerly. "I guess I'll just have to work harder to get him to like me."

Amy leans over to give me a small hug. "You don't need to worry about that, Bella. I don't think liking you is the issue here."

Before I can decode this statement, Lucas opens the door, arms filled with boxes, followed by the grumpy-looking Daniel.

"Between the four of us, I think we can get me packed and out of here today." Lucas frowns as he takes in the room. "Though, from the looks of things, you two have achieved next to nothing over the past hour."

"I wouldn't say nothing." Amy puts her arm around my shoulder and grins at my brother. "Bella and I have bonded some more. I'm so pleased she's here to stay."

At these words, I notice Daniel give a visible start and I grimace inside. I'm really going to have to prove my worth to him so he won't regret his decision and ask me to leave. Starting tomorrow, I'm putting into place Operation Perfect Roommate. It's going to be great.

CHAPTER 7

Bella

T HINGS WITH OPERATION 'WIN MY grumpy-but-oh-so-gorgeous roommate over' (the title of this plan may have morphed over the days) have not been going well. Everything I've tried to get him onside has only seemed to annoy him more. First, I thought being quiet and inconspicuous would work, but then he saw me tip-toeing past him in the hallway and he scowled at me. So, I moved to being that super-neat, always cleaning housemate, vacuuming and dusting like a maniac, but all that earned me was a few dirty looks. Nothing I did appeared to have the desired effect, which was to make myself indispensable to him.

"It's hopeless," I whine over the counter to my new friend Amelia, who has popped into Love, Lilly for lunch and a gossip session. She and I have become fast friends ever since we bonded over my fabulous new haircut and our mutual love of Pacey Witter.

"Why don't you try to just act like a normal person?" she asks as I hand her a coffee and one of Lilly's famous brownies. "You're pretty awesome when you're not acting all needy."

I laugh along with her, not taking any offense because what she's saying is true. I am acting like a crazy person, desperate for a boy to like me.

"Point taken," I say. "But I'm just going to try one more thing..."

Amelia groans. "What is it? I'm worried you've gone over to the dark side."

"Nothing too extreme," I assure her. "I'm going to cook him dinner tonight. It's the only skill he hasn't seen yet and you have to admit, a roommate who can cook is an instant winner. Is it not?"

She smiles and gives me a small fist bump before devouring the treat in front of her. "That actually sounds like a decent plan. And you know the way to a man's heart is through his stomach."

I quickly shake my head at her. "That's not what's happening here and you know it. I'm just trying to make him like me, so I won't have to move. There's no wanting to win anyone's heart."

My friend grins at me in an annoyingly condescending way and lets me get away with my blatant lie.

"So, what are you planning on cooking tonight?"

I detail the recipe I'd settled on after far too many hours of deliberation. Homemade gnocchi with a tomato and basil sauce. It's one I've made many times with my mamma and I'm feeling pretty confident that, after Daniel has tasted my cooking, he'll have to give in and accept me as his permanent roommate...and friend.

"That's a lot of pressure you're placing on one meal," Amelia tells me as she's saying goodbye.

"It's fine. I've got everything under control."

Three hours later, working in a kitchen that doesn't appear to have the basic cooking essentials, it turns out I don't, in fact, have everything under control. How have these men been able to live here without a stand mixer or a cast iron pan or even a rolling pin? Everything has taken me longer than expected, and by my current calculations, Daniel will be home soon (not that I know his schedule off by heart or anything) and not only is dinner not ready, but the kitchen is a bomb site. This is not the impression I was hoping to give on my last-ditch attempt to fulfil my operation 'best roomie' plan.

"What's going on in here?"

I jump a mile in the air and only just manage not to drop the open jar of passata in my hands.

"You scared me!" I say as I turn to look at him.

He's leaning against the doorframe looking delicious in a pair of worn blue jeans and a black t-shirt. His hair is wet from the shower I know he takes at the fire station before he gets home every day (again, not stalking his every move or anything).

"I'm cooking us dinner," I tell him in a voice that is filled with confidence I'm not feeling.

He looks around at the disaster that used to be his neat kitchen and smirks. A look I often see that I should take offence to; instead, it makes my knees wobble.

"Do you need some help?" he shocks us both by asking.

"Um, I know it doesn't appear so, but I have everything under control."

His doubtful gaze sweeps the room and I have to admit, things look grim. There's flour all over the counter and bits of tomato sauce dripping from the stove. But what does he expect? It's like cooking in the Flintstones' kitchen.

"How about I keep you company while you cook, then?"

My mouth drops open at this offer and I'm unable to form a cohesive response. Who is this Daniel and what happened to the man who spent the last week actively trying to avoid being in the same kitchen as me?

"Or I could just leave you to it?" he says, rubbing his jaw and looking uncomfortable, snapping me out of my overly long introspection.

"No!" I all but yell at him. "You stay. Sit. We can talk while I cook."

He grins at me, a smile so foreign on his usually solemn face that it has me a little breathless.

"How about you cook and I'll clean around you?"

Delighted by this opportunity to have him nearby and also to not have to clean up the mess I've just made, I agree instantly and we both get to work: me creating a culinary masterpiece (and some more mess) and him mopping up around me.

"So, how was work today?" I ask once I have the pasta rolled and cut into perfect gnocchi pillows.

Daniel sighs. "It was fine. Luckily no major events, just a few terrible car accidents that we had to attend. Those are always hard."

"But the risk to you is less in those situations?" I ask, wanting to know everything about his job, especially the parts where he's not putting himself in danger every day.

"Mostly, we are just called to the scene as protocol and aren't always needed. And today was one of those days. A good day," he finishes up, almost like he's talking to himself. "What about you? How's work going?"

I turn away from where he's wiping the flour off the bench top, a wide smile on my face, excited that my plan is working. *Look at us, bonding.*

"I love it there," I tell him in full sincerity. "Everyone is so nice to work with, especially Lilly, who I love. The customers are all so happy to be there. The space is so warm and inviting."

He gives me a warm smile of agreement. "I love it there, too. It's the sort of place you can go and just be. You know? With a good cup of coffee and a cookie, you can sit for hours and not notice the time. Lilly has done an amazing job with the space."

I must be gaping at him because he laughs and wipes his hand over his face in a self-conscious gesture. "What?"

"Nothing," I stammer, unable to tear my eyes away from his animated face. "I've just never heard you speak so much in one sentence."

He laughs at this. "I don't always have a lot to say."

"That I know to be true," I agree, laughing with him. "And hey, I've never seen you at Love, Lilly. Are you avoiding your favourite place because I work there?"

His cheeks heat up a little, and I watch in fascination as he shifts in discomfort. It seems he has been forgoing his Lilly treats because of me.

Before he can either confirm or deny this, the timer chimes in and dinner is ready.

"Saved by the bell," I tell him with a sly smile. "Do you want to set the table while I finish putting this together?"

Mr. Suddenly Agreeable does what he's told and before too long we are sitting together devouring the food in front of us.

"You know, from the state of the kitchen when I got home, I didn't think I'd be saying this, but this is the most delicious pasta dish I've ever tasted."

My entire body heats up at this compliment and I beam at him, pleased that my cooking has found a crack in his armour.

"You can thank my Nonna for the recipe. She passed it to my mamma before she died and then Mamma passed it on to me. It's been in my family for generations."

"And for good reason," he says through another mouthful. "It's amazing."

"Well, there's more of these sorts of meals in your future...if you'd agree to let me stay."

I hold my breath. My words have his hand paused mid-air, fork frozen halfway to his mouth.

"Is that why you've done this? Why you've been cleaning like a maniac? So I'll let you stay?"

"Well, yes," I say, noting his downcast expression. "I want to make myself both useful and indispensable."

"Isabella," he responds in a voice that is deeper than before. "I know I haven't been overly welcoming." I snort at this understatement and he smiles before continuing. "But you don't have to become my housekeeper to stay."

"I know that," I hasten to reassure him. "I just don't want you to have a reason to kick me out."

"Kick you out?" he repeats before swearing faintly under his breath. "OK, let's get one thing straight. You're Lucas's sister and that guy has been like family to me, so despite the impression I've been giving, there isn't a circumstance that I can envision where I will kick you out."

I feel the knot in my stomach that I hadn't known was there loosen and I reach over to squeeze his hand, sending tingles up my arm in the process.

"Thank you, Daniel," I say in a wobbly voice filled with emotion. "I'm so grateful to hear you say that."

He looks down at where my hand is holding his and then back up to my eyes, which are probably wet with tears, and I swear for a moment I think he's going to lean over and kiss me, but then he blinks and pulls his hand away. Moment gone, if it was ever there in the first place.

"I'm going to load these into the dishwasher and then head up to bed," he says, pointing to the now empty plates in front of us and standing up to move away.

"Bed?" I look at the clock on the wall. "It's only eight o'clock. Maybe we could..." I trail off, not wanting to ask him for more of his time, but also wanting all of his time.

"We could...?" he asks, his back to me while he washes the final pan in the sink.

"Watch some TV together?" I ask, feeling lame. Although he's been nice to me this evening, it doesn't mean he's suddenly my watch-TV-on-the-couch-friend.

He glances over his shoulder at me, and perhaps something in my face makes up his mind because where it had looked like he was going to say no, he surprises me by saying, "OK, what are we watching?"

And that's how I found myself fifteen minutes and a cleaned kitchen later, on the couch with Daniel watching *Dawson's Creek*.

"What is this show about again?" he asks as he struggles to follow along with the plot, given I've launched him into an episode halfway through season three (AKA my favourite season).

"It's *Dawson's Creek*. A show from the 90s about teenagers who talk and act like adults. I love it so much."

He looks over at me with an indulgent smile and nods. "I know this one. My mum used to love it."

"Well, she has great taste," I tell him.

"She did," he said in a low voice, causing my mind to come to a screeching halt.

DID? I search through my brain for any mention of Daniel's family in my conversations with Lucas and come up empty. Does this mean his mamma has passed away? I feel my heart break for him, wanting to offer him comfort for a pain I can only imagine.

"So, let me get this straight. Pacey is in love with Joey? And so is his best friend Dawson?" he asks, confused.

I sigh and put away my thoughts about Daniel and his mamma, focusing on the ultimate teen love triangle instead.

"Yes, they both love her. And why wouldn't they? She's smart and witty and so beautiful. Do you think she's beautiful?"

He stares at the screen in quiet contemplation while I hold my breath. If he doesn't love Joey, then we have a fight brewing in our very near future. "She's very beautiful," he finally agrees. "She looks like you."

We both freeze at this, the implications of his words reverberating around the room.

"I-I just mean, she has brown hair and blue eyes, like you," he stumbles while running his hands through his hair, his cheeks stained with red.

"Of course, I understand. Yes, we look similar," I agree, wanting to diffuse the awkwardness in the room, while my inner diva is dancing happily in my brain yelling, "He thinks I'm gorgeous!" over and over again.

"Well, that's me done for the night." He pushes up to his feet, looking around the room, actively avoiding my eyes. "Thanks for dinner. I'll see you around."

I smother a laugh at how uncomfortable he is and give him a little wave. "See you around, roomie!"

With a satisfied smile, I watch him leave and then settle back onto the couch to watch my show. The night had been a success; he loved my cooking and has no plans to get rid of me. As a bonus,

I think we may also be on our way to becoming friends. I'd say my mission to become the 'number one roommate' is now complete.

CHAPTER 8

Bella

D URING THE WEEKS FOLLOWING MY successful plan to squirm my way into Daniel's good books, I've settled into a routine of sorts. I spend most of my time either at work or out with friends. Yes, to my delight, I have found my friend-family here in Melbourne and I couldn't be happier about it. Both Lilly and Amy have embraced me into their lives, including inviting me to be a part of their book club (which I love). And Amelia has proven to be the ultimate girly girl, insisting we go shopping together, have lots of breakfast dates before work and many late-night messaging conversations. To think I've only been here for four weeks and I've already filled my life with a fun job and amazing people to spend time with; it's more than I'd dared to hope for when I bought my ticket here.

And to top it all off, my roommate and I seem to have reached a level of comfort with each other, where I'm no longer walking on eggshells, scared of annoying him and being shipped off to the nearest hotel (or Amy's place). He's been pleasant to be around, no longer scowling or grunting at me, and I'm taking this as a minor victory of sorts. So what if we aren't besties like I'd hoped. *Baby steps, Bella. Baby steps.*

The only downside that I can see from my decision to move to the other side of the world is the fact that while I'm over here, my favourite sport, my one true passion in life, Formula One racing, is taking place in Europe. Unfortunately, race times start at midnight Aussie time on a Sunday. And that's how I find myself here, right now, cuddled under a blanket, wearing my Ferrari team shirt, yawning and struggling to keep my eyes open. It's 11.55 p.m., almost time for 'lights out' and as I'm glued to the TV in front of me, I'm already dreading having to wake up for work in the morning. Really, there needs to be a better way to do this.

I'm just about to doze off, four laps into the already non-eventful race, with the pole sitter already miles ahead of the pack when disaster strikes.

"Charles. Box. Box. We have to retire the car."

"No, no, no!" I yell at the screen. Not again. What is wrong with this stupid team? Every week, something happens to one of the Ferrari cars. How are we supposed to win a championship with a car that breaks every two minutes?

I'm busy yelling this at the TV, in Italian—because it's easier to be angry in my native language—when a chuckle from the doorway has me gasping in fright.

"What are you doing?" I ask, my heart racing in anger and fear.

"What am *I* doing?" Daniel asks his eyebrows raised. *"I'm* not the one hurling obscenities at the television in the middle of the night."

I have the grace to feel shame for waking him up, especially when his work schedule is all over the place and he needs his sleep. "I'm sorry I woke you. I was trying to be quiet."

He laughs at this. "Trying? You were so loud that I'm pretty sure the neighbours are calling the police."

I glance out the front window nervously, hoping he's only joking, and then look back at the screen. Just in time to see the Red Flag being called because Charles Leclerc's car is stuck in the middle of the track.

"*Squadra stupida*," I mutter at the TV. *Stupid Team. They don't deserve my loyalty.*

"What are you watching?" Daniel asks as he takes a seat on the other end of the couch, too far away from me if I'm being honest with myself. Which I'm not.

"I'm watching my Ferrari team break the hearts of millions of Italians by being completely incompetent," I tell him in a huff.

He looks at me and then at the TV, a small frown wrinkling his brow. "You like car racing?"

Why does he sound so confused? Doesn't everyone? "Of course. I'm Italian." I say this to him like it explains everything. Which it should.

"But it's barely even a sport. What's got you so riled up?"

I gape at him, torn between throwing a pillow or a fist at his face. Barely even a sport!

"Please tell me you're joking," I plead with him, wondering if this is the moment when my little crush on him dies.

"I mean, not really. It's just a bunch of cars driving around in a circle for ninety minutes. I mean, what am I missing?"

I stare at him, speechless, while I try to gather my thoughts. There is so much to teach him and so little time.

"What you're missing is everything. There's so much more to it. Strategy, driver conflicts, team rivalries, cost-cap breaches and development budgets. It all comes into every weekend and then a win can come down to a difference of 0.004 seconds between two cars. It's the epitome of an elite sport."

"But it's...boring," he says, watching me with a hint of amusement, almost like he's enjoying baiting me in this way.

And I can't say I'm not taking the bait, because how can any sane human being not understand the brilliance of Formula One?

"It is *not!*" I shout at him, officially fed up with his ignorance. "See, look here. We've had a Red Flag because the stupida Ferrari car is so unreliable. Stupid team. Anyway, that means the race is neutralised and the race leader, who had been cruising towards victory, now essentially has to start again." I go on to explain the logistics of a re-start, creeping closer to where he is sitting so that he can see from my body language just how imperative it is for him to like my favourite sport.

"So, what you're saying is that the race leader, this Max guy, did all this hard work and now needs to start again?"

"Yes!" I exclaim, happy that he's getting it. "Isn't it wonderful?"

"Not if you're Max," he mutters, sitting forwards in his seat, his arms on his knees.

"True," I say. "But good for the one Ferrari driver left in this race. And if he gets off to a good start, we have a chance for a podium finish."

With my eyes glued to the screen ahead, I feel rather than see him scoot a little closer to me, the side of my body basking in the heat coming from his.

"Is it happening soon? The excitement?" he whispers sarcastically into my ear, making me turned on and furious at the same time.

"Yes," I hiss. "Just you wait."

We sit in silence as the cars get into position at the starting grid. I watch as they prepare for the restart and say a brief prayer that this one remaining car survives until the end of the race.

"It's lights out and away we go."

I hold my breath and grab onto Daniel's thigh, gripped by the action in front of me.

"Go, go, go!" I yell as the cars round the first corner, the Ferrari only just narrowly avoiding the path of one of the Red Bull cars. "Yes!" I scream as we take second place with a nifty overtake on the inside line. "That's it!"

Unable to control my excitement, now no longer needing to be quiet, I jump up and start doing a very pre-emptive victory dance. I know there's a long way to go, 57 laps to be exact, but this is a good start.

"That's it, keep it up. You can do it," I yell at the TV.

"Um, Isabella?" Daniel's deep voice brings me back into the room. I'd completely forgotten he was there for a second.

"Yes?" I ask, my eyes never leaving the screen. You just never know when things may go wrong.

"I thought we'd spoken about this," he says, forcing me to look at him to see what he's talking about. "About a certain dress code."

This now has my full attention as I look at Daniel looking at me. At my bare legs, more specifically. I'd come to watch the race in just my Ferrari team t-shirt and now the look on his face as he runs his eyes all over my body has me blushing the same colour as my shirt. Fiercely red.

"I didn't think you'd be here to see me," I tell him, keeping my tone hushed to not break the spell. To not take that look off his face.

"Either way," he says finally, blowing out a deep breath. "I think the ground rules must stay in place."

"And those are?" I ask, both curious and amused by his reaction.

"Pants are to be worn at all times in any common area," he says, his voice firm while his eyes travel back to where my t-shirt ends on my thigh.

"Got it," I tell him, feeling cheeky and also powerful. Daniel can't seem to look away from me and it's making my heart race faster than the cars on the screen. "Pants on at all times. What about tops?"

He splutters and starts coughing while I laugh and pat him on the back. "Just kidding, Dan. I'll be very respectful from now onward. Covered from head to toe."

"You don't need to go to that extreme," he mutters once he has his breath back. "But just some more material is what I'm asking for."

"Aye, aye, captain," I say as a crash in the race diverts my attention. "No! No!"

We both sit together and watch as they show the wrecked car, with the driver emerging unharmed and another Red Flag is called.

"See? So exciting!" I say to Daniel, hoping he's catching on.

"How about I take you to an Aussie Rules football game and show you a sport that's actually exciting?"

My breath catches at the casually issued invitation and I do my best to not appear overly eager in my response.

"I'd love that!" *Great. Good job playing it cool, Bella.*

He smiles at me, his dimple popping. "The next season starts in March. Do you think you'll still be here, then?"

I look at his handsome face, illuminated by just the glow of the TV and think to myself that being with him like this makes me never want to leave.

"I'll be here then," I whisper, loving his sunny smile in response. "Besides, the Melbourne Grand Prix is in March, so I'm definitely not going anywhere."

"So that's your reason to stay?" he asks, his voice deeper than before, his face closer to mine.

"It's one of many," I whisper back, caught up in the moment, wondering if he's feeling this 'thing' between us as acutely as I am.

"Good," he says in a satisfied tone, sitting back and taking his heat and the moment with him. "Then it's a date."

What's a date? I think as I watch him stand up and stretch, getting distracted by the expanse of muscled abs being flashed my way as his t-shirt rises.

"Date?" I finally manage to ask, my eyes lingering on the spot where his t-shirt meets his pants. "What date?"

Daniel smiles at me, a sweet smile that feels like it's filled with promise. "Next March. Izzy, I'm taking you to the footy."

With a little wave and that bucket of cold water of an announcement, he leaves the room. And I'm left to watch the rest of the race in a daze. Because I want Daniel to ask me out on a date for real. Here and now. And that's going to be a big problem.

DECEMBER

CHAPTER 9

Bella

I DIDN'T KNOW THERE WAS anything else to discover to make me love
Melbourne more, but then I met Snickers, the dog. I first saw
him when we went to Lilly and Oliver's place for dinner. He was a
blur of fur who had been put in a time-out outside after one too
many stolen treats from the kitchen bench. And then last Tuesday
night, after my now well-dissected and over-analysed midnight
meeting with Daniel, I attended Amy's book club and got to see
Snickers in all his furry glory.

I fell in love with him on the spot. Lilly and Oliver's dog is the
cutest thing I've ever seen and when leaving that night, I'd had to
force myself not to put him in my bag and kidnap him (or dog-nap
him, as the case may be). He's what they call a Spoodle (a poodle
crossed with a cocker spaniel) and is a soft bundle of chocolate
brown and caramel-coloured fur. Sure, he'd been quirky and
jumped at the slightest noise above a whisper, but once he got
used to being around me, he'd curled up on my lap and fallen asleep
instantly. And there he'd stayed for the entire evening, like a little
warm emotional support blanket.

So in love with him did I fall that I'd offered to dog-sit him this coming weekend, while Lilly and Oliver take a mini-break. It hadn't entered my mind that Daniel wouldn't approve. A point against my new status as world's best roommate, I guess.

"Please, Dan?" I ask, attempting to get him to change his mind. "He won't be any trouble."

He gives me a look filled with derision and snorts. "Have you met this dog? He's only trouble. Last week, Oliver told me Snickers stole his toothbrush, and they had to chase him around the yard for twenty minutes. And they never ended up getting it back. That is not a well-behaved dog."

I pick up my phone and show him the selfie that I took of the two of us together. In it, I'm smiling and Snickers is licking my eye. It's adorable.

"But look how cute he is," I try again. "And it's just for one night."

"No can do, Izzy," he says, making my heart jump at his nickname for me. I love that he calls me something different from everyone else. It makes me feel special. "I'm going to be away this Saturday night, so I won't be here to help you. And believe me, it takes more than one person to look after that fur ball."

My attention is now caught on the information that he's going to be away on the weekend and now I'm dying to know where he's going and with whom.

"You're going away?" I ask in my most casual tone.

"Yes," comes his oh-so-descriptive answer.

"Anywhere special?" I try again.

Daniel smiles at me, like he's on to my not-so-subtle attempts to be nosy. "Just going camping with a couple of my mates from the station. Leaving early on Saturday, I should be back Sunday night." He pauses and looks at me. "Are you going to be OK staying here by yourself?"

I bristle at the implication that I can't look after myself. "I'll be fine. Even better if I have a guard dog looking after me..."

He snorts again at this. "That dog jumps at his own shadow. I think you'd be better off with that lamp for protection."

With a laugh, I concede that both Snickers and the lamp are ineffective weapons and then call Lilly to tell her the bad news.

"That's OK, Bella," Lilly says after I've explained that the grinch Daniel won't allow Snickers to come over to play. "We'll figure something out. Maybe we can take him with us?"

"Not happening," I hear Oliver's voice faintly in the distance. "If we can't leave him behind, we'll have to postpone."

I feel terrible at the thought that these two will have to miss out on their couples' weekend and so I do something out of character for me: I decide to ignore specific instructions.

"Hey, Lil? I've changed my mind. I'll look after Snickers this weekend."

"But what about Daniel? Didn't he say no?" she asks, sounding puzzled.

"Well, yes. But I'm confident I can change his mind. And if not, well, he won't be here and what he doesn't know won't hurt him."

There's silence on the other end of the line, and I can almost hear the wheels turning in her mind. On the one hand, she doesn't want to be dishonest with Daniel, and on the other, she really wants to go away for a romantic weekend with her hunky husband.

"Sounds like a plan to me," she says eventually, getting on board with the subterfuge.

"Really?" I ask, shocked that she's willing to be devious with me.

"Bella, remind me to tell you the story of how I got Snickers in the first place. I didn't exactly have Oliver's buy-in on getting a dog that day, and yet here we are."

I grin to myself, loving Lilly's free-spirited ways and we make plans for Lilly to drop the dog off mid-morning, once Daniel had left for the weekend.

"You sure you want to do this? Snickers can be a bit of work."

I look at the photo of him on my phone and melt. "Of course I'm sure. How hard can one small dog be?"

Famous last words, I mutter to myself as I look at Snickers, who is now covered head to toe in mud. Not a single strand of his fur is the colour it once was.

"How did you do this?" I hiss at him, looking around to see only dry dirt and not a single patch of mud anywhere. "Like, where did you go to find all this mud?"

The dog wags his dirty tail at me and sits, offering me his paw.

"Don't try to win me over by being cute," I tell him as I put his leash back on his collar, regretting taking it off in the first place. "What am I going to do with you now?"

I've been asking myself this same question since Lilly left him on my doorstep (after Daniel had left to go camping, still unaware that I have become a dog-mum for the weekend). The moment I let him loose in the house, he ran from room to room, eventually emerging with one of Daniel's t-shirts around his neck and my shoe in his mouth. What followed was a 'game' of chase, where I attempted to retrieve our clothing and he ran away from me at the speed of light. After he tired of that and relinquished his treasured items, he went out back and started digging a hole. Knowing that Daniel wouldn't be pleased with this—and also, how would I explain all the random holes in the backyard?—I decided to take him for a walk to the local park. And it's that decision that led me here, to a dog that is covered in a now-dried thick coat of mud.

"Bath time it is for you, I guess," I tell him as we trudge home. Snickers barks in response and wags his tail some more, hopefully a sign that he likes baths.

I make my way through the side gate into the backyard and tie the leash to a tree.

"You sit and wait," I tell him in a stern voice while patting his head. "I need to find some sort of big bucket."

As I walk into the laundry, I google what sort of shampoo or soap I can use on dogs and then hurry to gather everything I need to get Snickers clean again. I find an empty rubber tub that looks about the right size and grab a bar of soap. After I've filled the bucket with water using the garden hose, I coax, pull and eventually carry the dog to his bath.

"You are more trouble than you're worth," I tell him after the third time he'd escaped from the bath. His slippery, soapy body is proving very difficult to grab a hold of and once he's out I have to chase him around the yard before carrying him back to the tub. The whole thing is both exhausting and an exercise in futility.

"If you stay still, I'll give you a treat," I say, watching his ears prick up. "Oh, so that's it. You'll behave for treats."

Snickers sits still and is a perfect dog for the rest of the bath time. It takes almost a complete bar of soap and all of my strength to get the mud off him, but once I'm done, he's back to looking good again. Well, as good as a drowned rat can look.

"I think I need to blow dry your fur," I tell him, my voice doubtful, because that seems like another painful task. "Because I can't let you roam around the house with wet fur, and if I leave you out here, you'll just get dirty again."

Decision made, I carry him into the house and over to the bathroom, where I place him on the toilet seat.

"Stay," I tell him while I grab my hairdryer. "Good boy."

Snickers barks in reply and I get to work, blow drying his fur and talking to him in a soothing voice to keep him in place.

"You're such a wonderful dog," I croon to him as I brush his fur and he licks my chin. "The best dog."

"Is he really?" a deep voice from behind me has me screaming in fear, ready to throw my hairdryer at the would-be assailant.

"Some guard dog you are," the same voice continues, while Snickers wags his tail and does nothing to protect either of us. *Daniel. I'm so busted.*

I turn around with what can only be guilt written all over my face to see him standing just outside the door, an amused grin on his face. "What are you doing here?"

"I think the bigger question is, what is *he* doing here?"

I bite my lip and look between the two men in the room, getting distracted by trying to figure out which one is cuter. Snickers has just had his hair done, so he's looking pretty good, but Daniel is wearing a tight t-shirt, so let's call it a tie.

"Izzy?" Daniel interrupts my thoughts, walking towards me and turning off the hairdryer. "I thought we agreed no Snickers here this weekend?"

"Yes, well, when I told Lilly I couldn't look after the dog, it sounded like they were going to cancel their plans. And I didn't want to do that. Lilly's been so good to me, offering me a job and inviting me into her life..." I trail off feeling bad for having lied to him. It's his house; he should be able to trust the person who's living in it.

"I'm really sorry I lied to you," I tell him. "It was wrong of me."

He looks at me, his gaze taking in my wet clothes and wild hair—it had been a hectic morning—and he does something that shocks me. He laughs.

"It's OK," he says, reaching over to pat Snickers, who appears delighted to have a new human to play with. "Lilly and Oliver have been good friends to me too, so I owe them."

I smile in relief and he holds up a finger to stop any further excitement from me. "But let's not make a habit of lying to each other. And sneaking men into the house."

My heart thumps at his words. Doesn't he know the only man I want actually lives in this house? I give him a wide smile of agreement.

"No lying and no secret men."

Daniel rewards me with his big grin, the one that seems to make a more regular appearance these days, and then he picks up the dog and walks out of the room, whispering to Snickers as he goes "What other trouble are you going to cause this weekend?"

A few hours and a lot of playing 'catch' with Snickers later, he's finally worn himself out and is curled in a ball on the couch next to Daniel. I've offered to make a conciliatory dinner to make up for the whole lying debacle.

"You haven't told me why you're home early," I call to him from my spot next to the stove. This is all feeling very domesticated of us: me in the kitchen, him on the couch watching sports.

"Oh?" he responds after a minute. "When I got to the station, a few guys had to cancel and then the whole thing kind of fell apart."

I walk to the living room and my heart literally goes pitter-patter when I see him snuggled up with the dog. The sight of this particular big, strong man gently patting a small fur baby has me melting.

"That's a shame," I say once I've got myself back under control. "You seemed to be really looking forward to it. Now instead, you're stuck here with me and that monster."

Daniel looks down at the dog snoring quietly next to him and then back up at me. "It's not the worst thing, being here with you two."

I take this as the highest praise and all but skip back to the kitchen, determined to cook him the best dinner he's ever had. Snickers and I have been the real winners here this weekend.

CHAPTER 10

Daniel

I WATCH BELLA LEAVE THE room and feel bad for lying to her. But it's not like I can tell her the truth. That I got to the station and decided I didn't want to leave her for the entire weekend, so I cancelled a camping trip I'd been planning for ages, just so I can spend time with her? I mean, there's no way I can let her know any of this.

"Snickers, I've got to get it together," I mutter to the little ball cuddled in beside me. "How did it come to this?"

I know the answer to this question. My carefully constructed walls started to crumble the night Bella cooked me dinner. I'd been doing so well to keep her at arms-length, ensuring we didn't spend too much time alone, only engaging in conversation when I absolutely couldn't avoid it...and then I came home and found her in a mess, trying so hard to be my friend. I could see it in her every expression. She so badly wanted me to like her—what a joke. Little does she know how far beyond like I am, that I'd only been acting like a jerk. And all of a sudden, I couldn't do it anymore. I couldn't continue to be the one to put that sad look on her face.

So, I'd offered to help in the kitchen and she'd looked at me like I'd hung the moon. And that was me done. My ability to keep away from her had disappeared and in its place is this desperate need to be around her all the time. Leading to the predicament I'm in now: cancelling plans with friends to sit at home on the couch with her.

"Stay away from girl dogs, little bud," I whisper to the dog. "Nothing good can come of it."

"What are you two chatting about?" Bella asks me from the doorway. Her face is flushed, and she has pulled her hair back into a small ponytail, her bangs pinned to the side. She looks messy and heart-stoppingly gorgeous. She doesn't need a single extra thing to look beautiful. Her beauty just is.

"Oh nothing, just guy talk," I say while nudging the dog to be silent.

"Well, if you can tear yourself away from our unwanted guest," she tells me with a little ironic smirk. "Dinner's ready."

And here's another thing, I think as I follow her back to the kitchen. Bella is not only gorgeous, witty and sassy, but she's also an amazing cook. It's like I never stood a chance.

"What have you cooked for me tonight?"

"Homemade pizza," she tells me with a cheerful grin. "I made the dough from scratch, just like we do at home."

I look down at the plate in front of me and see two giant, mouth-watering slices of pizza. "Where's the pineapple?" I joke, knowing from my time living with Lucas that this is the ultimate insult to an Italian person.

As predicted, her face flushes bright red while her jaw drops. Before she can get heated any further—I've seen what she's like with the Formula One—I laugh.

"I'm joking, I'm joking," I say as she throws a tea towel at my head, scowling at me as she sits down.

"You'd better be," she says, taking a bite of her pizza and letting out a little moan that has my stomach clenching. "Because not liking Formula One is one thing, but pineapple on a pizza? Well, that would be the end of us."

I feel myself choke a bit at her choice of words and take a big gulp of water, trying to not focus on my guttural reaction to the thought of us ending. Because that's ridiculous; we haven't even begun. As far as Bella's concerned, we're just roommates, maybe friends, and I can't seem to bring myself to take it further. My grief-stricken heart is still too scared to take the next step.

"So," I say, to change the subject. "Any plans for you and the pooch tonight?"

She smiles another big smile at me. "There's another Grand Prix on tonight. Snickers and I are going to watch it together."

I picture the two of them together on the couch and know I want to be there, too. Even if car racing is supremely boring, cuddling on the couch with Bella in that Ferrari t-shirt sounds like the perfect night in. Much better than sleeping alone in a cold tent in the woods.

"Sounds nice," I say instead of blurting out how much I want to join her.

"I would ask you to join us," she says, reading my mind, "but I know you don't believe Formula One to be an 'actual' sport, so I won't bother."

I shake my head at her cheeky smile and get up to clear the dishes. Little does she know that there will be three of us watching the race tonight, and I can think of nothing else I'd rather be doing.

At ten minutes to midnight, I head to the living room, followed by Snickers, who, over the course of the evening, has decided I'm his new best friend and has been by my side ever since. He even jumped into bed with me an hour ago, and we both lay there staring at the ceiling, waiting to hear Bella's footsteps in the hallway. Finally, it's race time. Something I never thought I'd hear myself say.

"What are you doing up?" Bella asks me from her spot on the couch.

When did that spot become hers?

"Snickers wanted to watch," I say, lifting the little guy in the air, using him as the perfect cover story.

"Well then, that dog has better taste in sports than you do," she says with a teasing smile, patting the couch next to her and beckoning us to come in.

Neither Snickers nor I need any further invitation, taking a seat next to her and inhaling her intoxicating scent. This alone is worth staying awake until midnight. I look over to see her tuck Snickers under her arm and admonish myself for being jealous of the dog. *Why does he get to snuggle with her?* I've officially lost the plot.

"Now pay attention," she says, drawing my eyes to her profile, as her gaze is fixed on the screen in front of us. "This race is being held in Monaco and is considered the pinnacle of the racing season. Every driver dreams of winning here."

"That means this race should be exciting, then?" I ask, enjoying watching how passionate she is about all of this. Her entire face comes alive when she's talking about it.

"You would think so," she says, turning to me with a slight frown. "But it often ends up being a pretty dull race. There's very little room to overtake, so it kind of ends up being a parade of cars going around."

"So, just a bunch of cars going around in a circle for ninety minutes," I tease her, provoking a predictably annoyed response.

"No. OK. Maybe," she says with a shrug. "Let's wait and see."

The three of us settle back into the couch, closer than we were before—I'm pretty sure I made that happen—and watch the start of the race. True to form, it's pretty uneventful and after fifteen minutes of watching cars zoom past, I decide to use this opportunity to get to know the woman beside me better.

"Tell me more about Lucas as a kid," I say, thinking it best to start with a simple question.

Bella gives me a warm smile as she takes her eyes off the race to face me.

"Luca was the best big brother growing up. Being a few years older, he spent a lot of time away from home studying, but I'd still consider him my best friend. I think I got my sense of adventure through him. Neither of my parents has ever left the country. They say 'Italy is the best place in the world. Why do we need to go anywhere else?'"

She says the last part with a thick authentic Italian accent, making me laugh.

"It always made me feel a bit bad about wanting more."

"More?"

"More than what our little village could provide." She gives me a sheepish look. "I stayed in Florence to go to university and then returned home to work with my parents. I think they just thought I'd marry someone nearby and eventually take over the family business."

I shudder internally at the thought of her marrying someone else. "What did you study at uni?"

"The sort of degree that gets you nowhere in life," she says with a light laugh. "I studied fine arts, thinking maybe one day I'd be an artist."

This is new information to me and I wonder why I'd never heard this before.

"And now you don't think this?"

She gives me a bemused look like she thinks my question is ridiculous. "Of course not. How many people actually make a living from their art?"

"Well, let me ask you this. Are you any good?"

She picks up her phone and starts scrolling. "Here, this is a painting that I did, hanging in my parents' house."

I look at the screen and am stunned by the picture in front of me. It's a landscape of an olive grove at sunset, the sort of painting you can see just about anywhere, and yet she has captured the beauty in a form that almost brings tears to my eyes.

"You did *this?*"

She smiles. Yes.

"Iz, this is amazing. You're truly talented."

Her face lights up at this praise and she takes back her phone, scrolling again and showing me a few more paintings that adorn the homes of various family members.

"You could make money from this," I tell her, poking her foot with mine to get her attention back from the TV in front of us. "You've got a gift."

"Do you really think so?" she asks, her tone wistful.

"I know so," I tell her, in awe of her talent. Just one more thing to add to the incredible woman she is. "Can you...can you paint something for me?"

"Seriously?" she squeals. "Because your bare walls have been driving me crazy!"

I laugh, looking around the room and acknowledging the expanse of plain white walls around us.

"My mum used to have photos of us up everywhere, and after she died, I couldn't look at them. They're all now in a box in a cupboard."

We sit together in silence after my revelation, while I try to sort out why I'd told her that. I never, ever talk about my mum with anyone.

"I'm sorry about your mamma," Bella says. Her gently spoken words soothing me. "And I'll paint you anything you want. I think it's time to get some colour back into your life."

With my heart thumping, I look at the woman sitting next to me, in her Ferrari t-shirt—and probably no pants, God help me—and I have to agree.

"I think I'd like that," I say, my voice also soft.

"Consider it done," she says, moving Snickers out of the way and inching closer to me. With her head resting on my shoulder, we both turn our attention back to the race and I say a silent thank you to whoever or whatever brought her here to me. Because she may be just the person to paint me back to life.

CHAPTER 11

Bella

THINGS BETWEEN ME AND DANIEL have improved so much that I can barely remember a time when we weren't this friendly. Most nights now we end up on the couch together, alternating between watching one of his serial killer documentaries and *Dawson's Creek*, which I know he secretly enjoys, given his frequent requests for 'just one more episode.' We have cemented our routine such that it feels weird to be spending the evening without him.

"But it's girls' night," Amelia says over the phone when I voice this revelation to her. "He can't come."

"I know," I agree while putting the phone on speaker and riffling through my cupboard, trying to find something to wear for the night ahead. Lilly, Amy and Amelia have decided it's time to introduce me to Melbourne's nightlife and have planned an evening out of drinking and dancing. "It's just weird, is all. I went from walking on eggshells around him to wanting to spend all my time with him."

"If you're not careful, that crush will blow out to something more," she says in a serious tone. Amelia has recently had her heart broken and is firmly on the anti-men train.

I pause in the process of trying on a sparkly black mini-dress. *Am I in danger of growing too attached to my handsome roommate?*

"It's not like that," I say with a shake of my head. "We're just good friends. And I've grown to depend on him."

"Sounds like you guys are already an old married couple. Dinner and couch together every night."

A grin fills my face at this very accurate description, and I can't help the warmth that fills my body as I think about our time together. Now that he's quit being a jerk all the time, Daniel is so much fun to be around.

"OK, enough about him. What do you think of this outfit?" I turn on my phone camera and show her the dress I'm considering. It's both short and shows a lot of my cleavage, and I'm not sure if I'm confident enough to pull it off.

"Damn, you look sensational," my friend says with a low whistle. "You're going to be knocking the men back with a stick in that dress."

The only man I want looking at me in this dress is Daniel, and if he were to approve, I wouldn't be knocking him back at all.

"Alright, I'll wear it. Can you come over and do my make-up?"

Amelia's face lights up at this request. She loves a good make-over.

"Give me fifteen minutes to get dressed and then we can sort out our hair and faces together. How does that sound?"

"Perfect. I'll get the wine ready."

After I hang up the phone, I take off my party dress and put on my regular clothes. *No need to be uncomfortable for longer than I need to be,* I think as I make my way downstairs to prepare a cheese platter for my friend.

"What are we watching tonight?" Daniel's voice startles me from the living room and I ponder getting him a bell to wear around his neck. He's always sneaking up on me.

"You're on your own tonight," I tell him, poking my head around the door and seeing him lounging on the couch, looking delightfully rumpled in a pair of basketball shorts and an old t-shirt.

My announcement has his head shooting up. "You're going out?"

"Yes, we're having a girls' night," I say as I walk to the kitchen. "So, you'll just have to pretend you hate watching *Dawson's Creek* all on your own."

"Girls' night?" he asks, following me into the room. "Which girls?"

"My friends," I tell him with a big smile on my face. I'm so proud of having made friends in such a short time. Granted, one of them is going to be my future sister-in-law; nevertheless, that doesn't always guarantee a good relationship. "Amy, Lilly and Amelia."

"Where are you guys going?" he asks with a slight frown.

"They're taking me out for a night of drinking and dancing. Apparently, I'm not a proper Melbournian until I've gotten drunk in Flinders Lane and grabbed a kebab from a food truck on the way home." I say this with a laugh because the whole thing sounds both ridiculous and delightful at the same time.

"Just the girls?" he asks, still with a strange look on his face.

What's he asking me? I wonder, trying to decipher his mood. *Is he annoyed I won't be spending the night with him tonight? Or is he anxious about who else I may spend it with?*

"Just the girls," I reassure him, subtly letting him know that the only guy I'm interested in spending time with is him.

"If you guys get stuck and need a ride home, just call me. OK, Iz? Anytime."

I reach up to kiss him on the cheek as I walk past, lingering a little as my lips brush the slight stubble on his jaw, causing my whole body to shudder in delight. If this is my response to just my lips lightly touching his skin, then I'm in more trouble than I thought.

Daniel's hand presses against my hip to hold me in place, our bodies almost but not quite touching.

"Promise you'll call if you need me," he repeats, his voice a little deeper than normal.

I look up into his warm brown eyes, which are closer than they've ever been, and I have the strongest urge to kiss him. In fact, I think I'm about to when—

"Bella, you here?"

Amelia's voice at the front door has us springing away from each other, Daniel's cheeks flushed a light shade of pink and my entire body vibrating with need.

"In here!" I yell in a breathless tone that sounds nothing like my own.

"Am I interrupting something?" she asks as she enters the room where we are standing, now far apart from each, the air thick with what almost was.

"No," Daniel says, walking over to the fridge and grabbing a beer. "You girls have fun tonight. And be careful." He says this last part while giving me a look.

"Yes, sir," Amelia says with a smile. "Don't worry, I'll look after your girl."

Both Daniel and I start at this description, while I feel a flood of warmth in my belly. Daniel's girl. It has the best ring to it.

"Shut up," I say as I drag her out of the room. "Don't wait up, roomie. We may be home late. These ladies have promised a night to remember."

Three hours later, this has proven to be true. But not in the way I'd hoped. It had all started well; Amelia had done my hair and make-up and I'd left the house feeling a million dollars. The look on Daniel's face as we'd skipped out the door to our waiting Uber had been worth every second that we'd spent getting ready. He'd seemed almost mesmerised by me as I'd floated by and the memory of his expression had kept me company ever since. We'd met up with Amy and Lilly at the first bar where they'd alternated between cocktails and shots and before we'd even gotten to the second place, the nightclub packed with trendy-looking people all tightly packed into a glamourous room, I was drunk. Not used to guzzling alcohol in this way, a wine with dinner more my usual speed, I'd opted to sit down at the bar once we'd arrived while the girls hit the dancefloor and that was the last I'd seen of them. It has been twenty minutes and there's no sign of them.

"What can I get you?" the friendly bartender, who'd been loitering in front of me for a while, now asks.

"Just water? Please?" I order with a half-smile, like I'm apologising for being so lame. Who goes to a club and orders water? Someone who can't hold her alcohol, that's who.

"Sure," he says, handing me a bottle. "Anything else?"

I shake my head and pay the exorbitant fee for something that should be free, hopping off my bar stool and going in search of my friends. Again. *Surely, they haven't left me?* I make my way around the dancefloor, through the middle of the dancefloor and around the dancefloor again, not seeing anyone. Just as I'm about to check the bathrooms, thinking that's got to be where they are, my phone pings in my bag.

AMY: Where are you? We're ready to go to the next place!

The next place? I think, looking at the time. It's already 1 a.m. Surely they don't want to stay out later than this.

BELLA: The next place? I'm ready to go home.

AMY: Really? ☹ OK. We'll come with you.

I feel bad for being a downer, but really, I don't want to drink any more. The effect of the heat inside this club and the alcohol is making my head spin. Just as I'm about to tell them to meet me outside, my phone pings with another message.

DANIEL: How's your night? Having fun?

What's he still doing up? I wonder as my heart rate picks up just from his one message.

BELLA: Ready to go home. The girls want to keep partying ☹

DANIEL: Want me to come get you?

My heart thumps harder at his immediate response, and I so desperately want him to come get me.

BELLA: No, you can't do that. It's late...

I hold my breath while I wait for his response. Which again is almost instantaneous.

DANIEL: Text me where you are and I'll come get you. Make sure the girls wait with you until I'm there.

I can't stop the stupid grin that is pulling on my lips at the thought of Daniel coming to get me. Of the man who once openly disliked me, now venturing out in the middle of the night to pick me up. I open the group chat and text the girls about my change in plans.

BELLA: Ladies, I don't want to ruin the fun, so Daniel is coming to pick me up.

AMY: OMG, Daniel is venturing out at night?

LILLY: Daniel is leaving the house??

AMELIA: Meet us outside. NOW!

With a laugh at their responses, I make my way out of the club, instantly relieved to feel the cool night air on my face.

"What's going on?" Amelia says as soon as they spot me.

"Nothing. He texted to see how the night was going and I told him I was ready to come home."

"So, he jumped at the chance to come and get you?" Lilly asks with a sly grin, while Amy smothers a laugh.

"It's not like that. He's just making sure I get home safely," I protest with a laugh of my own. These girls are so silly.

"He's just making sure you come home. To him," Amelia pipes up. "I saw the look he gave you when we left tonight. He was one second away from bundling you up and refusing to let you leave the house. If jealousy was a person, tonight it was Daniel."

"You have a wild imagination," I tell her while my insides do somersaults at her description. Because I'd felt the same way, that he hadn't wanted me to go out tonight. "He's just being a good friend."

"Well, don't look now," Amy says, pulling me in for a quick hug. "But your 'friend' is here to get you. Though I'm pretty sure in the time I've known Daniel, he's never offered to pick me up from anywhere."

"Me neither," Lilly adds with a hug of her own.

I give them all a little wave as I head to where Daniel has parked his car and is waiting for me. "Have fun! Don't drink too much."

"No promises!" they yell back in unison before bursting into laughter. Boy, they are so drunk.

I step into the comfort of Daniel's car and breathe a sigh of relief. Clearly, I'm not made to be a party girl.

"You doing OK over there?" he asks with a smile. Boy, he's so gorgeous.

"Hmmmm," I reply, leaning my head back and closing my eyes. "Thanks for coming to get me. I can't keep up with them, four drinks and I'm done for the night."

He chuckles and puts the car into gear, driving us away from the club.

"So, are you a true Melbournian now?" he asks after several moments of blissful silence.

I frown a bit, remembering my earlier words. "I think I failed," I tell him, my tone sad. "No food truck kebab."

"I can fix that." He changes lanes and takes a sharp right-hand turn down a side street. "Wait here," he tells me after parking next to a hole-in-the wall kebab store. *He's getting me a kebab?* I think as my mouth waters. I can imagine nothing better in my drunken state than a juicy, chip-laden, garlic sauce-dripping kebab.

"You're my hero," I tell him when he returns to the car several minutes later, his hands filled with two kebabs and a can of Coke. "You don't know how much I want you—I mean this—right now."

Grateful for the darkness inside the car, masking my fiery face after my slip-up—I just all but admitted I want him—I take my food and get to work demolishing it.

"So good," I groan around a mouthful. "Best food I've ever tasted."

Daniel laughs, his deep tone messing with my already spinning head. "You come from the land of the best cuisine in the world, and this back-alley lane kebab is the best thing you've ever eaten?"

I turn to look at him with a very serious expression on my face. "Yes, Daniel. This right here is amazing. You've made my entire night by getting me this. Thank you."

He looks at me, his expression hard to read in the dim light of the car, and then reaches a hand over to lightly stroke my cheek. Right next to my mouth.

"You have a bit of sauce right here," he says, his voice husky.

I feel all wobbly inside, this time not from the alcohol, and have to hold myself back from launching at him. That small touch, like many others we've exchanged in the last few weeks, has set me on fire.

"I'd better get you home," he says with a sigh, turning to put his seatbelt on and effectively breaking the tension between us.

Disappointed, I slink back in my seat with a frown. *Maybe the sexual tension I'm feeling is one-sided and all in my head?*

"You look amazing in that dress," he mutters a few minutes later out of nowhere.

I let out a small grin. *Maybe not.*

CHAPTER 12

Bella

W HAT IS A GIRL TO do the morning after drinking way too much alcohol? Christmas tree shopping! After waking to the unfamiliar effects of a hangover—thumping head, dry mouth, general wooziness—I decide the cure for all my woes will come in the form of Christmas cheer. Something that is decidedly lacking from this house.

"Daniel," I call out from the kitchen after guzzling a bottle of water and now nursing a coffee. "We need to go out."

I decide to be cryptic in my initial request because if my senses are correct, he doesn't seem like the get-into-the-festive-spirit type of guy.

"Where?" is his response from somewhere in the house.

"There's something we desperately need to get. It's time-sensitive," I yell back. How has he not realised it's three weeks until Christmas and the house is still undecorated? Granted, I'd kind of forgotten that it was approaching, the hot weather and lack of snow throwing me off somewhat. A summer Christmas is going to be the most fabulous novelty for me.

"I ask again, where do we need to go? And what do we need to get?" Daniel appears at the doorway of the kitchen, looking no worse for wear after our late-night escapades—unlike me. He's dressed in his usual faded blue jeans and a grey t-shirt. Why must he look so good in something so ordinary?

"Do you know what date it is?" I ask while discreetly wiping the drool from the corner of my mouth, surprised my dehydrated body has any extra liquid to spare.

"Um, the 7th of December," he says, looking at the date on the calendar hanging on the wall. One of the few things adorning any walls in this house.

"That means we have less than three weeks until Christmas," I tell him, downing the rest of my coffee and deciding to forgo breakfast. My late-night kebab is still threatening to make an appearance. "And we don't have a tree."

Daniel looks at me, his eyes doing that sweepy thing over my body, taking in my leggings and oversized t-shirt that keeps slipping off one shoulder, before settling on my face.

"I don't do Christmas," he finally mutters before turning and walking away.

Who doesn't 'do' Christmas? is the only thought in my head as I follow him down the hall and outside to the garage.

"What do you mean, you don't 'do' Christmas? It happens whether or not you're ready."

He pauses in the middle of picking up his toolbox and looks over his shoulder at me.

"Let me amend my statement. I don't like Christmas and I refuse to get involved in any of the festivities."

Stumped by this—because how is this even possible?—I try again. "But...but it's like the most wonderful time of the year," I say, literally quoting the lines to a Christmas carol.

With a sigh, his shoulders slump a little and he turns to me. "My mum used to love Christmas. She made a whole big thing about it. We would decorate every inch of the entire house. See over there?" he says, pointing to three big boxes stacked in the corner, up against the wall. "Those are all filled with her Christmas stuff. And with her gone..."

His words are like a dagger straight into my heart. How could I have not thought about this? About the fact that he'd lost his mamma and is all alone in this world. My heart breaks for him as I watch him stand up straighter, putting on his aloof mask and pretending like he just hadn't revealed a vulnerability to me.

"OK," I say, keeping my voice low and even, not letting a trace of sympathy appear in my tone. I know Daniel doesn't want people to feel sorry for him. "Would it be alright if I get a tree? Just a small one that I can keep in my room?"

I hold my breath as he looks at me, his head tilted, his expression tender.

"You don't have to keep the tree in your room, Iz. I don't hate Christmas. I just don't want to be involved in it."

"That's fair," I agree. "So, it'll be alright for me to decorate a tree in the living room?"

He gives me a small half-smile, so fleeting I feel I may have imagined it. "That's OK."

I walk forwards and wrap my arms around him in an impulsive hug of gratitude, knowing that he's trying to compromise to make me happy.

"Thanks," I say, giving him a squeeze, loving his tight hold of me in return. "I'll make sure it's the most unnoticeable tree in the world."

Daniel releases me—reluctantly?—and leans towards me with a small smile. "Get the tree that makes you the happiest, Iz."

My heart flutters at this and I force myself to take a step back. "That I can do."

A few hours later, after cajoling Amelia into taking me to the Christmas tree farm an hour's drive away, it turns out that the tree that makes me the happiest is also the biggest one known to man.

"It didn't seem this big before we had it cut down," I say as we stand in the parking lot, trying to manoeuvre the over-six-foot tree into her small hatchback.

"Maybe we can angle it in so that the top is sticking out of the front window?" Amelia says after we'd spent twenty minutes playing Tetris trying to get the tree into the car. So far, we've sucked at this game.

"I think that'd work. It just means I'll have to have the tree across my face as we drive." I say it with a laugh because I'm feeling a little delirious. *Maybe Christmas tree shopping while hungover wasn't the best idea after all?*

"Can we try?" she asks, sounding grumpy. Amelia also has a hangover and may be losing patience with the situation.

I sit in the front seat and help my friend thread the top of the tree through the back seats and out the passenger side window. With a triumphant squeal, I hear Amelia close the trunk of the car and I know we've been successful.

"We are masterminds," I say, through a mouthful of pine needles. "I knew we could do it!"

She murmurs something that is muffled by the forest covering my ears and puts the car in motion.

"I'm going to drive home slowly," she yells so I can hear her. "I can't see out the back or the side of the car."

That's no good, I think as I say a silent prayer to get us home in one piece. This Christmas tree better be worth it.

The look on Daniel's face when we get home makes me think maybe it won't be worth it. As we pull up into the driveway, he comes out of the garage, a look of horror on his face.

"Iz, are you in there?" he asks, the top of his head visible through the tree branches currently cutting off my air supply.

"Help," is all the oxygen I have left to say, the long drive home covered in tree officially wearing me out.

"What have you two done?" he groans while opening my door and pulling the tree out that way in what looks like an attempt to rescue me.

"I think this way's easier," Amelia says, having made her way to the back of the car and opening the trunk. "This is how we got it in the car; probably the best way to get it out again."

I hear Daniel muttering to himself, catching the words 'ridiculous' and 'crazy' in there, and I hope I haven't pushed him too far. He did say to pick the tree that made me the happiest, but perhaps I could have reined myself in a bit?

"On the count of three, we are going to pull. Iz, you cover your face."

With my hands over my eyes, trying to protect myself as best I can, I feel the tree being lifted off me and out of the car. *Halleluiah*, I think, stepping out of my door and stretching. That had been a very long drive home indeed.

"I can't believe you guys drove like that," he says with his hands on his hips, looking like the grump I'd met that very first day. "Do you know how dangerous that was?"

Amelia and I look at each other and shrug; it hadn't seemed like such a risk at the time.

"What can I say, Dan? Our girl here picked the tree she wanted, and we had to get it home."

When he looks like he's going to lecture us some more and officially ruin any remaining shred of Christmas cheer I have left, I step forward. With my hand on his arm, I give him a pleading look. "We didn't mean to do anything dangerous," I tell him, feeling his forearm flex under my fingers. "And we got home safely. We promise never to do anything like this again."

Amelia agrees with a cheeky grin on her face, her eyes bouncing between the two of us.

"Fine," Daniel relents. "Let's just get this monster into the house."

We watch as he lifts the tree, picking it up like it weighs nothing more than a feather, and walks into the house. I'm pretty sure we both sigh a little at this fine display of manliness before I pull my attention away from my roommate and back to my friend next to me.

"Want to help me decorate?" I ask as I notice her still staring towards Daniel's disappearing back. Well, his backside, to be precise. And who can blame her? His butt is prize-winning-worthy.

"I can't, Bella, sorry. It's not that I don't want to hang around and witness the wonderful sexual tension between you two," she says with a laugh as I poke her in the ribs, "but I have so many errands to run today."

I give her a tight hug. "Thanks so much for helping me today. It's my first Christmas away from home and I know the tree we picked is going to make it perfect."

She squeezes me back and waves goodbye, leaving me to face Daniel alone. I hope he isn't too upset with me. With a sigh, I decide to face the music. What's the worst that can happen? The tree's here now. It's not like we can just throw it out.

I walk through the open front door and stop short when I see the tree set up in the corner, the living room having been rearranged to accommodate it.

"When did you do this?" I ask Daniel, who is fixing the stump of the tree in a bucket of soil and water. Something I hadn't even thought to prepare.

"Do what?" he asks, distracted by the task at hand.

"The room," I clarify, gesturing to the couches that have been moved, along with the TV and the coffee table. He'd made it so that everything was now pointed towards the tree, making it the focal point of the room.

He gives me an almost sheepish look and then looks around the room. "This is how my mum liked to have it. So, I thought I'd sort it out before you got home, but if you want, we can put it somewhere else."

My breath catches at this, at the pure selflessness of this gesture, and I have to hold myself back from going over to him and kissing him senseless. The man who doesn't 'do' Christmas because it's too painful for him has taken the time to make it so that my Christmas is still special. I don't even think he understands what his actions mean to me.

"Thank you, Dan," I say in a voice that is wobbly with unshed tears. "You didn't have to do that."

He gives me an uncertain look before clearing his throat. "It's no big deal. I also got out Mum's boxes for you if you want to use them. You don't have to if you want to get your own stuff."

Once again, I feel tears clog my throat as I look at the boxes placed off to the side of the room. His mum's Christmas decorations and he's offering them to me.

"I would love to use them," I tell him, stepping closer to where he's standing so I can get a better look at his face. If it seems like it's going to be too much for him, there's no way I'll subject him to it. "But only if you're OK with it. I don't want you looking at the tree and it bringing you any sort of pain."

His eyes dart to mine and they are filled with sadness and something else. Something that looks a lot like hope. "I think my mum would love to know that her decorations are being used again. She'd hate to have them locked away forever."

I pick up his hand and squeeze it. "Then it will be my honour to use them. I'll make sure the tree is one your mamma would have loved."

Daniel's eyes fill with tears before he blinks them away. "OK, well, you're good to go," he says after clearing his throat and letting go of my hand. "I'm going back outside. Try not to break the house while I'm gone."

I laugh at his attempted joke to help lighten the mood then wait for him to leave the room before opening the first box to see what's inside. He wasn't joking when he said his mum loved Christmas. There is every type of Christmas decoration under the sun in here, and I can't wait to get stuck into it. With my Spotify Christmas playlist on blast, I begin the task of turning this simple tree into a masterpiece, determined to honour Daniel's mamma and her love for Christmas as I do so.

An hour later, I'm almost done. I've thread coloured lights through the branches of the tree, put up Christmas baubles in every colour and finished it all off with strands of golden and red tinsel. The total effect is bright and chaotic, not an ounce of colour coordination in sight. In amongst the boxes filled with generic decorations, I found ornaments that were clearly very personal to Daniel's family. One that looked like misshaped clay made by *Daniel, aged 5.* One that had *Daniel's first Christmas* written on it with silver glitter. And one that had a photo of the two of them together printed on it. As I'd carefully put these on the tree, off to the side so that they weren't in Daniel's face every day, I'd had to wipe away tears for the mamma who had so clearly worshipped her son and for Daniel who is grieving the loss of this wonderful woman. The process had left me a little heartbroken, and I can't imagine what he will feel when he sees it all put together in his living room.

I'm still partially regretting this whole endeavour, hoping that it won't cause him too much pain, when he steps into the room. To find me precariously perched on one leg, on a chair, trying to secure the Christmas star to the top of the tree.

"What are you doing?" he says, his tone angry and worried at the same time. He marches over to where I'm wobbling and puts his arm around me, holding me steady. "I thought you could at least do this without getting hurt."

I turn to look down at him, acutely aware that his arm is around my waist and it's causing me to forget how to breathe and offer him a weak smile. "I've been managing just fine. This is the last step."

He stares up at me, our eyes locked together, and then he shocks me by lifting me with one arm and gently depositing me back onto the ground.

"Let me," he says in that gruff tone he gets whenever we are in close contact. It's a tone that makes my toes curl.

I silently hand over the star and watch as he places it on top. Once done, he steps back and surveys the tree in front of him.

"You've done a great job," he says, making my heart sing with his praise. "My mum would have loved it."

I hear the sadness in his tone and I can't help myself. From behind I wrap my arms around him, pressing my front to his back, offering him silent comfort. With a deep sigh, he leans back into me. I glance at him and notice he's looking at the ornament with the picture of the two of them together.

"I can take it down if you want," I say in an urgent tone, kicking myself for putting it up in the first place.

"No—don't," he says quickly. "It doesn't belong in a box. *She* doesn't belong in a box." He turns around in my arms until we're facing each other. "Thank you for this."

"For taking over your living room and forcing a giant tree into your house?" I ask, keeping my tone light while I try not to cry at the grief I see on his face.

"For that," he says with his signature half-smile. "But mainly for bringing...the house back to life."

I put my head on his chest and let out a deep breath. "It's my pleasure, Dan. Your...*house* deserves to be happy."

I feel rather than see him nod and hope he understands what I'm trying to tell him. That he doesn't need to shut himself away from living his life forever, that his mamma would want him to be happy, and that I'm desperate to be the person to help him get there.

CHAPTER 13

Bella

AFTER DANIEL'S CONCESSION THAT CHRISTMAS does, in fact, need to be celebrated, I've been taking advantage and have been filling the house—slowly, slowly—with every Christmas decoration I can find. Over the past two weeks, I've been gradually adding to Daniel's mamma's collection, starting with the most adorable reindeer garden gnomes, which I found at a shop near the Love, Lilly café. The first day I brought Rudolph home and placed him out near the front door. When Daniel didn't say anything about it, I'd added the rest, day by day. Now we have Dancer and Prancer and the rest of the gang hanging out in the front yard, making it look so wonderfully festive.

When I'd completed that mission, I'd moved to the inside. There's now mistletoe adorning every doorway in the house—no secretly trying to trap Daniel in a kiss going on here—and I'd even managed to score a trio of Disney characters dressed in Santa costumes that dance and play Christmas carols when you press on them. They are noisy and oh-so-delightful. The last thing on my list is to hang twinkling lights around the front of the house. I'd gotten the idea from the neighbours across the street, whose house lights up so bright every night that I'm somewhat worried a plane may attempt to land on it. I'm not planning anything that extravagant, but a tastefully placed string of multi-coloured lights would really make the reindeer gnomes come to life (there's a sentence I'd never thought I'd say).

So that's how I end up here, on a Sunday afternoon, climbing up a ladder holding the edge of the roof with one hand and the string of lights in the other.

"Hmmm," I mutter out loud. "How am I going to do this?"

I look at the gutter in front of me and the lights in my hands, thinking the only way to attach these is to hammer some nails in and hope for the best. Knowing that Daniel has a fully stocked toolkit in the garage, I carefully make my way down the ladder (I'm not that fond of heights) and go to the garage to gather what I need. The sheer amount of stuff that Daniel has by way of tools leaves me slightly confused, but I'm finally able to find a handful of nails and what looks like Thor's hammer.

"This should be fine," I say to myself as I make my way back up the ladder, this time holding the hammer, the lights and the rail, with the nails in my mouth. Once up at the roof line, I again wonder how I'm going to do this, needing what looks like four hands to achieve a decent outcome.

"Izzy, what are you doing up there?" The angry voice has me wobbling on my perch.

"Im pmin mm mmms," I mumble through the nails in my mouth.

"What?" he asks, holding the ladder steady and glaring at me.

"IM PMIM MM MMMS," I mumble louder, earning myself an even icier glare in return.

"Spit out the nails and then get down here," he exclaims.

Oh boy, I've gone and done it. I've pushed him too far. With a silent sigh, I let the nails fall to the ground and chuck the hammer down while I'm at it—that thing is heavy! Taking careful steps, I make my way down the ladder, shuddering in delight as Daniel grabs hold of my hips to guide me down the final few steps.

"Now, explain to me why I can't seem to leave you alone without you attempting to kill yourself," he says once he has me safely back on solid ground.

"I'm hanging lights," I tell him in a feeble tone, pointing to the lights in my hands.

"And the nails? And the mallet?"

"Mallet?" I ask, confused and also distracted. He's standing so close to me and with his chest heaving in obvious annoyance, we're almost touching.

"That," he points to where Thor's hammer is lying on the ground.

I smile. "That's to use to hammer in the nails so I can hang the lights."

He takes a deep breath in and closes his eyes like he's praying for patience. "First of all, that's not a hammer." *It's not?* "And second of all, you can't put nails in the guttering. Seriously, I can't leave you alone for one second."

I won't argue this point because I'm not asking him to be away from me. In fact, I'd happily have him by my side all day, every day. I shrug my shoulders and gesture to the roof. "Then how am I going to hang these?"

"You're not," he grunts, moving away to pick up the scattered nails or—as he's muttering under his breath—'a tetanus shot waiting to happen'. "We don't need outside lights."

"But think about how nice it would look with the whole scene we have going on out here," I say, pointing to the gnomes who have been watching this all unfold. "They deserve to be illuminated every night."

"Isabella." Uh oh, *he's using my full name*. "We don't need the gnomes to be lit up. We don't need any of this."

I frown because what he's saying is true. "You're right, we don't need any of it. But it's so festive and it makes me happy."

This is a low blow. I know this because what I've learned over the past few weeks is that Daniel seems to like making me happy. A fact that keeps me warm at night.

"Can't you find something less difficult to make you happy? Like baking or reading?"

He's referring to the hobbies of Lilly and Amy, and I can't really blame him. Those things really are a lot simpler than having the spirit of Christmas thrown up all over your house.

"You're right," I tell him while slowly packing up the Christmas light, the epitome of a sad emoji come to life. "I guess we don't need the lights."

He looks at me, making a big deal about putting the lights back in the box, and sighs. "Here, give it to me," he says, putting his hand out to take them from me. "I'll hang them up."

I give him a beaming smile and pass the poorly packed box to him. "Thank you!"

"I'm doing this on one condition," he continues in a stern tone. "Name it."

"No more ladders. And no going into my toolkit."

Too easy, I think to myself. I'm not a fan of either. "Done."

I put my hand out to shake his, accepting the zap of electricity that buzzes whenever we touch, as he smirks at me.

"Don't think you played me, Iz," he says with a laugh. "I know exactly what you're doing."

I give him my most innocent eyes. "I have no idea what you're talking about. I'm just going to start dinner. Let me know when you're done."

And with that, I skip into the house, happy to have another Christmas mission on its way to being completed without having to climb that scary ladder again.

Thirty minutes later, I have a risotto on the stove and a glass of wine on the go.

"The lights are up, your highness," Daniel says as he enters the house through the back door. "And whatever you're cooking in here smells good enough to make the task I just completed almost worth it."

I laugh and grab a beer from the fridge for him. "It's almost ready," I tell him, handing over his drink and watching as he drinks half the bottle in one sip. He's so sexy when he's being manly. "But before we eat, I have something to give you."

He looks at me with raised eyebrows as I leave the room to get the present I had expressed delivered to me from Florence. I'd put a lot of thought into it, so I really hope he likes it.

"Here," I say, handing him the neatly wrapped parcel, complete with a bright red bow.

"What is it?" he asks, giving me a bemused look. "It's not Christmas yet."

"This is more of a thank you slash sorry for being an annoying roommate who often needs rescuing type of present."

He smiles at me and then carefully opens the present. I watch with my heart in my mouth as he takes out a Christmas bauble, made by a glassblower in my home village.

"I ordered it from home," I rush to tell him when he just stands there staring it at it. "We have someone in our village who does these custom-made. I thought, maybe, you'd like a new ornament this year. You know, like creating new memories to go with the ones your mamma has."

Daniel looks closely at the bauble, which has a hand-painted picture of him and Snickers on the front. I had sent a photo I'd taken of the two of them together on the couch, the weekend I'd snuck the dog over, and my talented friend had painted it on the glass. Truly, the two of them look adorable and I'm so hoping that he likes it.

"I love it," he finally says, his voice rough with emotion. "It's the best present I've ever received."

I look to see whether he's being sincere and am floored to see tears in his eyes. My stomach drops at the thought of upsetting him.

"Is it making you sad?" I ask as I move closer to him, stepping into his arms and leaning my head on his chest, listening to his heart racing.

"No," he replies, rubbing my back. "I'm just amazed that you did this. For me."

I look up and get lost in the expression on his face. "I just want you to be happy."

He traces a finger across my cheek and then places the softest of kisses on my lips. It is a barely-there, gentle pressing of his lips on mine. And it works to effectively steal my breath and my heart at the same time.

"You make me happy," he whispers, staring at my lips, both of us caught up in the emotion of this moment.

"Good," I say, clearing my throat and trying to gather my thoughts before I completely lose all sense of where I am and what I should be saying. "Because I have another favour to ask."

Daniel leans back slightly, his gaze narrowed. "What now?" he asks, his tone wary.

"Well," I draw out the word. "I may have volunteered us to host a BBQ lunch here on Boxing Day?"

He leans back even further, his eyebrows now drawn into a frown. That was quick. "You did what?"

"I was talking to Lilly and Amy and they mentioned wanting to get together for lunch on Boxing Day."

"And you offered our place?" I love that he calls it 'our' place. "Without telling me?"

"Technically, I did tell you," I say, reluctantly leaving his arms and going to where I'd placed a Post-it note on the kitchen counter a few days earlier. "See?"

He takes the note from me and reads it out loud. "Boxing Day BBQ lunch here. You're invited."

With a laugh that tells me he likes the call back to the notes he left me during the first few days after I'd arrived, he shakes his head at me.

"There's one small problem," he says, taking my hand and leading me out the back door. "Have a look around and tell me what you see."

I look at his smirking face and then scan the backyard with a sinking feeling. "You don't have a BBQ? How is that possible? My understanding is that every Australian has a BBQ."

He inclines his head. "Most do, but come on, Iz. You know me, why would I need a BBQ? I never have people over."

"But I so wanted to host a traditional Aussie BBQ," I say with a pout I can't hold in. This is turning out to be a disaster.

Daniel looks at me, lingering on my lips, before turning and walking back into the house. I follow a few steps behind him, noting him grab his car keys and head to the front door.

"Where are you going?" I call out just as he opens the door.

He turns to give me a long look before saying in that gruff tone of his, "I guess I'm going to buy you a BBQ."

I watch him leave and melt into a puddle on the floor. *He's going to buy me a BBQ.*

CHAPTER 14

Bella

I T IS THE DAY BEFORE Christmas when my homesickness finally sets in. Over the past seven weeks, I'd been so busy settling in, making friends, working hard and annoying Daniel that I hadn't given too much thought to my family back at home. I've Zoom-called with my parents almost every other day and have kept in touch with a few of my close friends and cousins via email, group chats and the typical social media updates, and this has made me feel close to them, even with them being half a world away. But there's something about the upcoming holiday that's making me miss them acutely. Even spending time with Lucas and Amy hasn't been enough to take the edge off, and so that's how I find myself sitting at the kitchen table, staring forlornly at the bright sunshine streaming through the window and wishing it was snowing instead.

"What's wrong?"

I look up to see Daniel watching me from where he's standing in the doorway. He had just come home from the night shift at work and must be exhausted.

"Nothing," I say with a sad attempt at a smile. "Just missing home a little more than usual."

He frowns as he walks over and sits across from me, helping himself to a sip of my coffee.

"That's natural," he says. "It's hard to be away from family at this time of year."

I wince as I think about his mamma and how he doesn't seem to have any family to celebrate with, and I try to pull myself out of the pity party I've been in.

"It is," I say. "But I have Lucas close by. And all of you. Really, I shouldn't be feeling homesick at all."

"But you are?"

I drop my chin, opting to be honest with him. "It just doesn't feel like it's Christmas Day tomorrow."

He looks around the house. It's so Christmassy that it now looks like Santa Claus and all his elves live here. He raises an eyebrow at me.

"I know, I know," I say with a small laugh. "The house is very Christmas-ready, but everything else is off."

"Like?" he probes.

"Well, the weather, for one thing. It's the hottest day I've experienced since I've been here, and tomorrow is going to be even hotter."

"Iz, it's summer here, we can't do anything about the weather," he says, being all reasonable and stuff.

"I know, but it's also Christmas Eve, and that's usually a big deal back at home."

Daniel pauses for a moment before replying. "If you were home, what would you be doing today? Tonight?"

"Well, we'd have all the family over. My cousins and aunties and uncles. We'd have a seafood feast for dinner to celebrate *La*

Vigilia di Natale, Christmas Eve, and then we'd all spend the night playing board games and watching old movies. And there'd be snow."

I say this last part with a childish pout, knowing I'm being unreasonable, but finding it hard to snap out of it. When moving here I'd imagined loving a summer festive season, but the combination of being so far away from my parents for the first time and the foreign nature of this continent and their customs has left me feeling melancholy. A feeling I'm not overly familiar with.

"How about the two of us cook up a seafood feast for tonight? And we can watch old movies together, if you want? I know I'm not a great substitute for your family back home, but it may make you feel better."

My heart doubles in size at his offer, amazed I'd ever thought this man to be grumpy and mean. "You'd do that? For me?"

He sighs like I'm asking a stupid question. "Of course. I love seafood and old movies."

I give him my happiest smile and get up to make a list of ingredients for dinner. If I want the feast to be like one my mamma and my ziettas would make, I need to get started now.

"OK, I'm going to get to the shops to buy what I need. If you're sure you want to do this?"

He grins a happy grin at me. "I can't wait."

And so, twelve hours later, after the biggest, most decadent seafood dinner, we're sprawled out on the couch watching *Dawson's Creek*.

"I thought the tradition was to watch old movies?" Daniel asks turning his head only slightly to look at me. We're both so full we can barely move.

"Shhh," I tell him. "We're almost at the best part."

We both turn and watch the screen and I hold my breath as Pacey shows Joey the wall he bought for her. He's like the perfect romantic hero; when Joey's art mural is vandalised and she's upset, he goes out and rents a wall for her to use as a blank canvas. To start her mural again. Pacey Whitter, he's so damn romantic.

"I don't get it," says the man next to me. "He's sixteen. How can he afford to buy her a wall?"

I sigh at this stupidly rational question. "That's not the point."

"It's not?"

"No. The point is that he's so in love with her that he's trying every grand gesture he can think of. And she's just too clueless to notice."

"Grand gesture?" he asks with a confused look.

Really, they need to teach this stuff to boys at school, so they can all turn out like Pacey.

"A grand gesture is when a man, or a woman, does something big to show the object of their affection that they care. It's in every romance book, dating back to the likes of Jane Austen."

"Huh, I've learnt something new today."

"Happy to be of service," I tell him as we watch the credits roll down the screen.

With a yawn, I turn to face Daniel. "Thanks for making this the perfect *vigilia di Natale.*"

He gives me a shy smile. "Did it make you feel less homesick?"

I stop and think about his question, realising that since he'd come home and offered to spend the day with me, my homesickness had all but disappeared.

"Yes. If we could wake up to some snow tomorrow, I wouldn't miss home at all."

With a smile of gratitude and a gentle kiss on the cheek, I wish him goodnight and head up to bed. Big day tomorrow, my first Aussie Christmas. Now I can't wait for the day ahead.

"Buon Natale!" I say to Daniel as I make my way into the kitchen the next morning, where he has a cup of coffee waiting for me. "Merry Christmas."

He sweeps me up into a bear hug—best present ever—swinging me around before letting me go.

"Merry Christmas, Iz."

"What time are we going to Lilly's place?"

Lilly and Oliver are hosting Christmas lunch this year and I'm so excited to see them all. I've been working hard on everyone's presents and I can't wait to give it to them.

"She said to come over around 11 a.m.," Daniel says, reading the details from a text message on his phone. "So, plenty of time to get hungry. I'm pretty sure Lilly is cooking us a feast."

We both look at each other with slight terror written on our faces, remembering the last time Lilly cooked for us.

"Maybe she'll be better at cooking a roast than a lasagne?" I offer with hope.

"Hmm, surely she can't mess that up."

We both frown at each other while I prepare myself for the worst, telling myself that Christmas is about more than just food. It's also about presents—and speaking of presents.

"Dan, I have a small present to give you," I say, walking towards where his wrapped gift is waiting under the tree.

He follows me, a slight frown on his face. "I thought we were waiting to exchange presents at Lilly's place?"

As a group, we'd made a plan to bring all the gifts to the lunch and open them together. To make it more festive.

"We are," I tell him. "But this is something I wanted to give you in private."

This has his eyebrows raising suggestively, causing my cheeks to heat up.

"Get your mind out of the gutter," I tell him with a laugh. "It's just something I thought you might want to open at home."

I bend down and pick up his gift, feeling nervous as I hand it to him. I've spent the last few weeks working on it.

Daniel slowly unwraps the present, while I watch on, wringing my hands.

"Do you like it?" I ask the minute the last piece of wrapping paper has fallen away. In his hands is a landscape picture I'd painted for him. It's of the Melbourne city skyline, painted in vibrant colours, and I'm hoping he'll like it enough to put up on one of his walls.

"I love it, Iz," he says in a hushed tone. "You're so talented."

"You really like it?"

"I do," he says. "I see this view every day, and yet the way you've captured it makes it look magical."

My heart races at his praise. "That's how I see it," I admit. "This city and all the people in it, it's all magical to me."

He looks between me and the painting again and then reaches over to brush his lips over mine. Another almost kiss that leaves me wanting so much more. "Thank you, Iz. I know the exact spot I want to put it."

I watch as he walks over to the blank space right above the fireplace, the spot I'd secretly chosen for it as well, and places it up against the wall.

"What do you think? Does this work?"

Tears fill my eyes as I see my painting hanging in the most perfect place in the room, and I nod.

"It's perfect."

"Then how about I get my hammer and some nails and work to getting this up on the wall? Unless you want to do it?" he asks with a cheeky smile.

"I think I'll leave the handyman stuff to you."

And so that's how I spend my first Aussie Christmas morning, watching my hunky roommate hang my painting and finally put some colour up on these blank walls. And with this, it feels very much like we are getting somewhere.

"Iz, are you ready to go?"

Daniel's voice calls me from the front of the house and I take one last look at myself in the mirror. Wearing a summer dress and sandals for Christmas lunch feels strange, but I have to say, I'm not hating this red maxi dress on me. It's form-fitting with a V-neck, hugging my curves and making me question where my inevitable food baby is going to fit. *Oh well, that's a worry for later in the day*, I think as I skip out of my room.

"Where are you?" I ask when I get to the front door without coming across Daniel.

"I'm outside."

Following the sound of his voice, I open the door and find that it is snowing. *What?* I blink to see if my eyes are playing tricks on me and when I open them again, the snow is still there. *Snow?*

"It's a Christmas miracle, Iz," Daniel yells from the other side of the yard where he's controlling the snow-making machine.

My jaw drops open and I rush forward. *How did he do this?*

"What have you done?" I ask as I twirl around the snow floating in the air. He's made me a white Christmas!

"You said you wanted snow, so I got you snow," he says with a wide grin, looking so boyishly happy it takes my breath away.

"I can't believe you did this," I say when I can catch my breath, my mind unable to fully comprehend what he's done. The whole front lawn is covered in snow and the effect is magical.

"It's no big deal," he says, coming up next to me and wiping the snow from my hair.

"It's a very big deal," I reply while taking his hands in mine and squeezing them. "You've made my day absolutely perfect."

Daniel goes still as he stands looking down at me and I watch as he slowly lowers his lips to mine. It's just a gentle kiss, like he's tasting me, and I lean all the way into it. We stay like this for what feels like just a split second before he sighs and lifts his head.

"I just want you to be happy," he says, repeating my earlier words back to me.

I look around the winter wonderland he's made for me, on this hot summer's day, and I can't imagine ever being happier.

"I love...this," I tell him as snowflakes coat his eyelashes. "Merry Christmas, Daniel."

He pulls me in for a hug, which lasts forever. "*Buon Natale,* Isabella."

CHAPTER 15

Daniel

"T HANKS FOR HAVING US OVER, mate," Oliver says, coming up behind me and tearing my gaze from Bella who is standing across the backyard chatting with her girlfriends.

"No worries," I say, looking at my friend. "You guys had us over yesterday. It's the least we can do."

And it's true. Yesterday, Lilly and Oliver had delivered an amazing Christmas Day, filled with carols and good cheer and so much food. When we'd arrived, after a glass of champagne and many hugs and kisses, we'd all opened our presents. Bella had surprised everyone by painting something special for each of them. For Lilly, she'd painted a picture of the outside of her café, complete with Lilly inside and Snickers sitting at the front door. And for Amy and Lucas, she'd painted a portrait of the two of them from the day they got engaged. The backdrop of Florence was stunning, but it's the look on our friends' faces, so in love, that Bella captured perfectly. She'd had everyone in tears with her extraordinary talent.

As for me, well, after getting the painting she'd done for me, I hadn't been expecting anything else. So, I was surprised when she presented me with one more gift. A Ferrari team shirt. Perfect to wear for the next time we watch Formula One together, she'd told me with that smile of hers, the one that makes me need to smile back. With the t-shirt in my hand, I'd been thrilled to present her the gift I'd been happily keeping as a surprise of my own.

"Two tickets to the Melbourne Grand Prix next year?" she'd yelled upon opening the present, promptly jumping up and down and shrieking with delight.

It was the best $600 I'd ever spent. Not that she needs to know how much I'd spent; regardless, the look on her face was worth every penny.

"You're burning the sausages," Lucas says now, bringing me back from my internal musings, which almost always are about Bella these days. She's completely infiltrated my mind.

I look down to see a plume of smoke coming from the grill in front of me and move into action. If I don't get myself together, I risk ruining the lunch that Bella has been so looking forward to.

"Thanks for looking out for Bella," Lucas says, watching me closely while I attempt to rescue the meat in front of me. "She'd told me about what a good roommate you are."

Roommate? I frown at the description. I want to be so much more than just her roommate.

"Though I don't remember you letting me decorate the house for Christmas last year, or buying me a snow machine," he continues with a knowing look.

I stop what I'm doing to try to gauge his reaction to the developments in my relationship with Bella. Is he upset that we may be moving towards more than just friends?

"If you looked like that," Oliver chimes in with a grin, pointing to where Bella is now sitting with Lilly and Amy, "maybe he would have been nicer to you."

I hold my breath and wait for Lucas to go into a protective big brother mood and am relieved when he just laughs.

"It's true," he admits. "Bella has always had a way of getting what she wants."

"It's not only because she's gorgeous," I come to Bella's defence, inviting shrewd smiles from the two men in front of me. "She's the kindest, most generous person I know. I do things for her because she's constantly going out of her way to make sure everyone around her is happy."

Lucas tilts his head to one side while giving me a longer, more measured look and I feel myself sweat. Had I revealed too much?

"You're right," he says with a grin. "She's kind-hearted, just like our mamma. Always putting everyone's needs before her own."

"Exactly, so I'm just making sure she's happy, too."

Lucas slaps me on the back. "I appreciate it, man. It's good to know you're here for her."

I take this as an unspoken approval and move the conversation on to more manly topics. We're a trio of men standing in front of a BBQ talking about our feelings. What has happened to us?

A few hours of watching cricket later, with my manhood firmly back in place, I stand with Bella at the front door to wave goodbye to our friends. Luckily, I hadn't ruined the hamburgers and sausages on the grill and together with the salads Bella had made and a few of Lilly's desserts, along with the four bottles of wine supplied by Amy, we'd had a wonderful Boxing Day lunch. Just like Bella had wanted.

"Oh my God," says the woman in question, the woman I'm getting addicted to. "I'm so full."

I sink onto the couch with a groan of my own. From the seafood feast on Christmas Eve, through Christmas lunch yesterday and the mountain of food we'd consumed today, I feel like I never want to eat again.

"Why did we eat so much?" she asks while patting her flat stomach. For someone so petite, she sure can eat a lot.

"Well, traditionally, we should have played a round of backyard cricket to work off some of the food," I tell her while leaning my head back and stretching my legs out in front of me. There's no way I'm moving from this spot anytime soon. "But neither you nor Lucas knows how to play. Amy and Lilly refused to play, so it would have just been me and Oliver. And that's just sad."

"It's because cricket is another one of your sports that makes no sense," she says, sounding indignant, a small frown wrinkling her nose. She's so adorable when she's on her way to getting mad.

"It makes more sense than your Formula One," I say to push her over the edge, rewarded immediately with that red flush that coats her cheeks when she's angry.

"Pfft, you know nothing," she says in a huff before she notices my grin and throws a cushion at my head. "Don't tease me, Dan. I'm too full to be angry."

I agree and let it drop, happy to sit with her on the couch and stare sightlessly at the TV in front of us. She's changed the channel from the cricket I'd been watching and I can see the opening credits for *Dawson's Creek* instead. She's so in love with this show.

"Not this again," I fake moan, knowing that I'll happily watch anything just to be near her. I've turned into the worst kind of sap over the past few weeks. Desperate to be near her, needing to make her happy.

"You love it," she mutters without looking away from the screen.

It gives me the perfect opportunity to study her unnoticed. Her hair has grown since her haircut and her bangs are now so long she has them swept to one side. She's dressed casually today in a pair of white shorts and a blue t-shirt that makes her eyes brighter. Her cheeks are more pink than usual, suggesting she either spent too much time in the sun or had too many glasses of wine, or both, and altogether she looks perfect. To me. For me.

"What are you looking at?" she asks, still not taking her eyes off Dawson and the gang.

I reach over and touch her cheek, happy to have a reason to touch her. "You've gotten a bit burnt in the sun today."

She touches her nose and winces slightly. "I never get burnt at home."

"You need to be careful; the sun here is harsh. Always remember to use sunscreen."

"Yes, Dad," she says, turning to me with a cheeky grin.

God forbid, I do not want to be considered a father figure to her.

"What are you doing for New Year's Eve?" she changes the subject while I take too long to figure a way out of the dad-zone. "Are you coming to Lucas and Amy's party?"

Every year for the past few years I had volunteered to work on New Year's Eve as part of my plan to hide away from everything festive. It had been working well, and they'd automatically rostered me on again this year, and now I was going to miss the opportunity to be with Bella on this one special night of the year.

"I'm working that night," I tell her, enjoying the look of disappointment on her face. Hopefully, it means she's upset not to be spending the night with me.

"That's too bad," she says with that smile of hers. The one that means trouble. "I guess I'll have to find someone else to kiss at midnight."

The thought of Bella kissing anyone other than me has blind jealousy raging through my body, and I have to work hard to hold it all in.

"Is that so?" I ask, managing to only half-strangle my words.

She looks at me and bites her lip like she's trying to decipher my words, my thoughts.

"I guess so?" she says, looking less sure and more flustered as I move towards her.

"You want to kiss someone else?" I ask as I stop within an inch of her face, her lips tantalisingly close to mine.

"Huh?" she says like she's lost track of the conversation. Which is fine by me because I'm done talking.

I reach one hand and gently move her hair from where it's covering her eye to behind her ear, letting my hand slowly caress her earlobe and neck as I do so. Bella's breath catches at this and I watch as she licks her lips, making them glisten in the late afternoon light.

"I'm going to kiss you now, Iz," I say, waiting for her brief nod before I crash my lips onto hers. The kisses before this have all been a gentle little tasting of her mouth on mine, but with this one, I want more. I *need* more.

I press my lips against hers and when she lets out a quiet moan, I take advantage, deepening the kiss, letting my tongue slowly dance with hers. It's an intense kiss, one that I feel with my whole body, and in this moment, I'm sure I never want to kiss anyone other than Bella, ever again.

Our kiss goes on and on, alternating between passion and sweetness, pressure and nibbling, and by the time we come up for air, I feel like I've been branded. That kissing Bella may have just changed my life.

"Was that OK?" I ask her when I get my breath back, a little embarrassed by how long it's taking me to find my sense of equilibrium.

"Not really," she says, shocking me into sitting upright, ready to apologise and beg for forgiveness. Had Bella not been as into that kiss as I had? "What I mean is, the kiss was amazing. A-Plus kiss, mind-blowing, in fact," she continues as she strokes my face, making me feel instantly better. "I'm just wondering why we've not been doing that this whole time?"

My entire body relaxes as I poke her in the ribs, tickling her and making her giggle. Literally the best sound in the world. "You had me worried," I tell her, my voice still not sounding 100 per cent normal. That kiss may have ruined me.

"I'm sorry," she says, giving me another brief kiss of apology, pulling back before I can deepen it. "I was only teasing. That kiss was more than OK, it was…" she trails off like she's trying to think of the words to describe what the kiss had been. I scramble my brain to help her and we both come up empty. I guess there are no words that are worthy of it.

"So, does that mean we can do it again?" I ask, pulling her closer to me so that she's sitting almost in my lap.

She pretends to think about it while I delight in just looking at her face up close. I have it so bad for this girl. Just sitting and staring at her is enough for me.

"Hmmm, maybe we can," she says with her cheeky smile. I have a catalogue of all her smiles. "After we finish this episode. It's my favourite."

I look up to see Pacey on the TV, no doubt doing something that will make Bella swoon, and agree. Gathering her close to me,

I tuck her in under my arm and enjoy the feeling of her body pressed against mine. I'd happily do anything to have her in my arms like this every night. Even if it means watching *Dawson's* bloody *Creek*.

CHAPTER 16

Bella

THE WEEK BETWEEN CHRISTMAS AND New Year's goes by in that blur where you never quite know what day it is. Everyone is off work, including me, thanks to Lilly closing the café for ten days, and so every day feels like a holiday. I wake each morning with that delicious feeling of knowing I don't need to be anywhere and that the whole day is mine to enjoy.

And enjoy them I have been. Including today, the last day of what has been the best year of my life so far. Today, I've been pampered with my friends. Amy had surprised me, Lilly and Amelia with a trip to a day spa where we've had massages, facials and now we're getting manicures. All to prepare for the party tonight, which according to Amy, my brother is busy setting up back at their place.

"He's such a good guy," Amelia says to Amy with a sigh. She's told me on many occasions how gorgeous she thinks Lucas is and I have a feeling she may have the smallest of crushes on him.

"He's not so bad," Amy agrees with a huge smile that tells me every time just how much she loves him.

"You didn't have to grow up with him," I say, wanting to dampen what's sounding like a Lucas lovefest. "He was so damn perfect all the time. It was impossible to live up to him."

"Now that, I can see," Amy agrees. "His ability to be good at everything can get annoying."

"And speaking of annoying," Lilly says, entering the conversation. "How's things going with Daniel? Has he warmed up to you yet?"

I feel my face heat up as I think of how far I've come in my relationship with Daniel since that first dinner party at Lilly and Oliver's place. When he had me convinced that he hated me.

"We kissed," I blurt out because I've been dying to tell someone. "A lot."

My friends all let out high-pitched squeals, frightening the customers around us and earning us disapproving looks from the staff at this very Zen-like day spa.

"Tell us everything," Amy demands, while the other two beam excited smiles at me.

I start with his change in attitude after I cooked him dinner, detail the Christmas decoration sagas and end with the unbelievable kiss on Boxing Day.

"It was like...nothing I've ever experienced before," I finish up, my entire body overheating just thinking about it.

"So, let me get this straight," Amelia says. "You have a 'mind-blowing' kiss on the couch, and then what? Nothing?"

"Well, no, not nothing," I say with a smile as I remember all the 'not nothing'. "There's been more kisses."

"Details," they demand.

I sigh and think about all the kisses we've shared since then. Like the one in the hallway the next morning, when I'd been walking to my room, and he'd grabbed me and gently pushed me against the wall, ravaging my mouth with the most passionate kiss. Or the one where I was outside in the garage, working on my next painting and he'd come up behind me, kissing my neck and working his way around to my mouth, causing me to drop my paint all over my clothes. Or how about the one where he'd woken me up from a nap on the couch with delicate kisses all over my face, like he was worshipping me. Each one has stirred something powerful inside of me and has me craving more and more.

"He's so romantic," Amelia says with a wistful look when I'm done.

"He sounds amazing," chimes in the lovely lady who is painting my nails and obviously listening to our conversation.

"He is," I agree, my face on fire at the thought of the entire room hearing these intimate details.

"But what does it all mean?" Amy asks, ever the practical one. "Are you guys together?"

I shake my head because I'm not sure. "We haven't spoken about it. And I think that's OK. Daniel's been through so much. Just getting him to open up to me this much is good enough for now."

Amy and Lilly agree, both of them knowing how much Daniel has had to endure over the past couple of years.

"I'm happy to go with the flow as long as it feels like we are moving forward."

"And does it?"

I think of Daniel hanging my painting on the wall and buying us tickets to the Grand Prix next year and I can't suppress my excited smile.

"It absolutely does. I can't wait for next year to start; I have a feeling it's going to be the best year yet."

I'm still high on this feeling when I get home to get ready for this evening's party. Thanks to the facial, my skin is glowing and won't require much make-up, and the nail technicians have left my hands and feet sparkling and party-ready. The only thing dampening my excitement is knowing that Daniel won't be there with me tonight, but I'm comforted by the fact that we live together and I get to see him almost every other waking minute.

"Are you almost ready to go?" Daniel calls out ninety minutes later. He's offered to drop me off at the party on his way to work, and I hurriedly buckle the strap on my heels before racing out my bedroom door. I don't want him to be late.

"Coming," I call as I walk as fast as these stiletto heels will allow, which isn't very fast. I had little need for shoes this fancy back home. "I'm ready."

I come to a halt in front of Daniel, arrested by the look on his face. He is slowly scanning me from the tips of my golden heels, over the expanse of my bare legs, up over the flirty skirt of my pale pink mini dress, trailing across the scoop neckline and the hint of cleavage, stopping on my carefully made-up face and freshly curled hair. And when he's done, his eyes make the trip back down again, like he's mesmerised and I'm thoroughly pleased by this reaction. It's like he's trying to absorb every inch of me and commit it to memory.

"You look…" he trails off, his jaw flexing as he stares at me.

"Thanks?" I say with a big smile, walking forwards to press a kiss on his jaw and put him out of his misery. "Do you like my new dress?"

I do a twirl in front of him, causing the skirt of my dress to flare ever so slightly, and he seems entranced by my legs. Which are looking smooth and bronzed, thanks to the careful application of my self-tanner. A tricky task that's paying off now.

"I love it," he says, pulling me closer and pressing an urgent kiss on my lips. "You look beautiful."

I lean back, gazing into his brown eyes, which are saying so much more than his words, and sigh. "I wish you were coming to the party tonight."

He gives me a pained look, taking in my dress again, a small frown on his face. "Believe me, I want to be spending the night with you, too."

With a reluctance I know we both feel, I pull away from him and pick up my purse. "We'd better get going. I think I'm already late."

Daniel takes my hands and we walk out of the house together. Once settled into the car, he turns on some background music and we sit in companionable silence. It's one of the most refreshing parts of being with him; we are equally happy talking as we are just being.

As we make our way to the party, I can't stop the thoughts that are racing through my mind. I told the girls earlier today that I'm happy with where I am with Daniel and our new status as friends who kiss, but if I'm being honest with myself, I want so much more. I want to turn the friendship we've developed over the past two months into something deeper, something to match the feelings I'm already having for him. And from the way he's been behaving, I sense he feels the same. Yet neither of us appears to be brave enough to take the next step.

"I think we should go out on a date," Daniel says, breaking into my mind and reading my thoughts.

Shocked, I turn to look at him and see that his gaze is alternating between the road in front of him and my bare legs. This dress has already paid for itself.

"You do?" I ask, my voice breathless with excitement.

"Yes." He shoots me a tight smile, his fingers tapping the steering wheel.

How could he think that I'd say no to a date with him? I'm just about ready to marry him at this point!

"OK," I squeak.

"Yes?" he asks with a slow grin.

"Of course. I mean, what about all the kissing we've been doing suggests that I wouldn't want to go on a date with you?"

He laughs and shakes his head. "I don't know. It's not like we've spoken about any of this," he says, gesturing between us.

"Because we've been too busy kissing." I bite my lip as I say this, knowing I'm drawing attention to my mouth and reminding him of all the kissing, earning a lovely, tortured groan from him in response.

"You are trouble," he says in his deep voice. *That voice is what's trouble.* "I knew it the minute you landed on my doorstep."

We park in front of Amy's house, where streams of people are entering the party, and I remain seated, not wanting this conversation to end.

"Is that why you were so mean to me?"

His head rears back ever so slightly and he turns to look at me with an apology written all over his face.

"Was I terrible?"

I pretend to think about it for a moment, drawing out his discomfort because he had been a little mean to me. "You weren't too bad," I admit, smiling when I hear his relieved sigh. "I mean, you tried to be mean, but my amazing charm clearly made it impossible."

In response to this, he pulls me over to his side of the car and places his lips on mine in a kiss that is filled with both apology and promise. It is tender, like he's worshipping my mouth with his own, and is over way too quickly.

"Maybe I can skip the party and come to work with you?" I whisper as he pulls his lips away, leaving his hands on my face and stroking my jaw gently with his thumbs.

"There's not a chance in hell I'm taking you to the station looking like that," he replies in a raspy voice, sounding all jealous and swoony.

"OK, fine. I shall just have to enjoy this party without you," I tease as he gets out to open my door for me.

"Don't enjoy it too much," he says, helping me out of the car and pulling me to him so that our bodies are pressed together.

With another kiss filled with everything I'm feeling for him, I say goodnight and walk towards Amy's house and a party I have no inclination to attend now. I feel Daniel's eyes follow me and as I get to the front door, I turn to see him standing at his car, watching me with an expression of adoration and annoyance.

With a smile, I give him a small wave. "I'll miss you," I call out as he's getting in his car.

This stops him in his tracks and he turns, surprising me by blowing me a kiss. "Happy New Year, Iz."

Happy New Year, I think as I enter the party. If I'm spending it with you, Daniel, it's going to be a very happy new year indeed.

CHAPTER 17

Bella

T HE PARTY IS IN FULL swing when I enter the house and I quickly scan the room, trying to find a friend.

"You made it," Amy says, sweeping me into a hug from behind. "What kept you so long?"

"This dress," I say with a smile, turning around to show it off properly. "I'm pretty sure Daniel was reluctant to part ways with me looking like this."

"Smart guy," she replies as we both laugh. "You're a bit of an evil genius, teasing him with this knock-out look."

"And it worked," I confide in her as we walk towards where they've set up a bar, filled with buckets of beer and champagne. It's going to be a big night. "He asked me out on a date!"

"He did?" she said, her voice an octave higher than normal. "That's so exciting."

"What's exciting?" Lilly asks, coming up next to where we're standing, looking gorgeous in a pair of tight leather pants and a slinky top. Amy obviously had a hand in dressing her tonight, or else she'd have turned up in jeans and a t-shirt.

"Daniel asked Bella out on a date."

"Ooh, that's amazing. You must be so excited."

I think about the butterflies that took flight when he asked me the question and haven't settled down since, and grin at them. "I'm beyond excited. This could be the beginning of something real."

Amy and Lilly exchange a glance. "You really care about him, don't you?" Amy asks.

"He takes my breath away," I tell them, feeling my cheeks heat up at what I'm revealing. The depth of my emotions for their friend.

"Then I'm glad he found you. Or you found him. Because there's not a single person I know who deserves to be happy more than Daniel."

The three of us look at each other with tears in our eyes, knowing the pain he's been experiencing since the death of his mum.

"What's going on here?" Lucas asks, pulling Amy into his arms and kissing her on the temple. They're so affectionate with each other, I love it. "You guys look like you're at a funeral. It's a party!"

"Very true," Lilly says, finishing the rest of her drink and filling up another. "Here Bella. Tonight is the night to celebrate. And we have so much to be happy about."

I take my glass of champagne and cheers with my brother and my new friends, thinking back to last New Year's Eve, when I'd gone to church with my parents and then played board games with two of my cousins, heading to bed before midnight. My life couldn't be any more different now and I'm so proud of myself for doing something scary to make the life I want.

Still, I need to pace myself tonight, I think as I instantly feel the effects of the bubbles going straight to my head. I walk over to where I've just spotted Amelia chatting with Sammi and Madi, two more of our book club friends.

"I love your hair," I say to Amelia after I've greeted them all. Both Sammi and Madi are fantastic girls and I can't wait to get to know them better. "When did you do that?"

Amelia has changed her hair colour from platinum blonde to fire engine red and she looks amazing. Seriously, that girl can pull off any look.

"This morning," she says with a grin. "I decided 'new year, new me'."

"Well, you look amazing," I tell her, linking my arm through hers, so happy to have met her the first week I got here.

"Where's that gorgeous roommate of yours?" Sammi asks with a grin.

I squash the immediate flame of jealousy that ignites at the thought of another woman thinking that Daniel is gorgeous, because hey, he is, and let her know that he's working tonight. "Apparently, it's a busy night for firefighters, something to do with all the fireworks gone wrong."

Madi and Sammi both laugh at this while Amelia frowns, looking behind me. "Um, Bella. Are you sure he's working tonight?"

I turn to follow her gaze and find myself staring at Daniel, who is standing in the doorway, looking determined.

"I think perhaps he decided there's something more important at this party," Amelia says while poking me in the ribs. "Clearly, all those fires can wait."

With a smile to acknowledge I heard her, I give them a small wave and float away from where they are all grinning at me, heading straight towards where the man who had invaded all my thoughts is standing.

"What are you doing here?" I say when I get to him, loving how he takes hold of my hand and pulls me to him.

"Apparently, I was too distracted to be useful this evening," he says with a wry smile. "My captain got me to switch with someone who could focus on the job."

I shake my head in confusion. "What happened?"

He takes me into the hallway and presses a quick kiss on my lips like he can't help himself. Like it's been too long since we've kissed. Which, to be fair, it has been.

"When I got to the station, I couldn't seem to stop thinking about you and this little dress," he says, squeezing my hips and making me yelp. "And my captain took one look at me and told me to leave. Said I'd worked too many holidays these past couple of years and I deserve to enjoy this one."

My heart breaks as I look at him, at this beautiful man who had chosen to work on these special days in an attempt to ignore them. To work through the pain and loneliness, literally. And I thank his kind fire station captain for being so generous to let him have this one back.

"So, here I am," he says, resting his forehead against mine in such a tender gesture it has my eyes smarting with tears.

"Here you are," I whisper back to him, happy to be in this little bubble, just the two of us enjoying a moment together in amongst the craziness of the party. "But I thought you didn't like parties."

Daniel had expressed to me many times how much he'd prefer a night on the couch over a night spent making small talk with strangers. He's an introvert who comes alive only with the people he knows and trusts the most.

"I don't," he agrees. "But I do like you."

My knees shake at this admission, and I move closer to him, looping my arms around his neck and placing a kiss on the side of his mouth. It's all that I'm allowing myself to do, because if I start kissing him properly now? Well, what I want to do to him wouldn't be appropriate for this public setting.

"I like you too."

"Hey, man." My brother's voice has us springing apart. "I didn't think you could make it tonight."

We both turn to look at Lucas with what I'm sure are identical expressions of guilt written across our faces. Not that we're doing anything wrong, but I don't want my brother to find out that I'm dating his friend by stumbling upon us canoodling in his hallway.

"Um," Daniel says, his face flaming red. *He's so cute.* "I switched my shift."

"Good news," Lucas says with a smile, looking between the two of us. "Because Bella here was miserable without you."

This has my eyes shooting to his and sure enough, he's smirking back at me. I should've known that he'd be onto us. Hell, he'd probably figured us out before we had.

"Uh, great," Daniel says, still looking unsure, standing about a metre away from me with his hands in his pockets.

"Relax, man," Lucas says with a big smile. "I'm a protective big brother, but I know I have nothing to worry about here. You're a stand-up guy and Bella is a grown woman. If you make each other happy, then you'll hear nothing about it from me."

I release a relieved breath at the same time as Daniel, feeling even happier as I feel his arms wrap around my waist from behind.

"Thanks, mate. I appreciate it."

Lucas's eyes go to where my hands are covering Daniel's, and he can't suppress a small grimace.

"Maybe just refrain from too much PDA in front of me?"

I shake my head and lean my body back against Daniel's. "We will if you will," I say, referring to the constant kissing and cuddling I've had to endure between him and his fiancée.

"Fair enough," he says with a laugh. "When you're done out here, come outside. It's almost midnight, and we can see the city fireworks from our backyard."

We watch Lucas's departing back and I turn to Daniel with what I know is a huge smile on my face. At this rate, I may as well get used to smiling this big because everything seems to be working out perfectly.

"That went much better than I'd thought," I tell him.

He rubs his hands together, looking relieved. "Your brother is cool and we're friends, so I was hoping he wouldn't have a problem with this. With us."

"There's an us?" I say, my tone light but hopeful.

"I hope so," he replies, pulling me flush against him. "I'd like there to be an us."

With a happy squeal, I give in and kiss him the way I've been wanting to for the last ten minutes. With all my heart.

"We'd better go outside to see the fireworks," he says several minutes later when we both emerge from our kissing haze, his voice rough with emotion.

"Yes," I reply, sounding somewhat vague. Because I'm pretty sure we'd just been creating fireworks of our own with all the kissing.

He takes my hand and leads me outside, where we are instantly enveloped by our group of friends. With Daniel behind me, holding me tight, and Amy next to me squeezing my hand in delight, I watch as the sky explodes in a multitude of colours. It's the most breathtaking display I'd ever seen, and I watch enthralled for five full minutes, marvelling that this is how I'm welcoming in the new year. Surrounded by great friends, in the arms of the man I'm falling in love with.

"Happy New Year, Iz," he says to me once the fireworks have finished and everyone is cheering and singing and drinking around us.

"Happy New Year," I reply, hugging him tightly to me.

"Last year on this night, I couldn't fathom welcoming in another year. Because it meant another one without my mum. Another year alone in this world," he says to me in a quiet voice, his story for my ears alone. "And then you knocked on my door…"

"And?" I prompt when he seems unable to finish his sentence.

"And my world started turning again," he admits, looking into my eyes, his voice filled with sincerity. "For the first time since my mum's diagnosis, which turned my life upside down, I thought maybe there is a light at the end of this dark tunnel."

He stops again and I can't help it; I kiss him with my whole heart, his words filling me with every emotion possible.

"You've helped bring me back to life," he says so quietly I almost miss it in the chaos of the surrounding party. "And now I have something to celebrate this New Year's Eve."

My heart thumps at his display of vulnerability. How had I ever thought this man to be aloof and grumpy? He is the most extraordinary man I've ever met.

"I travelled across the world to have an adventure, to see and learn new things," I whisper back. "And then I met you. Daniel Richardson, you are the most incredible human being I've ever met and I'm thankful every day that when I knocked on your door, you let me in."

He laughs at this and then using one finger he lifts my chin, pressing a brief but passion-filled kiss on my lips.

"We have so much to look forward to," I tell him when I've caught my breath.

"We do, Iz. That we do."

JANUARY

CHAPTER 18

Bella

"**W**HY DID YOU LET ME drink so much?" I moan from my foetal position on the couch. Head forward, eyes closed, temples throbbing. "How am I going to face all that sunshine at the beach?"

Daniel laughs from somewhere nearby. I'm not sure where because currently my eyelids are welded shut.

"I told you that last shot of tequila was a bad idea," he says in an amused tone.

Clearly Mr. Designated Driver is feeling fine and full of life this New Year's Day. That's very contrary to my current state. I've only been in Melbourne for two months and yet in that time, I've experienced two of the worst hangovers of my life.

"You'll have to leave me behind," I say, lying back down on the couch with a whimper. "I'm not going to make it."

I feel his hands on my head, gently stroking my hair and relieving some of the pressure. *Ooh, that feels good.*

"Iz, we leave no man behind," he says with a chuckle. "Here, take this Advil and drink this bottle of water. You'll feel better once you're breathing in the sea air."

I take the offered tablets and down it with a full bottle of water, wondering who'd exchanged grumpy Daniel for Mr. Sunshine.

"Don't you Aussies know that the first day of the year is for sitting on the couch, eating leftovers and napping?"

He gives me a look and shakes his head. "You only did that because it's cold and gloomy over that side of the world on the first day of the year. Take a look outside. You won't see a more perfect beach day than this."

I look out the front window, shielding my poor sore eyes from the glare and have to admit he's right. The sky is a bright shade of blue and cloudless, and the sun is beating hot, accompanied by a gentle breeze. *Damn these Aussies and their beautiful weather.*

"Plus, you've been dying to get to the beach. There's no way I'm letting your little hangover stop you from coming today."

"Little hangover," I mutter as I force my aching body off the couch and towards the front door. Clearly, he has never gone head-to-head drinking with Lilly before.

"This better be worth it," I grumble as I sit down in the passenger seat, sunglasses firmly in place, praying for the paracetamol to do its job. "And yes, I know, I sound like an ungrateful brat and I will apologise for this behaviour later. When I no longer feel like a piece of roadkill."

He laughs at me again—it seems that hungover-Bella is hilarious—and then leaves me in peace for the twenty-minute drive to the nearest beach. According to Amy, it's important to get there early on New Year's Day because the beach gets busy with everyone wanting to celebrate the start of a new year with a beachside picnic. *Damn these Aussies and their incessant need to be outdoors all the time.*

"OK, Iz, we're here," he says, waking me from my power nap. Already I feel better, which is a miracle given just a few minutes ago I'd felt like death warmed up. "You're at the beach."

I look out the front windscreen and gasp. The view in front of me is nothing short of spectacular. Miles and miles of white sand, crystal blue ocean that goes on forever, hitting the horizon in a blending of magnificent turquoise and brilliant aqua. My hands itch to grab my paintbrush, eager to capture these colours on canvas.

"You like?" Daniel asks after I'd been sitting and staring in silence for several moments.

"I love," I tell him in a hushed tone, my hangover all but forgotten. "It's like nothing I've ever seen before."

I'd been to the coastline of Italy on multiple occasions and it has its own special kind of beauty, but the rawness and ruggedness of this beach in front of me is unlike anything I'd ever experienced.

"Well, come on. What are you waiting for?"

I look up and take his hand, keen to get my feet on the sand and my body in the ocean.

"Bella, Daniel! Over here."

We look over to see Lucas, Amy, Lilly, Oliver, Amelia, Sammi and Madi already set up about 500 metres from where we're standing.

"Coming!" Daniel calls back, taking my hand and walking over to the group, carrying a beach umbrella and a cooler filled with drinks and snacks for the day. For my part, I'm carrying a bag with a couple of beach towels and a book and am feeling underprepared for the day ahead.

"Welcome," Lilly says when we reach them, looking way too spritely for the amount of drinking she'd partaken in last night. "Take a seat."

I look around in awe at the setup. In the middle of everyone are three giant picnic rugs that look specially made to be sand-resistant—how handy is that?—with two big beach umbrellas on either side. They have scattered a few beach chairs around, with several coolers already opened, filled with drinks and sandwiches. These people are no rookies; they have everything sorted for a full day at the beach.

"Hi guys," I say, taking a seat and running my hands through the sand. It's so fine, so unlike the pebbled beaches we have at home. "It's gorgeous here."

The group looks around like they are taking it in for the first time, accustomed as they are to the beauty of the beach around them.

"It is," Amelia agrees. "But be warned, the water is always freezing cold."

The girls in the group all laugh. "It doesn't matter how hot the weather is, that water comes straight from Antarctica, and it's freezing."

Great! I think as I pull my summer dress over my head. A dip in some cold water will help clear away the tequila cobwebs from my head. As I'm tossing my cover-up onto the picnic rug in front of me, adjusting my small bikini top, which is the same colour blue as my eyes and I love it, I notice Daniel looking at me. And when I say looking at me, I mean scalding me with his eyes. Like if we weren't in public, my cute bikini wouldn't last long on my body.

"Maybe you also need a dip in some cold water?" I whisper to him with a cheeky grin, giddy at the way he makes me feel when he looks at me like that.

"Between that bikini and your dress last night, I may have to live in a bath of cold water," he whispers back, while pulling me closer, his hands caressing my lower back. "Do you buy these things to torture me?"

I pretend to think about it. "Maybe?" I say because it's true. I'd absolutely bought this bikini with Daniel in mind. "Are you saying you don't like it?"

"I'm saying there's very little material to like…and I love it."

I reward his honesty with a light peck on the lips, earning some cheers and groans from our friends around us.

"You two aren't going to be all lovey-dovey all day, are you?" Amelia asks with a pained expression. The girl really is anti-relationship at the moment.

"And I thought we talked about PDA," Lucas adds, looking at where Daniel's hands are moving, towards my butt.

Daniel snatches his hands back.

"We did," I say, taking his hands and putting them firmly back on my hips. "And remember we concluded that what's good for you is good for me?" I look pointedly to where he's holding Amy close to his chest and send him a wink.

"Fine," he mutters, turning away from us. "I'll just bleach my eyes out when I get home."

Everybody laughs at this and then gets back to the tasks at hand. The boys are setting up what looks like a game of beach cricket, with the help of Sammi, Madi and Amelia, and the rest of us are edging our way down to the shoreline, attempting the first swim of the day.

"Izzy," Daniel calls as I'm hopping across the hot sand, now understanding why everyone else keeps their flip-flops on—this sand is giving my feet third-degree burns. "You need to put sunscreen on."

I turn to look at him and frown, torn because I'm almost at the water's edge and I'm dying to cool off, and the desperate need to have that man rub sunscreen all over my body.

"I'll be fine," I yell back, choosing to cool off first. "I'll do it later."

"Iz, you'll burn," I hear him shout before I am hit by the first wave and a thousand freezing-cold needles. They weren't kidding. This water is frigidly cold.

"Woah," I squeal as I emerge, dripping wet and turning into a popsicle. "Why is it so cold?"

Amy and Lilly shake their heads at me and laugh while they continue to make their way slowly into the ocean.

"There's a skill to it," Amy lectures me as she inches her way closer to where I'm getting pounded by waves. "You have to let your body acclimatise bit by bit."

I watch, fascinated as they take a good five minutes to reach waist-high deep in the water and then plunge underneath, emerging triumphant and not even a bit cold. *Huh.* Looks like there's a method to their madness.

"And now that we are wet, the key is to not stop moving," Lilly says as she jumps up and down. "Keep your body temperature up by staying in constant motion."

What a lot of rules to just go for a swim in the ocean, I think as I follow their lead, diving into waves and body surfing back to shore. And it works as well. Pretty soon the water feels warm and I'm too busy having fun to think about anything else.

"So, you and Daniel are a proper item now?" Lilly enquires as we bob up and down, letting waves crash over us as we have a quick gossip session.

I wipe the water from my eyes and smile. "He told me I've helped bring him back to life."

Amy lets out a whistle at this. "Has he told you what happened with his mum?"

"Yes," I say. Daniel and I had stayed up talking on the couch a few nights ago and my heart had broken when I'd heard his story. "I know the whole tragic story. It seems like his entire world came crashing down."

Amy nods while Lilly gives me a sympathetic look. "It was pretty traumatic. And I can tell you is that after his mum passed, he shut himself away from life. His grief was all-encompassing."

"We tried to help as much as we could," Lilly adds with a sad frown. "But he was resistant to all of our offerings of friendship. Most of the time, he'd only tolerate us."

"And now look at him," Amy says pointing to the group playing cricket on the beach. "I don't think I've ever seen him this animated, this happy, in all the time I've known him."

I look to where she's pointing and see Daniel catch the ball and throw it up in the air with glee. It seems that is a good thing because the next thing I see is him running to hug Lucas while Oliver watches on with a sour expression. And during it all, Daniel has a mile-wide smile.

"He does look happy," I agree. "He's so much more open now. So affectionate and thoughtful. I've never met anyone like him before."

"You sound like you care about him a lot," Amy says as we all start to shiver. Our keeping warm methods have failed us.

"I do," I say, shading my eyes to stare at him playing the strange game on the beach. "And I think he cares for me, too."

"Oh, he does," they both say at the same time.

"That boy is a smitten kitten," Lilly adds with a grin.

"Then I vote we get out of this ice bath and get our lovely men to warm us up."

The girls both whoop at this suggestion and we all make our way back to the warmth of our towels and the scorching sun. *This is the life.*

"Sunscreen, now," comes a growly voice from next to my ear as I'm lying on my front, trying to get the feeling back in my fingers and toes.

"Let me warm up a bit," I whimper back, trying and failing to suppress a shiver. I'm pretty sure my whole body is a shade of blue.

"We told you the water's cold," he points out, lying down next to me and pulling me closer, the warmth of his body effectively working to thaw mine. "You have much to learn about the ways of living down here."

I open one eye and look up at him from where I'm now nestled against him, chest to chest. "Will you teach me?"

His tender look travels over my face and a small smile flitters across his. "Will you listen?"

I nod, my head bumping against his biceps.

"Good, then first lesson. The Aussie sun is sharp and if you're not careful, you'll get burnt. You need sunscreen."

With a grin, I snuggle in closer to him, finally feeling warm and oh-so-content. "OK, just let me rest here for a minute. Please."

I feel rather than hear him sigh. "Fine. Warm up and then sunscreen."

He draws me closer still, wrapping his strong arms around me while I close my eyes again, leaning into the comfort of his body next to mine.

"Sure, sounds good."

And then, just like that, I fall asleep.

CHAPTER 19

Bella

"YOU LOOK LIKE A BOILED lobster," I mutter to my reflection in the mirror. Turns out Daniel was right and I was oh-so-very wrong to put off applying sunscreen, and I have the red, raw skin to prove it. Why don't I ever listen? Where a few hours in the Italian sun leaves my skin a lovely, bronzed colour, the same amount of time in the sun Down Under has left me red and splotchy. And in pain; anything touching my raw skin is causing me an endless amount of discomfort.

"What am I going to wear to help this situation?" I ask my reflection, noting that the person in the mirror is seriously lacking in answers today. "The least amount of material, it is," I say out loud, defiantly breaking the house rules—surely, they must be redundant now—and putting on my shortie pyjama set. The soft cotton feels just about manageable on my poor skin.

"Iz? Are you OK? You've been in there for like an hour," Daniel calls from the other side of the bathroom door.

I take a deep breath before letting him in, knowing that I'll be in for a big fat 'I told you so.'

"I'm a monster," I say after he's opened the door.

He stands there staring at me, a smile fighting to make an appearance on his face. "You're not a monster," he replies, gently stroking my flaming cheek. "But maybe you'll listen to me next time?"

I give him a look of defeat and hang my head in acknowledgement of his question. The Australian sun has beaten me and I know when to surrender.

"Come on, I've got some aloe vera after-sun lotion, which will help."

I follow him to his bedroom where I watch as he riffles through his top drawer, coming up with a tube of lotion I hope will soothe my burning skin.

"Here, this will help," he says, handing it over and taking a step back, running his hands through his hair and looking everywhere but me. Maybe the sight of me wearing my small clothes sitting on his bed is a bit too tempting for my roommate? Perhaps I don't look as bad as I'd thought.

"Let's go to the living room and get the AC on. You'll feel better once your body temperature is back to normal."

With a sigh, I stand up to follow him back out of his room, when really I'd wanted to stay and have a look around. It's the first time I've been in here and I'm curious to see what fills his most personal space.

"Iz? Are you coming?"

Daniel looks at me from the doorway and I nod, hoping that I'll be visiting his room again soon.

"Why don't you get started putting on that lotion, and I'll get us a cool drink," he offers after he's turned on the AC and made sure I'm settled on the couch. The man may not know it, but he's a born caregiver.

"Thanks," I say, watching him walk away. "Nothing alcoholic," I add, hearing him chuckle in response and smiling to myself. I love the sound of his laughter.

I turn the TV on, find *Dawson's Creek* on Netflix and lean back on the couch, applying the after-sun lotion to my face. *Oh boy, does that feel good.*

"Better?" Daniel asks as he sits down next to me, handing me a glass of lemonade with so much ice. The outside of the glass is sweating with condensation. My dehydrated body is suddenly dying to drink the whole thing in one go. Too much sun coupled with a hangover has left me feeling like a dried-up prune. *Sexy.*

"Can you do my back?" I ask once I've downed the lemonade— sour just like I like it—and I've finished moisturising the rest of my body. "I'm pretty sure that's where the sunburn is the worst."

"That's what you get for falling asleep on your front," he says in his grumpy, now deeply appealing tone.

"OK, I get it. Sun bad. Sunscreen good. Now, can you please help me?"

I place the aloe vera into his hands and turn around to face away from him, presenting him with my magenta-coloured back, complete with what is going to be the most horrendous tan line I've ever had. I wait patiently for him to lift my top up and once he starts, I then wait impatiently for him to apply the lotion. And when he does, every nerve ending along my spine comes alive. Sunburn all but forgotten, all I can focus on is the feeling of his rough hands on my skin.

"So good," I accidentally say out loud.

He chuckles. "You like?" he asks, his voice a little unsteady—like he may not be unaffected by having his hands on me.

"Hmmm," is all I can find to reply as he gently rubs lotion along my back, over my shoulders and back down along my sides. If I wasn't already burnt, this would have done the job of setting my skin on fire.

"All done," he says after the fastest ten minutes of my life. *Surely there's more skin he can rub?*

I shudder as he pulls my top back down and places a kiss on my neck, just above my shoulder. Gah, his lips may be my kryptonite.

"You can turn around now," he says with a smile clear in his voice. "Your man Pacey is on the screen, no doubt about to do something swoon-worthy."

This has me turning around quickly and, sure enough, there he is, trying to convince Joey to give him a chance. To love him more than she loves Dawson. And seriously, is there any competition? Dawson sucks.

"She's so blind," I say to Daniel, who's pretending to scroll through his phone with one eye on the TV in front of him. "How can she not know that the perfect guy is right in front of her?"

"Sometimes people are deliberately blind to these things, because if they acknowledge their feelings, then they also have to acknowledge the potential to get hurt."

I turn to Daniel and see that he's looking at me, his eyes darting between mine like he's looking for something. Answers? Reassurance?

"I get that," I say, inching closer to him and resting my hand on his leg. "Really being with someone takes a great deal of courage. And I know Joey will get there eventually. When she feels safe enough to trust him with her heart."

We are talking about the show, but I hope he can hear what I'm saying. That he can absolutely trust me to look after his heart if he's brave enough to give it to me. And it would seem like he is able to decipher this coded message because, as soon as I've finished my sentence, he's reaching over to pull me into his lap and his lips are on mine.

Sigh. *I could kiss this man forever*, I think before I lose the ability to think at all. Such is the masterful way he kisses me.

We kiss slowly at first, like our lips are getting reacquainted with each other and then it builds to something more. It's like we can't get close enough. We can't taste enough. We can't breathe enough of each other in. And just as we're about to move beyond just kissing, there's an alarm going off in my head. Or is it his? *How would I be able to hear an alarm in his head?* I think as he gently picks me up off his lap and places me back on the couch next to him.

"That's my work phone," he says, his voice deep and filled with regret. "I have to take it. It only rings when there's a Code Black level emergency."

I wave him away, too caught up in the aftereffects of that kiss to comprehend what he's saying. Who needs words anyway when you can just have mind-blowing kisses? Through this haze, I listen to Daniel speak in urgent tones to someone on the other end of the phone. Then he's back in front of me, a dark frown on his face.

"There's been a major incident on the freeway, seven cars involved, so I've been called to the station to be on standby, just in case."

"That's awful," I say, snapping out of my lust-filled daze. "I hope everyone is OK."

He grimaces in reply. "I've got to go. I'll be back as soon as I can."

I walk over to give him a hug, squeezing him tight and giving him some of my strength. Going to these sorts of accidents must be so traumatic and I hope for his sake that he's not needed at the scene of the crash today. That he can start this year trauma-free.

"You go. I'll be here waiting for you," I say as I watch him rush to the door, waving a harried goodbye before he leaves.

Humph. *Not exactly the end to the day I'd been hoping for,* I think as I get myself another glass of lemonade and a packet of chips to snack on.

"Looks like it's just going to be you and me, Dawson," I say to the TV screen as I press un-pause and get lost in the world of teenage angst. I know it's all a bit ridiculous, and I've seen it all before, but I can't help but get sucked in every time.

I'm halfway through the second episode of the evening—the one where Joey has to know that she's in love with Pacey—when my phone rings. A call from Mamma.

"Buon Anno," I say as I answer the phone. Happy New Year.

"Bella?" My mamma's shaky voice on the other end of the line has the hairs on the back of my neck standing up. Something's wrong.

"Mamma?" I say, my tone urgent, sitting up on the couch, my whole body at attention. "What's wrong?"

"I t-tried to call Luca," she starts, her voice wobbly with tears. "But he's not picking up."

"Mamma, I'm here on the line. What's happening?"

"It's your papa," she says. Words that have my heart bottoming out. Papa? "He's collapsed again."

"No," I whisper. My papa had survived a stroke over two years ago and has recovered since then. This can't be happening. "Tell me what's going on."

My mamma details the events of the day, her sentences broken up by tears. "Your papa had woken up with a bit of a headache this morning. We'd thought it was because of the vino from the night before. And then just before lunch, he just keeled over on the couch. I called for the ambulance straight away, like last time, and now we're at the hospital and they tell me he's had another stroke, that they won't be able to operate this time and I don't know what's going on. I need to talk to Luca, but I can't get a hold of him…" She sobs this last sentence, while I feel tears dripping down my face.

"It's going to be fine, Mamma," I tell her in the strongest voice I can muster. "Just like last time. The doctors will look after him."

"You need to find Luca," she repeats, like finding Lucas will fix this for all of us. "He'll know what to do."

"OK, I'll get him to call you. And we are coming now, Mamma. You just hang on 'till we get there, OK?"

I hear her sob, and I can barely hold myself together. We're so far away and she needs us. Papa too.

"OK, Mamma?" I repeat when she doesn't answer. "And you call if you hear anything from the doctors?"

"Si, yes, Bella. I will."

"I love you, Mamma. You give Papa a kiss from us and tell him we'll be there when he wakes up."

"OK," she says, her voice still wobbly but stronger now.

I disconnect the call and with shaky hands, I dial Lucas's number only to reach his voicemail. *Dammit, Lucas. Where are you?* Without a second thought, I call the only other person I can think of to help me through this.

"Izzy?"

The minute I hear Daniel's voice, I burst into tears, my grip on my emotions officially gone.

"Iz?" he says, his voice urgent. "Isabella? What's wrong?"

I take a deep breath in and try to compose myself. "It's my papa. I need to find Luca."

"OK, Iz. Just slow down and tell me what happened."

I stumble my way through the details of what my mamma had told me over the phone, ending with a hiccup and more tears. "I have to get home, Dan. I need Luca."

"I'll find him," he says, making me sag onto the couch with relief. "I'm on my way home. We'll figure this out together."

My heart races at this offer. "You can't leave, what about the emergency?"

"We have downgraded it. I was about to head home, anyway. Are you going to be OK until I get there?"

I look around the room feeling lost and helpless and alone. "I'm not sure?" I say, my voice breaking again. How am I going to get through this?

"Call Amelia and tell her what happened. Keep her on the phone with you until I get there."

I silently agree while wiping the tears from my face.

"Iz? Can you do that?" he asks when I don't respond.

"Yes, I'll do that."

"I'll be there soon. And we'll get through this together."

After I hang up the phone, I get up to pace around the room, my nervous energy not allowing me to sit still. *Daniel is coming home and we're going to get through this together,* I repeat to myself over and over again. Because if I allow myself to think of anything else, I may just fall apart.

CHAPTER 20

Daniel

WITH A MUFFLED CURSE, I put my phone in my pocket, hurrying to my locker to grab my bag, almost sprinting out the door and to my car. Thank god they had downgraded the Code Black level emergency and the surplus of firefighters had been told to go home, so I can leave work and get to Bella.

I groan out loud as I think about her voice over the phone; listening to her cry and not being there to comfort her almost killed me. She'd sounded so small, so filled with worry and grief, and the only thing I can think to do is to find a way to make it better.

"Come on, Lucas, pick up," I say as I dial his number. I'd plugged my phone into my Bluetooth to allow me to drive and talk at the same time.

"Dammit!" I swear again as his phone goes to voicemail. "Lucas, where are you?"

I hang up without leaving a message and call Amy, hoping she will pick up.

"Daniel?" I'm relieved to hear her voice pick up after three rings. Thankfully, one of them has a working phone. "What's up?"

"Hey, Amy. I need to speak to Lucas. Is he there with you?"

Something in my voice must have put Amy on high alert. "What's wrong?"

"I really need to speak with Lucas. Please, Amy," I add when it sounds like she's going to ask more questions.

"OK, he's right here."

I hear some muffled sounds before Lucas comes on the line. "Dan? What's up?"

I pause for a second, knowing my words are going to deliver a blow to Lucas, wanting to give him a few extra seconds before his world crumbles. Again.

"Bella just called me. It's your dad." I go on to explain everything I'd learnt from Bella, stressing that it's not the worst-case scenario and that no news is good news. Lucas is silent until I'm done and then he's all action. Given his role working as a doctor in a trauma unit alongside Amy as the chief nursing officer at Melbourne's biggest hospital, he is the best person to take control in this situation.

"Can you stay with Bella while I get things sorted?" he asks, going straight into solution mode. "I'm going to call my mamma and then book flights for us to leave tonight."

"OK," I get in before he continues, talking over the top of me, a man on a mission.

"Just make sure she's packed and ready. I'll send you the flight details. Can you drive her to the airport?"

I feel the wind knocked out of me at the thought of Bella leaving tonight, heading back to Florence to the unknown facing her on the other end and my own grief surfaces, threatening to overpower me.

"Of course, man. Whatever you need. You just take care of what you have to. I'll look after Bella."

"Thanks, I know you will," he says before rushing off the phone to call his mamma. I only hope she has some good news for him when he gets through to her. For Bella's sake, I hope for a miracle.

I force myself to drive the speed limit despite wanting to floor it to get home sooner and after another eight long minutes, I'm finally home, my seatbelt unbuckled and half out the door before the car is even in park. My only thought is to get to that girl inside. My girl.

"Iz? Where are you?" I call out as I open the door, rushing in and finding her on the couch, staring at her phone with a vacant look on her face.

"Izzy?" I crouch down in front of her and take her ice-cold hands in mine. She looks at me, her face soaked with tears, and I feel the wind knocked out of me. Her sadness is my kryptonite. "Iz, has anything happened? Have you spoken to your mum?"

She shakes her head as more tears spill down her cheeks, and I have to close my eyes against the pain those tears are causing me. "There's no change. Papa is still unconscious," she says in a small voice.

I pull her into my arms, settling her on my lap as we sit on the couch. Her small body shudders as she cries while I wrap myself around her, trying to shield her from this hurt.

"That's good, no change? It means he has gotten no worse," I say, trying to find something to help her.

"I guess," she replies, looking up at me with a hint of hope in her expression. "Last time he had a stroke it took him a while to wake up, and he was OK then."

"So, maybe it's the same this time. And he's at the hospital with doctors working on him. He's in the best place."

Her brow furrows, while her front teeth gnaw on her bottom lip. "Did you get through to Luca?"

"Yes, he's calling your mamma now. And he's booking you a flight home for tonight. He's going to send me the details, and I'll take you to the airport. You don't need to worry about doing anything."

Bella sighs against my chest and I hold her closer, wanting to absorb her pain and make it my own. Not wanting her to have to go through any of this.

"I guess I should pack," she says after several minutes.

"I'll do it. You just rest."

Her cheeks flame at this, a wonderful sight to see some colour on her pale cheeks. "You're not packing my underwear, Daniel Richardson," she says through a watery smile. "That will not be how you see my underwear for the first time."

I smile back at her, marvelling at how she can manage to find any humour at this moment, and press a gentle kiss on her lips.

"How about we do it together?"

She gives me another small smile and I help her up from the couch, pulling her in for a tight hug, kissing the top of her head and sending a quick prayer to whichever god is listening to spare her from anything bad that may be coming her way.

"Bella? Are you here?"

We both look up to see Lilly letting herself into the house.

"Amy called and told me what's going on. I've come to help," she says, walking over to envelop Bella in a hug. "I've brought brownies," she adds, holding up a box in her hand, like the baking angel she is.

"Thank you," Bella says, crying against her shoulder. "I can't seem to keep it together."

"You don't need to," Lilly says, patting her back. "You just need to put one foot in front of the other. We'll take care of the rest."

I watch as Bella's shoulders sag with relief and I mouth "thank you" to Lilly from behind her back. In this moment, I'm so grateful for this tightly formed support network we've created amongst us.

"OK, how about I help you get packed, while Daniel heats up the brownies? Once we're done, we can have them some with ice cream while we wait for Lucas to call."

Both Bella and I agree to this course of action and I watch the two of them head to Bella's room with a lump in my throat. I can't get my thoughts straight. The only thing I can do is try to hold it together until she's gone. Then I can examine how this is bringing back every nightmare I'd experienced with my mum two years ago.

As I'm putting the brownies in the oven to reheat, knowing that these may be just the thing to get Bella through this awful wait for any news, Lucas sends me a message.

LUCAS: Booked flights for me, Amy and Bella. Leaving at 12.15 a.m. You'll need to be at the airport at 10 p.m. at the latest. Make sure Bella remembers to pack her passport.

LUCAS: Thanks, man.

I look at the clock on the wall. It's already 9.00 p.m., which means we'll need to leave in the next fifteen minutes to get to the airport on time. My stomach clenches at the thought; only a few more hours with Bella before she leaves for who-knows-how-long. I don't know how I'm going to deal with another person I love leaving me. If we had been together more than two minutes, maybe I could offer to go with her, but our current relationship status makes it hard to know where I fit in her support system.

"We're done," Lilly says, coming into the kitchen and breaking through my thoughts. "She's just freshening up and then she'll be down."

"Good," I say as I allow Lilly to serve up three bowls of brownie and vanilla ice cream. "Because we have to leave soon."

"I hope they land to hear some good news," she whispers, watching the door to make sure she's not overheard.

"That's going to be the longest flight imaginable," I reply with a heavy heart. Those 24 hours in mid-air, not knowing what awaits them when they land, will be almost unbearable.

"Whatever happens, we'll all be here for them," she says, pulling me in for a side hug, perhaps sensing my inner turmoil.

"Yes," I say as Bella enters the room and steals my breath away. She does that every time she enters a room, but right now, in this moment, knowing that she's leaving, just looking at her is making me breathless.

"These look amazing," she says to Lilly, sitting at the table and taking a bite. "I know I serve these every day and have tried them so many times, but tonight they look even better."

"It's my re-heating skills," I tell her with a crooked smile, running my hand over her hair and placing a kiss on her forehead. I can't help myself; I need to touch her while I still can.

"We need to leave as soon as we're done here," I tell her as we all finish the generous helpings in front of us. "Lucas has you guys on a midnight flight, so we have to get you to the airport."

The mention of Lucas and the flight ahead has tears filling Bella's eyes and I have to hold myself back from picking her up and running away with her. Far away, where all of this hurt can't find her.

"OK," she says, her voice barely a whisper. "I guess we should go."

"You two go. I'll stay here and clean up," Lilly says. "I'll lock up after I leave."

I nod my thanks and take Bella's hand. We walk into the hallway together, where her suitcase is waiting. The same suitcase that she'd arrived on my doorstep with only a blink of an eye ago.

"Bella, we'll be thinking of you." Lilly pulls her into a hug, tears in her own eyes. "We all love you."

"Thank you, Lilly," she replies, squeezing her new friend back before taking a deep breath and looking at me. I can see her trying to bundle up her courage. "Let's go."

We drive to the airport in silence. I know my thoughts are too jumbled to work through with a conversation, so I can only imagine what's going on in Bella's mind. With one eye on the road ahead, I see her checking her phone every thirty seconds and can feel her anxiety as acutely as if it were my own. I'd been there in her shoes, waiting for that call that may or may not come and upend your world.

"I'll call you," she blurts out. "When we land? I'll keep you up to date."

I pick up her hand and press a kiss on her knuckles. "OK," I say simply. "You can call me anytime."

Bella tilts her head, yes, squeezing my hand in return and I continue, trying to make sure she understands what I'm saying. That I'm here for her, completely. "You call me day or night. For whatever. Anything you need, anything at all, you call me."

She smiles and tilts her head acknowledging what I'm saying. "I will."

I park the car in the short-term parking and we spend just one more minute looking at each other. For me, I'm trying to memorise her face as it is now, not knowing when I'm going to see her again, or the person she may be when I do. I know for a fact that losing a parent can change a person, and I'm hoping against hope that this doesn't happen to my beautiful, sweet Bella.

"We'd better get inside," she says, opening the car door with obvious reluctance. She knows that this will probably be the easiest part of the next few days.

"I don't know if I can do this," she says after I've taken her suitcase out of the trunk and set it in front of her.

"You can do this," I try to assure her. "So far, you just know that your Papa is unwell. That's it. Don't let your mind go anywhere else."

She presses her face against my chest and I hold her close. We stand like this for several more minutes before she pulls away. Squaring her shoulders, she gives me a half-smile.

"You're right. He'll probably be awake when we get there and scolding us for making an unnecessary trip to see him."

"Exactly. And it will just be a few days with your family before you come home."

"Home?" she says, looking between me and the airport in front of us. Perhaps wondering which is which?

We walk to the departure gate, where we find Lucas and Amy, both looking pale and stressed.

"Thanks for getting Bella here," Lucas says as I watch Amy pull Bella into a hug, both of them with matching tears in their eyes.

"You'll keep me up to date," I say to Lucas. "Let me know if she needs me."

He nods, his face pinched with worry. "Will do, Dan. Ladies, we need to get going."

Bella turns to me with wide eyes as I take her hand to walk her a few paces away, trying to get a few more seconds of privacy.

"I-I..." she starts before trailing off, looking lost again. "I'll call you."

"OK," I say before placing one last kiss on her lips. One last taste. "I'll be here."

She gives me one final squeeze before turning back to join Lucas and Amy, the three of them heading through the double doors and out of sight. I stand and watch for several moments longer, knowing that she's gone, but unable to move from my spot. The love of my life has just left me for an uncertain future and I feel like she has taken my heart right along with her.

CHAPTER 21

Bella

T HE NEXT 24 HOURS PASS in a blur of anxiety and tears. Our flight
had a stopover in Doha, where Lucas spoke to Mamma and
confirmed there'd been no change in Papa's condition. Both Amy
and Lucas assured me that this isn't bad news, but the worried look
they'd exchanged afterwards had left me even more on edge. *Come
on, Papa. Wake up!*

After another flight to London to catch our connecting flight
into Pisa, we then take a ninety-minute train ride to arrive finally
in our village, where our Uncle John is waiting to pick us up.

"Welcome home," my uncle says as he ushers us into his car,
helping Lucas pack the suitcases into the trunk. "We'll go straight
to the hospital, where your Mamma is eager to see you."

"How is she?" Lucas asks from his spot in the passenger seat.
Amy and I are sitting in the back, holding hands, exhausted from
the gruelling journey.

"Your Mamma is strong. She's coping well. Mostly she just sits
by his bedside, talking to him. Waiting for him to open his eyes."

"And what are the doctors saying? It's been hard to get a straight answer from Mamma."

My Uncle Rob turns to look at Lucas while we wait for a red light to turn green.

"As you know, your Papa has had another stroke. The doctors don't know how bad it is yet. I think it's just a wait and watch. We'll know more when he wakes up."

If he wakes up, I think as I feel Amy squeeze my hand. I look at her and can see the same concern on her pretty face.

"I know your Mamma will be happy to see the three of you. Your Papa too, when he opens his eyes…" Uncle Rob trails off and we sit in silence for the rest of the trip to the hospital. Each lost in our own thoughts about what awaits us when we get there.

"Here we are," my uncle says as he pulls up in front of San Giovanni Hospital, the closest hospital to my parents' house. "You go in and I'll park the car and meet you up there. He's in the ICU, same as last time."

The three of us emerge from the car, rumpled and travel-worn, and rush through the hospital doors. Lucas takes the lead and we follow behind, opting to take the stairs to the third level to get there as quickly as possible.

"Lucas. Bella."

We both look up to see our mamma in the hallway outside of what must be Papa's room, looking at us with relief plastered on her face.

"Mamma," I cry as I rush into her arms, desperate to be held by her and to offer her my comfort. This is where I've needed to be since the minute I heard the news.

"My Bella, I'm so glad you're here," she says, smoothing my hair and clasping me to her.

"How is he?" Lucas asks as Mamma lets me go to fold him into another tight hug. "Any change?"

Mamma shakes her head, her lips in a tight line, like she's only just holding it all together.

"I'm going to talk to the doctors, find out more," Lucas says, taking charge, completely at home in this environment.

"OK, the nurses over there will direct you to the right people," Mamma tells him while pulling Amy into a hug. Poor Amy has been watching this all unfold, trying to follow along the rapid-fire Italian dialogue. "You two can come and sit with Papa."

I take in a shaky breath and follow my mamma into a room—not too dissimilar to the one Papa was in last time—and am shocked by the sight in front of me. He is hooked up to three different machines, all buzzing and beeping sporadically, and he looks so still, so lifeless that I feel my tenuous control over my emotions break.

"It looks worse than it is," Amy says, putting her arm around my waist and anchoring me to remain upright. "These machines are just monitoring him; all the noise means that your Papa's body is still doing what it's supposed to." Amy working as a nurse in the same hospital as Lucas, means I know I can trust what she's saying, and at this moment I'm so grateful to have her by my side.

"Here, Bella. Sit with your Papa. Talk to him. Let him know you're here."

I do as my mamma asks, taking a seat next to the bed and picking up his cold hand in mine.

"Papa? It's me, Bella. I flew across the world to see you, to talk to you. So you'd better open your eyes and make it all worth it. OK?" I hold my breath and wait for any sort of response; an eye twitch, a hand squeeze, anything to let me know he hears me. That he's still here with us.

When he remains still and silent, I look at Amy for guidance.

"Keep talking to him, Bella," she says in a low voice.

And so, I do. I spend the next hour telling him all about my life in Melbourne. About working with Lilly and figuring out the crazy public transport system. I tell him about Snickers and our weekend together, about the Christmas tree debacle and the snow machine. About the day at the beach and the now-faded sunburn. I tell him all about Daniel.

"So, you see, Papa, you have to wake up and meet this wonderful man. Because I know you'd love him. He's the best man I've ever known, other than you and Lucas."

When I've run out of words and am emotionally spent, I put my head down on the bed next to this man I've loved so completely my whole life and I do the only thing I have left. I pray. For a miracle. For a way to bring him back to all of us.

We spend the next five hours like this, with Mamma, Lucas and I alternating who sits bedside, keeping vigil. Amy has managed the flow of the vast amounts of family members visiting, while keeping us filled with coffee and snacks. And through it all, my papa has remained still, eyes closed.

"Amy, you need to tell me the truth. The longer he remains like this, the worse it means. Is that right?"

She gives me a pained look, taking a moment to study me, perhaps to assess how much she should share.

"It's not a great sign, Bella," she finally says, putting her arm around my shoulder and pulling me close to her. "But we can't give up hope. Your Papa is strong. If anyone can wake up from this, it'll be him."

I sniff and try to put on a brave face, while I feel my heart disintegrate in my chest. In every worst-case scenario I'd played out in my head over the past 36 hours, I don't think I'd ever truly thought that we could lose him.

"Thanks, Ames," I say before standing up on shaky legs. "I'm just going to get some fresh air. Call me if anything happens."

She tilts her head in agreement, understanding my meaning—call the minute even an eyelid twitches—and I exit the ICU, heading for the gardens that surround the hospital. Once outside, I take a deep breath in and try to reign in my emotions. It will not help anyone if I fall apart now. With a better mindset in place, I pull out my phone to text Daniel. I know he's been worried about me and so I've been trying to keep him up to date as best I can.

BELLA: Still no change.

He replies instantly, almost like he's been watching the phone, waiting to hear from me.

DANIEL: OK. How are you?

BELLA: Hanging in there.

I wait for a text response and am startled when my phone rings in my hand instead.

"Izzy?"

My body reacts to the sound of his voice, feeling both soothed and comforted at the same time.

"Hey," I say, trying to keep the wobble out of mine.

"Talk to me," he says.

And so, I do. I tell him everything I'm feeling. My fears about what each passing hour of no-change could actually mean for my papa, my worry about what this is all doing to my mamma, and how I don't know what I'll do if the worst happens.

"I don't know how to exist in this world if he's not there," I tell him, my voice breaking as I cry again.

Daniel sighs down the line. "I know, baby. I know."

We sit on the phone in a silence broken only by the sounds of my tears.

"Whatever happens, you'll get through it," he says at last, forgoing any empty platitudes and telling me what I need to hear. "We'll get through it."

His words give me the strength to wipe my face and go back inside. Comforted by the knowledge that I'm not alone and there's a man on the other side of the world willing to catch me if I fall.

"I better go," I tell him now. "I'll call you later?"

"You call me whenever you need," he says.

And then, just after we've hung up, I hear the ping of a text message from Daniel. I open it up to see a photo, a selfie of Daniel with Snickers, with an accompanying message that reads: *We're both here for you.*

I let out a choked laugh as I look at the adorable image in front of me. Snickers has his face pressed up against Daniel's and they both appear to be laughing. Two of my other favourite guys hanging out together, sending me their support and for the first time in days, I'm able to smile. And it's enough to get me through the rest of this horrible day.

For the next few days, we live in limbo, gathered either at the hospital or back at my parents' home whenever we need a few hours of rest. As expected, our extended family has come out in droves; the house is filled with aunties and uncles, cousins and friends, neighbours and customers from the deli, all offering food, comfort and a soft place to land. Every time I need to take a break from Papa's bedside, a cousin is ready to drive me home and an aunty to feed me when I'm there. And through it all, my mamma has been a beacon of strength, never leaving her husband's side. She's barely slept in days, refusing to go home with one of us, stating that she has to be there, that he needs her.

"Just take a few hours to sleep in an actual bed," Lucas tries to reason with her, after we arrive to find her asleep in the chair next to Papa's bed.

"I'm fine," she says, rubbing her eyes and then taking Papa's hand in hers. "Did you talk to the doctor?"

Amy and Lucas exchange a look that has my stomach clenching with fear.

"Mama, we need to talk," he says, his voice muted and so very sad.

"Lucas, you're scaring me," she admonishes him. "What's happening?"

Amy squeezes her fiancé's hand and makes her way out of the room. "I'm going to get you all some coffee."

We watch her leave and then turn back to Lucas, who is running his hand over Papa's hair.

"Mamma, Bella," he starts before swallowing deeply and drawing in a deep breath. "The doctors have run some more tests and they've confirmed that Papa is in a coma. And that he may not wake up from it."

His words seem to reverberate loudly as I feel the room start to spin.

"What are you saying?" Mamma asks, her already pale face now devoid of colour. "He has to wake up."

My brother wipes at the tears that have gathered as he walks over to wrap his arms around Mamma before turning to pull me into the hug.

"The damage from the stroke is more extensive than last time and they can't know for sure whether it is too extensive."

I feel Mamma's legs give way and take a step back to let Lucas catch her, watching as he places her in the nearby chair and calls out for the nurse. Through a daze, I see the nurse and Lucas check Mamma's blood pressure and pulse as she cries, and I try to make myself wake up from this nightmare. *Surely this isn't really happening.*

"Bella?"

I turn my head to see Amy offering me a coffee and a sympathetic smile.

"What can I do? How can I help?"

My head is spinning and I can't seem to catch my breath. She looks at me and then guides me out into the hallway, sits me down in a chair and tells me to take in deep breaths.

"That's it, Bella. Just breathe in and out. Focus on that."

As my heart rate slows and I feel more centred, I turn to my almost sister-in-law and ask her to explain everything to me. How can it be that he may never wake up? She gives me a sad smile and explains what's taken place in a language I can understand, letting me know why the doctors are no longer sure that he will ever regain consciousness.

"I'm so sorry it's not better news," she says as I break down again. "But you can't give up hope."

She embraces me and we remain like this until Lucas comes out of the room, looking like he's aged fifteen years in the last four days.

"You OK, Bella?" he asks, putting his arms around me and Amy.

I squeeze him back, trying to let him know that I'm here for him, too. That he doesn't have to be the strong one for all of us.

"What happens next?" I ask while fearing the answer.

Lucas looks away from me, a lone tear trailing down his cheek. "Now we wait."

My broken heart breaks again at this and I feel like I want to crawl out of my skin. "For how long?"

He looks at me with equally broken eyes. "For as long as it takes. And we pray he comes back to us and we don't have to say goodbye."

I look at him, completely at a loss. I will never be ready to say goodbye.

CHAPTER 22

Bella

F OR THE NEXT TWO DAYS, we don't leave my papa's bedside. Mamma, Lucas and I are a tight unit, surrounding him with so much love. Mamma tells us stories of their time together when they were first married, before we were born, when he used to bring her flowers every day and take her out dancing each Saturday night, even though he hated to dance. She tells us about when we were first born and how Papa would be the one to wake up with us in the middle of the night. He would walk us around the house and sing to us until we'd fall back asleep. She tells us about how much he loved to watch Lucas play in his soccer team and me in my school plays, how he'd brag to all the customers at the deli about his amazing kids who were going to change the world someday.

"He is so proud of both of you," Mamma says now as she strokes her husband's cheek. "You, Lucas, he's always raving about how smart you are. And that there's no one in the world more qualified to be a doctor than you."

Lucas lets out a little laugh and shakes his head.

"And you, Bella, oh boy, your Papa has worshipped you since the day you entered this world. He saw you for the first time and that was it. You could do no wrong."

My eyes fill with tears at this because it's true. If there was a picture of a daddy's girl in the dictionary, it would be me.

"He was so proud of you moving to Melbourne and taking control of your life. I know that he loved hearing all the stories you both told us, the pictures you both sent. He'd show anyone who crossed his path the pictures of his brave kids making a life for themselves in Australia."

Lucas and I exchange a sad smile. Papa had been so supportive of us making a life for ourselves, even if it broke his heart to be away from us.

"I wish we'd been here," Lucas says vocalising the feeling I'd had inside this entire time. We should never have left him.

"Don't be silly," Mamma shushes him. "He wanted the best for you both and you would never get that here. The two of you were meant for something bigger and he knew it. And you would never have met Amy if you'd stayed here. Don't forget that."

He looks into the hallway where Amy is standing guard, the perfect, most supportive partner a person could ask for and gives us a sad smile.

"True," he agrees with an emotional look on his face. It's the look he always gets when he's thinking about Amy.

"I just want more time with him," I speak up with a catch in my voice. "I still need him."

Mamma comes over to hug me. "I know, my Bella. I know."

And so, we continue to sit and wait for him to come back to us.

"Bella, you need to look after yourself."

I look up to see Amy by my side and blink. *What time is it? What day is it?* We've been existing in this artificial space, bathed in fluorescence lights for too many days now. I've completely lost track of time.

"When was the last time you ate something?"

I try to think about what my last meal was and come up empty, and yet the thought of eating anything makes my stomach roll. The longer my papa remains in a coma, the worse my own body feels in response. It's like I'm slowly fading with him.

"Come on, let's get some fresh air," Amy says as she takes my hand and pulls me to my feet. I look to where my mamma is sitting, still holding Papa's hand. She waves me off.

"You need to move around, stretch your legs, Bella," Mamma says with a small smile. "I'll be here."

I kiss her on the cheek and gently pat my papa's leg before following Amy out of the room. The brightness of the sunshine highlights how long it's been since I've been outside and once the crisp winter's air hits my lungs, I'm grateful to have been forced to do this.

"Thanks, Amy," I say as we stroll around the hospital gardens. "I needed this. I was going a little crazy in there."

She smiles at me. "The first rule of looking after someone is that you have to take care of yourself. It's like they say on the plane, 'Put your own oxygen mask on before helping others.' You won't be any good to your family if your body gives up."

"I know," I say, while rubbing my hands against the cold. How had I already forgotten how the winter weather bites here? "It's just that I don't want to be away from him...just in case."

"You have your mum, Lucas, and me. We're all in this together."

I agree with this and we fall into silence, both lost in our thoughts, me still struggling with everything that has happened these past few days. *How did I go from being sunburnt and kissing Daniel on the couch to this nightmare?*

"Oh, and I spoke to Lilly, and she says to take all the time you need. That your job will be there for you when you get back."

Two days ago, when we'd gotten the news that Papa may not wake up, I'd asked Amy to call Lilly and let her know the situation. That I don't know when I'm coming back. Or even if I'm coming back.

"That's so nice of her," I say with a rush of affection for my boss and friend. "But she doesn't have to do that. Who knows how long I'll be here? She can't hold the position for me indefinitely."

"She knows, but she's happy to hold off filling the position until we know more. Let's just give it some more time. You need to have all your options open if you can."

I nod, because that makes sense, and the knowledge that I'll still have a job to go back to gives me some hope that maybe my life will one day go back to the way it was.

"Thank her for me when you speak to her. I know I've been sending texts to the group chat, but I really need her to know how much I appreciate this."

Amy smiles. "I will. And just so you know, everyone at home loves you and is thinking of you. Especially one particular young man, who, according to Lilly, is completely lost without you."

This brings another smile to my face, a rarity this week. "Daniel. He's been my lifeline through this whole thing. I'd be lost if I couldn't talk to him every day."

"So, you guys are serious?" she asks.

It's the question I'd been avoiding like the plague. How can I be serious with a man who lives on the other side of the world? A place that, depending on what happens in the next few days, I may never call home again.

"I don't know, Ames. I mean, I'm crazy about him, but everything is too up in the air at the moment. Just before all this happened, I thought we were on our way to being very much 'something' but now..." I trail off as the possibility of losing my papa and Daniel at the same threatens to overwhelm me.

"OK, let's not get ahead of ourselves," Amy says, perhaps noticing that I'm close to breaking again. "One day at a time."

One day at a time, I repeat to myself as I feel my pocket vibrate. A call. Please don't be bad news.

"Izzy?"

I blow out a relieved breath and show my screen to Amy to let her know who's on the line.

She gives me a small wave and turns to walk back to the hospital, giving me some privacy to talk to the man who has been consuming every other thought in my head.

"Iz? Are you there?"

"I'm here," I say.

"How's your dad? Any change?"

I give a sad shake of my head, even though he can't see me. "No, still no signs he's going to wake up." I try to keep the tears out of my voice, knowing that it upsets him to hear me cry.

"And you? How are you holding up?" his deep voice sounds filled with concern.

"Amy says I need to put my own oxygen mask on first," I say.

"What?" he sounds alarmed. "You need oxygen?"

Perhaps I should have explained my metaphor to him first. "No, sorry. I just mean that I need to look after myself better so that I can be there for the people who need me."

"And who's looking after you?" he says like a man who desperately wants that job.

"I have tonnes of people here to look after me," I reassure him. "Family, friends, Lucas and Amy. I just need to let them."

"Promise me you will," he says. "You're kind of important to me."

My heart thumps at this and I feel a sense of warmth inside for the first time in days. "Only kind of?"

I hear him chuckle. "Eh, you're not too bad to have around."

"You just want me home so you have an excuse to watch *Dawson's Creek*." I'm teasing him and it feels good. To not feel stressed and worried for just one moment.

"What would you say if I had finished season three without you?"

"I'd say you're in for a world of pain," I tell him while letting out a little laugh. I knew he loved that show! "And then I'd ask what you thought of that season finale."

"Well, you're right. That Pacey is the king of a grand gesture."

"I know right," I say and then spend the next five minutes dissecting every scene in that episode. Because it is by far my favourite.

"Thank you," I say after I've run out of adjectives to praise the wonder of Pacey.

"For what?"

"For taking me out of my life. Even if it's only for a few minutes."

"I wish I could do more," he says, his voice so sincere it makes the ever-present tears spring back into my eyes. Does one ever run out of tears? Because I feel like I've shed a lifetime's worth.

"I wish you were here." The words slip out in a moment of pure vulnerability.

There's a silence over the other end that rings loudly and lets me know I may have overstepped the boundaries of our newly-formed attachment.

"Ignore me," I rush to say when he doesn't respond. "I think I'm just delirious. And I need to eat; perhaps my blood sugar is making me say stupid things?"

"Iz—" he tries to interrupt my ramblings.

"Dan, forget I said that. I'm sleep-deprived and can't be held accountable for the words that come out of my mouth."

More silence greets this.

"OK?" I ask, determined to fix this.

"OK, Iz. I understand," he finally says.

"Good." Relief. "I'd better get back and let Lucas go home to get some rest."

"You get some rest as well," he says, that concerned tone back in his voice.

"I will. I'll call you later. Tomorrow?"

"Call me whenever you need me. I'm here."

With a deep sigh, I hang up feeling better and worse at the same time. Better, because hearing his voice is the highlight of my day. And worse, because what if I'd just scared him away permanently?

Twenty-four hours and four unanswered phone calls later, it appears that maybe my neediness has scared Daniel away. Because, why else, after being so supportive since my papa's collapse and everything that followed, would he suddenly stop picking up when I call?

The first time he didn't pick up I'd thought maybe he was at work and sure—he can't be available for me twenty-four hours a day. The second time? OK, he's busy. But once the third and fourth calls had gone unanswered, I'd started fearing the worst.

"I mean, what else can it be?" I ask Amy during our now regular walks around the garden. She'd made a point to come and get me and take me outside as often as possible, and the benefits for both my mental and physical health have been tremendous. Just fifteen minutes out of that sunless/airless room and I feel a thousand per cent better.

"I'm sure it's not what you think," she says with a smile. *What's she got to be smiling about?* "He's probably just busy."

"Or I've gone and freaked him out by moving too quickly. We're not even a couple yet and I'm asking him to fly to Italy to hold my hand. So stupid."

I've been mentally kicking myself in the butt for that comment since the second it left my mouth, and now that he's ghosted me, it seems like it's been a well-deserved butt-kicking.

"It's not like you guys aren't close. He's been putting out very clear signals that he's into you," Amy says, being all rational and not understanding at all the gravity of the situation.

"Being into someone usually involves a few dates, some handholding and kissing. Not being asked to support someone through the worst days of their life."

Amy goes to interrupt me but I'm on a roll.

"And also, what if everything I'm going through is bringing up all his own grief from losing his mamma? I've been so selfish in my trauma that I haven't even thought about what having to help me through this is doing to him."

"Bella, you're spiralling," she says, taking my hands in her and turning me to face her. "You're not being selfish, you're being human. If Daniel can't handle hearing about what's happening here, then he's a grown man and he can tell you that. You've done nothing wrong. Daniel will call you back and you need to calm down." Amy says this last part in a tone that feels like a slap in the face. The sort of slap that a person needs when they're bordering on being hysterical.

"Thanks," I say once her words have settled into my mind. "You're right. It's just that I…need him. I really need him."

"I know," she says, her voice sympathetic. "And he'll be back. I promise."

I look into her sincere eyes and even though I don't believe her—I think Daniel's run for the hills—I agree. It's not like my love life is a priority right now, anyway.

"You good to go?" she asks after giving me a short but firm hug. One that I gather strength from. "I think you should go back to your parents' house tonight, eat a proper dinner and sleep in a bed. Me and Lucas will stay here with your Mamma and we'll call you if we need you."

I reluctantly agree to this because, although I don't want to be away from the hospital just in case anything happens, I also desperately need a shower and to sleep in a bed.

"You'll call me?" I ask again.

"We'll call."

A long shower, a pair of my most comfortable pyjamas and a bowl of pasta later, I'm on the couch attempting to keep my eyes open to watch some mindless TV. I don't have it in me to concentrate on the drama of Dawson's Creek tonight, so I switch it to some reality TV show where all the contestants are wearing bikinis and looking for love.

"Good luck to you," I say to the screen in front of me while checking my phone again and seeing no messages from Daniel. "Love isn't all it's cracked up to be."

And speaking of cracked up, it would appear that I'm officially losing it if I'm talking to the television and lecturing these happy shiny people to give up on love.

"Ignore me," I say to the beauty on my screen who's currently in a love triangle. "I'm just bitter because I drove away the one man who could have been my everything."

With a sigh, I turn it all off and decide to go to bed. Who knows what tomorrow will bring; I need to get some proper sleep.

As I'm making my way to my room, turning off lights as I go, the doorbell has me jumping out of my skin. I don't think I've ever heard the doorbell ring before in this house; everyone we know just lets themselves in.

"Coming," I call out, curious and somewhat alarmed at who would be at the door at 9 p.m. With some trepidation, I open the door and am floored by the person standing in front of me.

"Hi Izzy."

It's Daniel.

CHAPTER 23

Bella

"WHAT ARE YOU DOING HERE?" I ask as I blink rapidly, trying to make sense of what's in front of me. It can't be real; my frazzled brain has finally snapped.

"You asked me to come," Daniel says, his hands in his pockets, looking unsure. Like perhaps I wouldn't want him to be here.

"But—but," I stammer, still in shock. "You can't really be here."

"The thirty-hour total flight time says something different," he tells me with a crooked grin. "Can I come in? It's freezing out here."

I spring back to life, pulling him inside, wheeling his suitcase in behind him. Once I close the front door, I lean back against it, feeling the need to have something solid to hold me up.

"What did you do?" I ask again because this, him being here, is like a dream. At any moment, I'm going to wake up and he will have disappeared.

"I know it's a bit much," he says, running his hand through his hair. "But you sounded so upset and like you needed someone to be here for you. And the next thing I knew, I'd booked a flight and was on a plane. It all happened so fast."

"Is that why you haven't been answering my calls?"

He takes my hand and squeezes it. "My phone's been in flight mode for the last day. I had to rush to catch my connecting flight—did you know there's no easy way to get here? That you have to go through London, then Pisa and then the train trip?"

I laugh at his utter dismay over the arduous trip to get from Melbourne to my doorstep. "I'm well aware that it's not easy. But how did you even find me? This house?"

"Amy," he says. Ah, that explains her smiling face this afternoon. She knew he was coming. "I called to ask both Lucas and Amy if they thought it would be appropriate for me to turn up like this and they were both OK with it."

As they should be, I think. *Given what a basket case I've been, I bet they're happy to have someone here to look out for me.*

"So, let me get this straight," I say as I step closer to where he's standing, placing my hands on his chest just to double-check he's not a mirage I'd conjured up in my sleep-deprived state. "I say that I wish you were here with me and you just get on a plane and come over?" Even as I'm saying this out loud it sounds eerily similar to what I did just a few months ago. Jumping on planes seems to be our theme.

He gives me a sheepish look. "When you put it like that, I sound a bit nuts."

"You don't," I object. "I was the crazy one to even ask you."

Daniel puts his arms around my back and pulls me closer until we are touching chest to chest. It's blissful. "Are we arguing over who is the crazier person?"

I laugh and plant a kiss on his lips. "I promise you, in that argument, I'll always win."

He kisses me back, a gentle kiss that tells me without words how much he cares and how much he missed me, and I kiss him back with the same sentiment. It's only been a week and I've missed him like crazy.

"So, you're here," I say as I come up for air.

"I'm here. For as long as you need me."

This has me holding him tightly as the emotions from the past few days through to his showing up on my doorstep pour out of me. I lean into him and let myself cry. I'm so tired.

"I got you," he whispers in my ear.

Sigh. He's got me.

After Daniel has showered and eaten one of the several pasta dishes left by one of the many aunties who have been cooking up a storm as a way to show their love, we are cuddled up on the couch, Daniel in a lounging position with me half lying down next to him, chatting about everything and nothing. It feels good to just be normal again.

"So, I see you and Snickers are besties now," I say as I run my hand over his chest, garnering a little groan of appreciation from the man next to me.

"He's not so bad," he admits. "When he's not being a pillow hog."

"You let him sleep in your bed again?" I ask, my eyes wide with shock.

"Lilly dropped him off a few days after you left. She told me he's a wonderful emotional support animal and that he'll help me not feel so lonely."

"And did it work?"

Daniel makes a hand gesture that says so-so. "He's noisy, like you. So that helped with the silence you left behind. And he's not so bad to cuddle."

"Better than me?"

He shifts me so that I'm almost lying on top of him. "There's no one I'd rather cuddle with than you."

I place my head on his chest with a sigh. "So, no need to be jealous of the dog?"

"I wouldn't go that far. He sheds less hair than you." This has been a big source of angst for Daniel since I moved in: my hair everywhere.

"It's the price you pay for being with someone with such luscious hair," I remind him with a slight poke in the ribs.

"I guess? I just don't know how it ends up in places like in the honey pot. Or wrapped around my toothbrush."

"I like to keep you on your toes," I say, loving that he's here with me and we are having this ridiculous conversation.

"What's happening for the rest of tonight? Are you going back to the hospital?" he asks after we've sat in a comfortable silence for a while.

"No, Amy and Lucas insisted I come home for the night. Which made sense given they knew you were arriving," I say, marvelling at how they kept this a secret from me. "I'll be going back first thing tomorrow morning."

"Do you...I mean, would it be...?" he trails off, looking uncertain again.

"I'd love for you to come with me. Meet my mamma. And my papa."

My heart breaks a little as I say this last part. This isn't the way I'd hoped for my parents to meet Daniel and I can only hope that they will have a chance to get to know each other under better circumstances. If my papa ever wakes up.

"Are you sure?" he asks, running his hand over my hair in a soothing motion. "I can just wait here for you? Or in the hospital café? I don't want to get in the way."

I look at him closely to see where this is coming from. "If being in a hospital is too hard for you, you don't have to come."

He shakes his head. "That's not it. I just know what it's like, the waiting, the uncertainty. I don't want to overstep."

"Daniel, you flew over thirty hours to get here because I asked you to. I think 'overstepping' is well in our rear-view mirror now."

"OK, then I'll be happy to be with you tomorrow. And meet your mamma and papa."

With that settled, I lie back down next to him on the couch. And with a yawn, I close my eyes, grateful that he's here and that sleep is finally coming to get me.

The next morning, with Daniel by my side, I approach the hospital in a better frame of mind than the previous days. Maybe today will be the day we get our miracle?

"Dan," Lucas says from where he's pacing the hallway outside of Papa's room. It's such a common occurrence I'm surprised he hasn't worn holes in the floor. "Thanks for coming."

"How's Papa?" I ask, interrupting the pleasantries to get an update. "I'm guessing from the lack of messages that there's been no change?"

Lucas shakes his head, his mouth drawn down into a frown. "No change. The doctors are going to run some more tests today, and then we may need to make some decisions."

I feel a chill fill my body. *Decisions?* Daniel squeezes my hand in support and I move closer to him, taking comfort just from his nearness.

"What sort of decisions?"

"Bella," he starts in a hushed voice. "He can't stay like this forever. So, the doctors will do another scan, and then we can talk. No need to worry about it now."

Typical Lucas, always trying to shield me from the worst-case scenario.

"Why don't you go in and see Mamma? I'm sure she'll love to meet Daniel."

I've told Mamma all about Daniel over the past few days and I'm pretty sure she's already in love with him. The snow machine story sealed the deal; she's a true hopeless romantic, my mamma.

"OK," I agree while giving Lucas a pointed look. "But you will let me know more about these 'decisions' we have to make. I need to be prepared."

Lucas nods and draws me in for a quick, but fierce, hug. "We're in this together. And we'll be there for each other."

With a pit in my stomach, because that didn't sound promising at all, I take Daniel's hand again and enter the room.

"Hi, Mamma," I say in a soft voice, going up to the bed and kissing my papa on the cheek. "Look who came to visit."

Mamma looks up with tired eyes and her face lights up when she sees the man standing next to me. I've shown her so many photos of Daniel that she recognises him immediately and the pure joy on her face in meeting him just makes me love him and the fact that he came all this way to be with us, even more.

"*Buongiorno,*" he says looking nervous and so-freaking-adorable. "*Che piacere incontrarla.*" It's nice to meet you. *When did he learn Italian?*

Mamma looks at me with raised eyebrows and smiles. "It's nice to meet you too," she says in broken English. Mamma's been practising her English so she can communicate with Amy, and now Daniel, it would seem.

"Can I get you something to eat? Or drink?" he offers in English. Looking relieved to not have to continue in Italian.

"No, no. You two sit and talk to Papa. I'm going to stretch my legs."

We both watch as she places a kiss on her husband's lips before walking to the door. "I'll meet you later?" she says to Daniel before she leaves.

"*Si,* yes," he replies, granting her one of his wide smiles.

"I didn't know you could speak Italian," I say after Mamma leaves and we've taken the seats next to the bed. "Why didn't I know this?"

"Because I don't," he says with a laugh. "I just listened to an 'Italian for Dummies' podcast on the flight over here. Thought I'd need it to impress your family."

I look at him, dumbfounded by this gesture. He spent a thirty-hour flight learning a new language just to impress the people I love the most.

"I'm just glad your mum can speak a little English because, after that brief conversation, I was all out of words."

We laugh together while I hold myself back from kissing him senseless. *When will he ever stop surprising me with his thoughtfulness?*

Once I have my emotions back under control, I turn to the man lying in the bed next to us. So still, just like every day since we've been here.

"Papa, I'd like you to meet Daniel. He's the guy I've been telling you about."

Daniel shoots me a questioning glance before he focuses his attention. "It's nice to meet you, sir."

We both wait for a moment, like we're expecting a response, before I continue. "Papa, Daniel flew all the way here to meet you. So now would be a great time for you to wake up."

More silence, more nothing.

"Please, Papa. Please. You have to wake up."

Daniel takes my hand and runs his lips over my knuckles. "Your daughter's right, Mr. Mancini. I flew all the way here to see you. So, it would be great to talk to you, to hear all your stories about our Bella here. But if you need to rest some more, to get stronger, that's OK too. We'll wait."

I look at him, talking to my papa like he's known him forever, and my heart pinches. The words that are coming out of Daniel's mouth sound like ones he's had to say before. And I feel terrible knowing that he's probably had to say them to his own mamma. In the worst circumstances.

"In the meantime," he continues while I watch him with my heart in my eyes, "let me tell you what I know about your daughter. I have to say, you've done well to have lived with her for so many years. She's so noisy, and she's terrible in the mornings, and what's with all the singing she does when she thinks no one's listening? Your daughter is beautiful, but boy, is she tone deaf."

I let out an indignant snort and kick him in the shin. *How dare he criticise my singing?*

"And what's with the sport she watches? Formula One? That Ferrari team doesn't seem to be any good."

With bated breath I look at my papa's sleeping form, knowing that if anything is going to get him up and fighting, it's someone insulting his beloved team Ferrari. Still nothing.

"It was worth a try," I tell him with a sad smile, knowing what he was trying to do. To bring some levity into the room. "But, if you say one more bad thing about Team Ferrari, we're going to have a problem."

He grins at me. "Noted."

We sit together for another hour, talking to Papa about our lives in Melbourne, filling in the silence and willing him to wake up.

"How's things going in here?" Lucas asks from the doorway. He'd gone home to shower and change and is looking better than he did earlier that day.

"No change," I say, hating those two particular words.

"Why don't you take Daniel out for a few hours? Show him around *Valle delle Stelle*. I'm sure he'd love a tour."

Daniel shakes his head. "I'm not here to be a tourist. I'm here for support. Just ignore me. I don't want to get in the way."

"I think it'd be a great way to get Bella out and moving. Maybe even eat something?" Lucas says, giving him a pointed look like I'm not in the room and can't see what he's doing. He wants to let me have a few enjoyable hours before we have to face 'decisions' later today.

"I'm happy to do whatever Bella wants."

I look between them, feeling torn. Because part of me wants to take Daniel around the village and show him where I grew up, what makes me who I am. But the other part doesn't want to leave this room.

"It will be good for you, Bella," Lucas says. "Remember, you need to look after yourself."

This decides it for me. I can't have everyone worried about me when there's so much else to be concerned about.

"OK, we'll go out for a few hours. Have some lunch. Then we'll be back."

Daniel takes my hand to help me out of my seat.

"You'll call us..." he says to my brother as we exit the room.

"Of course."

The sunshine is almost blinding as we step out of the hospital and walk to the car I'd borrowed from a cousin. It's a benefit of having family close by; they're all ready and willing to help in a crisis.

"We don't have to do this, Iz," Daniel says from his seat in the passenger seat, gripping the seatbelt as I zoom us away from the hospital. He doesn't realise this yet, but I drive a bit like a Formula One driver—the faster, the better.

"No, it's good. I need to get out of there. The waiting is suffocating me."

"I know that feeling well," he says, looking out of the window with a pensive expression. "When my mum was in her last days, and the morphine was the only thing keeping her alive, I sat with her for hours on end. Those four white walls felt like they were moving in on me; every day they got closer and closer."

My mind races at the thought of Daniel sitting alone in a room with his dying mum, and I can't imagine what he must have gone through. Alone.

"I wish I could have been there with you," I tell him after I've gotten my voice under control. The image of Daniel in that room is now one that I think will haunt me forever.

"I wish she could have met you," he replies with a sad look on his face. "You're both so similar. She would have adored you."

We sit in silence after this, too many big emotions filling the space between us. What I wouldn't give to have met his mum. For her to be alive and waiting for him back at home.

"Here we are," I say when I've found us a parking spot in front of my parent's deli.

"You drive like a maniac," he tells me as he unravels himself from the small passenger seat and stretches. "I think you should stick to public transport when we get home."

My stomach plummets at the mention of 'home', the idea that I'll be going back there soon. With him.

"Come, meet my aunty," I say in place of addressing the enormous elephant in the room. That I don't know if I'll be returning home with him. "She's looking after the deli this week."

When my papa went to hospital, the family got together and made a roster to ensure the deli could remain open and fully staffed. The generosity of these people, my people, takes my breath away.

"*Zia Anna*," I say when we enter the shop. "This is my friend Daniel. From Australia."

My aunty looks him up and down and starts fanning herself in a dramatic fashion.

"*Lui e magnifico*," she sighs. He's gorgeous. "*Delizioso*."

I grin because she's so right. He is delicious.

"I'm just showing him around the village for an hour and wanted to say hello."

She looks at Daniel, who is rubbing the back of his neck and looking embarrassed—clearly understanding the Italian word for 'delicious'—and pulls him in for a big hug.

"*Benvenuto*," she says. Welcome.

"*Grazie*," he replies, hugging her back and giving me a look over my shoulder. A look that is pleading for rescue as my aunty holds on for several seconds too long.

"OK, Zia," I say, my smile bigger than it's been in a while. "You can let him go. We're going to walk around town. We'll come and say goodbye before we head back to the hospital."

"You take care, little Bella," she says, pinching my cheeks like I'm ten years old again. "And tell your mamma not to worry about the deli. We're looking after everything."

I tear up and squeeze her with another hug. "*Grazie, Zia. Grazie.*"

With a last wave, we leave my family business and I take Daniel on the promised tour of where I grew up. As we walk around, hand in hand, Daniel shivering in the cold that he says is 'unlike anything he's ever felt before', I point out all the landmarks that make this place so special.

"It's like a movie set," he says, looking around with wide eyes, taking in the small shop windows, the small laneways, the cobblestone footpaths; all so alien to the urban Melbourne city architecture. "It's so gorgeous here. I don't know how you could have left."

I look around this place I've called home my whole life through his eyes and can admit that with the last dusting of snow on some rooftops and lampposts that it looks magical.

"It is beautiful," I agree. "But what you see here, everything within your eyeline? That is it. That was my entire world."

He does a 360-degree turn. "Huh."

"Small, right?" I say as I wave to the fourth person I know on this street. "Stiflingly so."

Daniel looks at the people roaming around at a slow pace, many stopping to chat on the footpath, most with a cheerful smile or greeting.

"Small isn't bad," he says finally. "When it's filled with so much goodness."

He's right, I think as I greet another cousin with a kiss and a hug. This place is filled with only goodness. And love.

"But it is cold," he continues, his breath coming out in plumes of smoke, his Melbourne winter jacket not cutting it in the thick of this European winter. "Let's find somewhere inside to eat."

I chose the perfect little café that sells coffee and pizza to die for. Once we've settled in, order placed, I sit back in my seat and stare at him. His cheeks are red, as is the tip of his nose, and his hair is a tousled mess. He looks tired after the gruelling journey to get here and yet, to me, he looks utterly perfect. Or as my aunty pointed out, *delizioso*.

"What's going on in there?" he asks, tapping me on the forehead before running his hand down my cheek.

"Just admiring the view," I tell him, delighting in the blush that blooms on his cheeks. He's even hotter when he's embarrassed.

"Hmmm," he says, sweeping a glance over me. *Gosh, I hope I don't look as bad as I feel.* "I think I have the best view."

We lean forwards at the same time, a kiss needed to punctuate this delightful flirting, and just before our lips can touch my phone blares to life. I jump back to take it out of my bag and, with a sinking feeling in my stomach, I answer the call.

"Lucas?"

CHAPTER 24

Daniel

I WATCH WITH MY HEART in my mouth as Bella answers the call from her brother. When I see tears run down her cheeks, I reach over and grab her free hand in mine, my mind going to the worst news.

"He's really awake?" she says in a shaky voice, her words reverberating between us. *What?* "He's, OK?"

I squeeze her hand in encouragement and then get up to cancel our food order so we can get out of here and to the hospital as soon as possible. With some hand gestures and broken Italian, I manage to explain the circumstances and—not surprisingly given the smallness of the village—

the waiter knows the Mancinis and their situation and is waving us away with a 'go now' gesture.

With a grateful smile, I hurry back to where Bella is putting on her coat, her phone still pressed up to her ear.

"What does that mean?" she asks as we make our way outside and down the path to where we had parked her car. She listens intently to what her brother is saying and then turns to me with a bright smile. One that I haven't seen in far too long. "OK. We're on our way back now."

She hangs up the phone, throws it into her bag, and then turns and launches herself at me. I catch her in my arms, lifting her up and twirling her around. Her excitement is contagious.

"He's awake!" she exclaims as I place her feet down on the ground. "Lucas says he opened his eyes and seems to understand what's going on around him."

I squeeze her and kiss the tip of her cold nose. "That's incredible news."

"Yes," she says, her voice breathless. "Lucas is trying not to get my hopes up, but it's a good sign."

"Absolutely. It is a good sign. It's the best."

"Let's go then." She lets go of me and walks around to the driver's side of the car. Once we're buckled in, she stops and takes a deep breath. "I can't believe he's awake," she says, almost like she's talking to herself. "I'd been preparing for the worst."

I don't tell her that I'd been doing the same, that it was part of the reason that I'd hopped on a plane to be with her. And I'm so unbelievably happy that she won't have to deal with that fate.

"Well then, let us get to the hospital. I'm looking forward to meeting your Papa properly."

Bella places a small kiss on the side of my mouth, pulling back to smile at me, before she puts the car into gear and zooms off towards the hospital. If I thought she was a fast driver before, well now that she's got somewhere to be, her foot barely touches the brake pedal. I hold on tight and pray that we get to the hospital in one piece.

"You can breathe now," she says with a dry chuckle as she slides into a parking spot so tight that has me sucking in my breath, sure that she's going to hit something. "I'm actually a really good driver."

"If you say so," I mutter as I let go of the door handle and flex my fingers. I'd been holding on so tightly that my knuckles are sore from my efforts.

We enter the hospital together and she takes my hand, pulling me towards the stairs, the simple gesture tugging at my heartstrings. This here is an important moment for her family and she's including me with them.

"Come on," she says as she runs up the stairs.

I follow behind, keeping close, making sure she doesn't stumble. Bella hasn't slept or eaten properly in days. There's no way I'll not be right behind her ready to catch her if she falls. Both literally and figuratively.

"Mamma!" she yells as we open the doorway to the ICU and see her family in the hallway, all weeping in each other's arms. "What's happened?"

"Nothing, Bella," Lucas says quickly, correctly reading the panic on her face. "We are just waiting for the doctors to do an assessment. But Papa is still awake. He's conscious and alert…"

He trails off and looks between his mum and Amy, who all look relieved and anxious at the same time. How is that even possible?

"So, why are you all crying?"

I take her hand in mine in case the news isn't entirely good.

"Your Papa is awake," Amy says, biting her lip and looking at Lucas. "But he's not able to talk or move…yet."

Bella sags against me and I put my arm around her to anchor her in place.

"What does that mean?" I ask when Bella doesn't seem like she's able to.

"Nothing, yet," Amy answers. "He's just woken up after a coma. It could take a while for everything to settle into place in his brain."

"So, still good news, then?" I ask, pulling Bella even closer, aware that she's shaking now.

"It's great news," Lucas says, giving Bella a reassuring smile. "Papa is awake. He's aware of his surroundings. He's able to nod his head and answer questions to let us know his brain function is OK. We just need more time to see whether there is permanent damage."

I watch as Bella walks over to where her mum has been listening to the conversation unfold. Mrs Mancini has a determined look on her face as she takes her daughter into her arms.

"My Bella, this is the best news. Your Papa has come back to us."

This seems to break the dam in Bella and she sobs into her mother's arms. I force myself to look away, unable to watch her cry so deeply. Even the sound of her tears is ripping me up inside.

"Dr Lucas Mancini?"

We all look up to see the doctor exit the hospital room, wearing a neutral expression. I listen and try to translate the rapid-fire exchange in Italian in front of me, keeping a close eye on Bella's face. Mostly, she seems to take in whatever the doctor is saying and it's calming her down. A fact I'm grateful for.

"The doctor is pleased with the tests he's run so far," Lucas translates for the benefit of me and Amy. "And he thinks Papa will be able to talk again soon."

My heart beats fast at this bit of good news, delighted for this family that they will get their patriarch back.

"The paralysis is a different story," Lucas continues, causing everyone to deflate a little. "It may be permanent."

The implications of this seem to settle between us, before Bella's mum speaks up, her voice strong and clear.

"*Finche la sua mente e forte, il suo corpo seguira.*"

I look at Bella to translate for me and she does so with tears in her eyes.

"As long as his mind is strong, his body will follow."

We all sniffle at this and I marvel at how strong this woman in front of me is. She's spent seven days fearing the worst and now she's got her husband back. She's happy to take whatever he's able to give.

"So true, Mamma," Lucas says as he draws her close to his side. "Whatever happens, we're just happy to have him back."

They turn to where the doctor had been waiting for them to digest the news, asking about the next steps, and I watch another conversation take place that I don't understand.

"We need to be careful not to wear Papa out," Bella says as the doctor leaves us. "So, only two people to visit at a time and we need to keep the conversations short."

Everyone agrees as it's decided that Bella's mum is to visit first, then Lucas and Bella and, if there's time, Amy and me.

"I don't need to go in," I say to Bella quietly as we wait in the hallway. "It should be family."

She pouts a bit at this. "No, I need you to meet him. I need him to know you're here."

I can't and don't want to argue with her, so I give in, putting an arm around her shoulder and letting her lean on me as we wait. For her to see her dad awake again after so long, and for me to meet the father of the person who means more to me than anyone else in the world.

It's not until later that evening that the subject of the future comes up. After spending time with Bella's dad, whose eyes are the same colour as the woman I love and seemed to twinkle as he looked between the two of us, we arrive back at the house to have dinner with Amy and Lucas.

"Amy is going to try to get a flight home tomorrow night," Lucas says as we sit down at the table to eat. There's so much food in front of us, it's like they catered the dinner for forty people instead of four.

"I don't think I can take much more time off work," Amy says almost apologetically. "And now that your dad is out of the woods..."

"It makes sense for you to go home," Lucas says, placing a kiss on her temple. "I'm going to stay on for a bit longer to assess the situation here."

I feel Bella's gaze on me and I look up to see her eyes locked on mine.

"Um, maybe I'll try to book the same flight as you, Amy?" I say, unsure of what my place is here now that things seem to be stable. I don't want to overstay my welcome. Especially if Lucas's fiancée is thinking it's time to go home.

"That'd be great," Amy replies with a relieved smile. And I can't blame her. Doing that journey home alone wasn't something I was anticipating with much enthusiasm.

"Do you have to leave so soon?" Bella asks in a small voice, making me want to retract my previous words and offer to stay forever.

"He probably has to get back to work, Bella," Lucas answers for me. "And besides, we don't know how long we'll be here sorting everything out."

She bites her lip and offers a weak smile. "Of course."

"I can stay," I say in a loud voice, causing everyone to look at me. "I have lots of leave and my boss has told me to take as much time as I want. If you need me, I can stay."

She blows out a deep breath and sits up straighter, like she's gathering up the last of her strength. "Lucas is right. We don't know how long this will take. You can't stay here forever."

With my eyes, I try to tell her I can, that I will, but the conversation seems to have moved on and the moment passes. It's not until later that night, as she's setting me up in her bedroom, that the topic comes up again.

"Bella, nothing's set in stone. I can stay as long as you need me."

I can see her resolve waver before she pulls it back in. "You can't. I don't know when I'll be able to leave. Or if I'll be able to leave."

This last part has me reeling. In all of this, I'd never fully considered the idea that Bella wouldn't be coming home to me.

"You may not come back?" I ask, trying to keep the hurt out of my voice.

She gives me a pained look and shakes her head. "I don't know what's going to happen. If my Papa has permanent damage, then who will be here to help Mamma? It's not like Lucas can stay. He has a job, and he has Amy..."

My heart deflates as I take in what she's saying. That perhaps there's nothing as important for her to come back to.

"Of course," I agree now instead doing what I really want to, which is to beg her to come home. With me. "You do what you need to for your family."

She bites her lip, a gesture that shows how uncertain she's feeling. "You understand?"

I finish making up the single bed where I'll be sleeping tonight—Bella sleeps in her parents' room—giving me a minute to regain my composure.

"Of course, I understand," I say finally, giving what I know is a tight smile. It's the best I can do in these circumstances. "There's nothing more important than family. And believe me, you need to treasure them while you can."

I say this last part with a hollow feeling in my chest, the sort of pain that had been commonplace in my life before Bella showed up.

"You look after your family," I say again when she continues to stare at me, with sadness on her face.

"But then, who's looking after you?"

I reach over and place a small, but tender peck on her lips. The lightest of touches before I pull away, holding back all my emotions.

"I don't need to be looked after. I'm used to looking after myself."

We wake the next morning to more good news: Bella's dad started talking during the night, showing that his vocal cords haven't been impacted by his paralysis.

"It's significant progress," Lucas tells us over breakfast. "We're going to see him today. Spend some time with him before Amy leaves later this evening."

At some point during the evening yesterday, Lucas had booked flights home for both me and Amy. Leaving from Pisa at 11.30 p.m., meaning I have less than twelve hours to spend with Bella before we have to say a possible permanent goodbye. I'd grappled with the idea of raising us trying a long-distance relationship but squashed the thought almost immediately. It's not like Melbourne and Florence are close neighbours. I have the thirty-hour journey home to prove it. It all feels a bit hopeless, living an entire world apart.

"I think you should take Daniel out and show him a bit of Florence before he leaves," Lucas says to Bella now, perhaps sensing the tension in the air. "It'd be a shame for him to come all this way and not see anything."

Before I can protest, Bella is agreeing. "We can see Papa first thing, then I'll drive him into town. You and Amy can meet us there and they can take the train to Pisa from there?"

They both start working on the logistical details while all I can focus on is the fact that I'll be leaving and she'll be staying. I don't care what I'm doing today, as long as I'm with her.

"Are you sure you don't want to stay close to the hospital?" I ask Bella as we clear away the breakfast dishes. "I don't mind staying here."

She shakes her head, a look of determination on her face. "Lucas assures me that Papa is going to be fine. That he's on the road to recovery, even if it's a slow one. So, I want to spend this day with you, to show you around. To make it special."

The way she's framing it is almost like she's planning a day for us to remember; in case we spend no more days together after. It makes the pit in my stomach widen to a crater and I have to force myself not to break down and beg her to come home with me. To not be selfish and demand she be mine forever.

"OK," I say instead. "I'll finish packing and then we can go."

Thirty minutes later we are saying goodbye to Bella's parents in the ICU. Her mum is hugging me tightly, murmuring "Thank you" over and over again. And her dad is smiling at me, a big smile filled with gratitude. Their warmth and affection have me leaving them with a lump in my throat and I can only hope that I'll get to meet them again someday. In better circumstances.

"You ready to go?" Bella asks after she's kissed her dad a dozen times and extracted a thousand assurances that they'll call if they need her.

"Let's go."

She drives us along the highway at full speed, pointing out landmarks and noteworthy places along the way. Now that the situation with Bella's dad has improved, I can observe Florence through the eyes of a tourist, and even here in the dead of winter, with everything damp and misty, the place is stunning.

"I don't know how you ever left," I tell her after we cross into Florence city and she looks for a place to park. "It is so beautiful here."

"Melbourne is beautiful too," she argues. "Just a bit newer."

I look around at the Florentine architecture and don't necessarily agree. It's like this city is straight out of a fairy tale. Light lemon-coloured buildings with red rooftops are everywhere. In the middle of it all is the imposing structure which Bella informs me is *Cattedrale di Santa Maria del Fiore*. Or Duomo for short. It stands high above the skyline of the buildings surrounding it and with its white, pink and green patterned walls and its Tuscan red dome, it's magnificent.

"It's the third biggest church in Europe," Bella tells me like a little tour guide as we stand out the front, staring at the building. "And if you want, we can climb to the top. You'll get to see a panoramic view of the entire city from up there."

I can't help the grin that crosses my face at this offer. Having never been to Europe before, now that I'm here playing tourist for the day, I want to see everything.

"Let's go."

We climb up the 463 steps (Bella being the tour guide again) to get to the top and once there, the view takes my breath away. Or maybe it's the woman standing next to me that has me feeling breathless—but whatever the reason, I'm enthralled.

"It's incredible," I tell her after we've done a complete circle and taken in every vantage point. "The buildings look like they're cascading, all towards the river."

"It's pretty special," she agrees, taking my hand and leaning into me, both of us savouring the moment.

"So," I say before I can let myself get caught up in the reality that this may be our last day together. "What's next?"

She smiles. "Follow me."

For the next two hours, we walk until our feet ache. We spend thirty minutes in the *Galleria dell 'Accademia*, where we marvel at the wonder of the Statue of David (which is awe-inspiring in real life), walk around the outside of the impressive *Uffizi Gallery* (which we don't have enough to go through) and end up on the *Ponte Vecchio*, a bridge that I didn't even know I knew. Every single part of the tour is filled with one spectacular building, structure, monument or view and by the time we stop for a re-fuelling snack, I'm in love with this city.

"What do you think?" Bella asks after we've ordered gelato at one of the oldest and best gelato shops in Florence, *Vivoli Gelato*.

"I think it's too cold for ice cream," I tell her as I attempt to regain the feeling in my hands and feet. Most of the day we'd been so busy sightseeing that I'd barely noticed the freezing temperatures, but now that we've stopped for a breather, my Aussie body is ready to protest the cold.

"Psst, it's never too cold for ice cream."

"Bella, if you can see your own breath," I say, pointing to the mist cloud coming out of her mouth, "I'd suggest it may be a little too cold for ice cream."

"Just you wait, mister. It'll so be worth it."

And she's right. When our ice cream arrives, Nutella flavoured for Bella, white chocolate for me, I have to agree that any temperature is fine to eat this ice cream, because it's incredible.

"Maybe we can franchise this place and open a shop in Melbourne," I say with little thought as I devour the ice cream cone in my hand. So good.

Her smile drops as I say this and I realise what I've done. I've spoken of the future, of Melbourne, a topic we'd been successfully avoiding all day.

"Yeah, maybe?" she says while pushing away her gelato cup like she's lost her appetite.

"Hey." I tip her face up to mine and wince when I see tears in her eyes. After this past week, I'd be happy to never see Bella cry again. "What's wrong?"

"It's nothing," she says with a sniffle. So definitely not nothing.

"Talk to me."

She gives me a long look, her gaze filled with questions, before she takes a deep breath. Almost like she's steeling herself for what she's about to say.

"I don't think I'll be coming home." I sit in silence. "To Melbourne," she clarifies and I feel wounded. Because, although she'd raised this possibility earlier today, I don't think I'd let myself believe it would actually happen.

"You can't rule it out, though?" I say, trying to keep the desperation out of my voice.

She sniffles some more and shifts her gaze away from me. "I can't figure out how I'd be able to leave my parents. From what Lucas has said, Papa has a long recovery ahead. I know that Mamma will need to be there to help him, and I'll need to be here to help her..."

I close my eyes against the pain her words are inflicting on me and feel myself drawing away from her. Like I'm putting up the barriers that I should've kept in place from the minute I met her.

"I get it," I begin before my voice gives out. Clearing my throat, I try again. "You need to be here for your family."

"But what about you? Us?" she blurts out, looking as miserable as I feel.

I attempt a smile and fail. "I don't think I can do long distance with you, Bella. I think it would be too hard."

Her sad frown tells me she'd already thought the same thing.

"I guess it's just a matter of timing," I tell her when I've got my voice back under control. The hollow feeling in my chest is making even just breathing difficult.

Bella leans over and loops her arms around my neck, pulling me close and nuzzling into my chest. We sit like this for a while as I try to rationalise my way out of this. We are from two different worlds; clearly, we were never meant to last.

"I-I-thank you, for everything," she says. Her words sounding like a goodbye.

I muster up all my strength and shift away from her. My suit of armour back in place. If I'm going to be able to leave this woman behind knowing that she won't ever be following behind me, then I have to put that shield back around my heart.

"Maybe we can keep in touch? As friends?" she says as I increase the distance between us. Both physically and emotionally. "And perhaps one day, I'll come and visit?"

I shake my head, now unable to process even a friendship with her. "Let's just say goodbye now and then we won't have any hurt feelings down the road. You know...in case circumstances don't change."

She looks crushed when I say this but nods. "I'll keep you up to date with my Papa's progress?"

I swallow and agree to this because, as much as this all hurts now, it'll be nice to be a part of a medical emergency with a happy ending.

"We still don't know what the next few weeks will bring," she says with a sense of urgency as we head towards the train station where we're meeting Amy and Lucas. Where we're going to say goodbye. "Maybe I'll be able to come back?"

She looks at me, her blue eyes wide and a little frantic and I understand her emotions completely. I'm barely hanging onto mine.

"Maybe," I agree to placate her when we both know that the road ahead is filled with too many unknowns to make any sort of predictions. "But let's not make any promises."

With one tear rolling down her cheek, she gives me the saddest smile. "I-I," she stammers. "I'm so happy I met you."

I clench my teeth to stop myself from breaking down. "And I'm happy I met you," I get out. "I hope for a full recovery for your dad."

She gives me one last hug before we walk towards the platform, where Amy and Lucas are also hugging goodbye.

"I'll miss you," she says in place of goodbye.

I bob my head because I'm out of words. This is a cruel twist of fate, one that allows her to get her dad back but keeps her from me in the process.

"Bye, Bella." I give her one last kiss and then walk away, not allowing myself to risk looking back.

Once again, I'm losing someone I love and I'm not sure how I'll survive it this time around.

CHAPTER 25

Bella

"HAVE YOU HEARD FROM HIM since then?" Amelia asks me as I detail that final, heart-wrenching goodbye with Daniel over a week ago. In the days that have passed since then, I've been unable to talk about it for fear of losing it. I've only just managed to get through the story today without breaking down into sobs.

"Not a word," I say. "He didn't even turn around to wave goodbye. And since then, it's been silence."

"That's really weird, given the fact that he flew all the way to Italy just to be with you."

In my mind, I know this is true, that Daniel, through his actions, had given me every sign that his feelings for me were real and meaningful. But what I also know is that his trauma makes it hard for him to open himself up. The fact that I had to leave him too must have hurt his heart greatly.

"He's sent a few emojis," I amend my earlier statement. "When I've updated him with news of my Papa's progress. The odd thumbs up and smiley face. But that's it."

"How are you doing with all of this?" she asks with pure sympathy in her voice. Amelia may not be a fan of relationships in general, but I'm pretty sure she had been ready to hop on the Belliel (Danella?) bandwagon.

"Not great," I admit. "There's only so much a person can take, you know? And between my Papa and Daniel, I feel like I'm drowning."

"But your Papa is doing better?"

I think of the progress he's made over the last week, regaining some movement in his hands and feet, and I feel a buzz of optimism. Things are going in the right direction; it's just moving at a snail's pace.

"He is," I say. "Lucas has organised for him to be moved to a rehabilitation clinic close by, where they will focus on getting him more mobile. Well, as mobile as he'll get."

Lucas and the doctors taking care of Papa had been very clear that a full recovery back to his old self is off the table and that he will need some form of help for the rest of his life. It's a fact that is weighing heavily on every decision I make. I need to be here for my parents, giving back to them everything they've ever given to me.

"And that's why you won't be coming back? Because you have to stay to help?"

My heart hurts at this. At the thought that I won't ever be moving back to Melbourne. To my new friends. To Daniel.

"It's too early to know for sure. Lucas thinks Papa will be in rehab for a few months and then he'll be back at home with Mamma. But we won't know what that will look like. Best case is that he'll regain some movement, but I can't see how that will ever be enough to provide the kind of help Mamma will need."

"Lucas is coming back, though?"

I hear the pointed question in her voice and I try to ignore it. The ever-present wondering of why he gets to leave, but I have to stay. And the answer is, I don't have to stay, but there's no way I can leave. Not after everything we've just lived through. My heart and my conscience won't allow it.

"He's got Amy and a job. It's a simple decision for him."

Amelia makes a non-committal noise over the phone and I hurry to end the call, knowing that I can't have any more people trying to convince me to be selfish and put my needs first. I've heard it from Amy, Lilly and even Lucas. I just can't keep fighting them, especially when my heart isn't in it.

"I'll call again soon. Give my love to the girls at the book club."

Just another thing to miss, I think as I head to the kitchen to prepare dinner. I loved those nights with the girls, gossiping about men and love and life, all under the guise of talking about books. It's one of the millions of things I'm going to miss about the life I had been creating for myself.

"You OK, Bella?" Lucas asks as he enters the room to find me staring into space, lost in my miserable thoughts.

I sigh. "I'm OK. How did things go at the hospital?"

If I think that I've had a rough time over the past two weeks, Lucas has had it worse. He's had to keep us all from falling apart while also juggling a myriad administrative duties. I don't know how he's managed it, but I know we would be lost without him.

"Good," he smiles while pulling me in for a side-hug. "Papa is more alert today, and he's slowly regaining feeling in his extremities. So, the paralysis is most likely only temporary."

Tears fill my eyes as I take in this news. Just seven days ago we'd been preparing to decide about end-of-life care and now our papa is one step closer to being OK. It's a miracle.

"That's great," I say as I chop the prosciutto for the Carbonaro I'm making for dinner. It's the simplest dish I can think of, one I can make with my eyes closed. With my mind as scattered as it is tonight, it's the best that I can do. "Is he ready to be transferred?"

Lucas pours us both a glass of wine and takes a seat at the kitchen table with a sigh. He looks as tired as I feel.

"Yes, they are happy to move him there tomorrow. And that's when the hard work will begin. He's going to need a lot of therapy to get him back to 'normal'."

Lucas uses finger quotation marks for the word normal because we know no matter how hard Papa works, he won't ever get there completely.

"Still, it's a good day."

"It is," my brother agrees. "And yet you look like your heart is breaking."

I turn my back to him so he can't see the tears welling in my eyes. I'm a freaking crying machine these days.

"It's just overwhelming, you know?" I say, keeping my voice steady. "It's been a big couple of weeks."

I can feel his eyes burning into the back of my head and I refuse to turn around, knowing my face will give me away.

"So…I've heard Daniel is a complete mopey mess," Lucas says a few minutes later out of nowhere, causing me to jolt and almost drop the carton of eggs in my hands. "Amy said she saw him at Love, Lilly today and he's a different man. Back to the person we met after his mamma passed."

This snaps what's left of my tenuous control over my emotions and I let out a sob. My pain, I can deal with, but the thought that I'd hurt Daniel like that—that I'd caused him to revert to that person who was so sad and so lonely and closed off—is too much to bear.

"Bella," Lucas says as he pulls me into a firm hug. "What are you doing? Why are you breaking both of your hearts?"

I sniffle against him and try to pull myself together. The anger his words are invoking helps because it sounds like he thinks this is something I'm choosing to do. Which it's not. It's something I have to do. For our family.

"I'm not trying to break anyone's heart," I say, my voice stiff as I push him away. "You know one of us needs to stay. That Mamma will need help."

"Has she said that?" he challenges me with raised eyebrows, being all Lucas-the-know-it-all.

"She shouldn't have to," I throw back at him, feeling my cheeks heating with indignance. "Papa won't be able to help in the deli for at least six to twelve months and that's the best-case scenario. You were the one to tell us that. He may never fully recover. And then what? Mamma has to take care of everything on her own?"

He reaches over to smooth my hair back in a placating gesture and I swat his hand away, not willing to be placated.

"I'm not sure you realise, but Mamma isn't alone here. In fact, she's the least alone person in the world. There's literally an entire village of family and friends here to help if she needs it."

"But that can't last forever. People come out to help in times of crisis. Mamma will need help for months, maybe years."

"So that's your plan? To stay here indefinitely?"

I feel my body shudder at the thought, and I try hard to hide it. This is my home and I love my parents dearly, so why does the thought of being here with them make me feel so panicked?

"If they need me, then yes. That's my plan."

Lucas's face softens. "And what about what you want, Bella? What about you and Daniel?"

My heart thumps at the sound of his name and I feel myself getting dizzy. *How is it that I have to choose between the people I love the most in this world?*

"We were barely a couple," I say, my voice dull. "I'll get over it."

His mouth twists as he watches me lie. "Will he?"

I leave his question hanging in the air and get back to cooking dinner. Because either answer to that question leaves my heart broken.

Five days later, after we've said a tearful goodbye to Lucas, I finally get a moment alone with my mamma. By now it's been almost three weeks since that phone call that had us sprinting to get here and I only now feel like we are catching our breath. Our papa has settled in well to the rehab facility and every day both Mamma and I spend the hours he's not in physical therapy talking to him, reading to him and sometimes just sitting with him. He's in good spirits, keen to hear all the stories from my time Down Under, wanting to know all about the latest team Ferrari news, lamenting the fact that Italy didn't make the soccer World Cup and loving all the general gossip from the village. It's the times that I'm with him that make my decision to leave Melbourne, to leave Daniel, almost worth it.

"So, my Bella," Mamma says as we both sit down on the couch with equal amounts of weariness in our bodies. Most days, we are exhausted by the time we get home. And that's without the added work that the running of the deli is going to add, something neither of us has spoken about yet. "Lucas tells me you plan to stay."

I look at her, shocked. *How is this something she needed to hear from Lucas? Surely it was a given that I'd be staying!*

"Of course, Mamma. I'm not leaving you and Papa."

"Do you want to stay?" she asks, always direct and never letting me get away with anything. Even if what I'm trying to get away with is looking after her.

"I want to be here for you and Papa," I reply, side-stepping the question.

"But what about your life in Melbourne? That was your dream."

"Dreams don't have to come true," I tell her with a sense of sadness. "And besides, it's not about me. You need me."

She gives me an amused look. "I do?"

"Of course. You'll need to be with Papa at rehab, and you'll need someone to run the deli while you're there. And then when he's back home, he may not be able to help as much as he used to. You need me."

With a gentle hand, she pushes my now over-grown bangs out of my eyes and places a kiss on my forehead. It soothes me instantly, as only a mother's touch can do.

"My Bella, I love you, but my baby, I don't need you. Have a look around. I have so much help, I'm knocking them back."

"But-but." I start to explain that this help won't always be here and she puts a hand up to stop me.

"Bella, your Uncle Rob will manage the deli moving forward. And your cousins Greg and Bruno both want to work there after school and on the weekends to earn money to save for a car. I'm actually at a point where there's not enough work to give them all."

I stare at her in silence. What is she saying?

"After your father had the stroke last time, we put a plan in place, should something happen to one of us. We know we can't work at that deli, just the two of us forever, so we called a family meeting and asked if anyone would want to step in if or when we can no longer do it. Turns out, there was almost a fight for who wanted it more."

"There was?" I'm dumbfounded by this information.

"Your Uncle Rob offered to buy out half the business if anything like this were to happen again, so it means that I'll still have a place to work, but it won't be something I have to worry about. It's a win-win because he wanted to retire to something simpler and closer to home."

Huh.

"Last week we went to the lawyer's office in town and completed the paperwork. Your Papa is thrilled; he's been wanting to do less with the deli and move towards retirement, anyway. This has now just sped up the process."

She gets up to make us some tea while I digest everything she'd just told me. The deli is now in safe hands, Mamma still has a place to work with a steady income, they've made a tidy profit from what I can understand by selling half of the business and now Papa can focus completely on getting better once he's home. No more deli stress!

"Looks like you've got it all sorted," I finally say as we sit back down with our cups of tea. "But that doesn't mean you don't need me. What about emotional support? What if Papa were to get sick again?"

I say this last part in a low voice, almost a whisper, because I don't want to put even the thought of it out into the universe.

"I have a full support network here, Bella. You know that. You've lived here your whole life. If something happens to one of us, it happens to all of us. I don't need you to give up your life to hold my hand."

"But what if I want to be here with you and Papa?"

She looks at me closely and then smiles a secret smile. "If I believed your heart was here with us, Bella, I'd happily have you stay here with me forever. But it's not here, is it?"

I start to nod but end up shaking my head because there's no point lying to her. She's seen the way I look at Daniel.

"I love you and Papa..." I trail off, taking a moment to regain my composure. "And I'm scared to leave again. Because I don't think I'll ever forgive myself if something happens to one of you and I'm not here to help. To just be here."

Mamma pulls me into her arms and strokes my back. "Bella, sad things are a part of life. Even if you had been here, you wouldn't have been able to prevent what happened to your Papa. You can't allow the fear and the guilt to hold you back from living your life to the fullest."

She pulls back and looks me in the eye. "Your Papa and I have lived a long, happy life together. We've experienced every joy imaginable; we've raised two wonderful children and now we want you to experience all of that joy for yourself. We never want to be the reason you are unhappy, and if you stay here and give up the chance to be with that wonderful man, you will regret it."

I feel my whole body sigh as her words sink in. She's giving me permission to go and live the life that she's been lucky enough to have with Papa. She loves me enough to let me go.

"And if the worst happens again, then you and Lucas just come home and we work it out. Like we did this time," she continues in her practical, no-nonsense way. "It's the way life works, my Bella. We get older and get the privilege of watching our children live their best lives. And that's what you were doing in Melbourne. You were happy. You were becoming the person you were meant to be."

"Does Papa agree? That I should go back?" I hurt at just the thought of leaving them. "Doesn't he want me to stay and be close by?"

"He wants you to be happy," she says in simple terms. "And we know you will be the happiest in Melbourne. With Daniel."

I blush at how much my parents must have observed during those two days Daniel was here with me. I thought everyone was too stressed to notice us.

"In fact, your Papa is surprised you haven't left already. He's already planning a trip to Melbourne for your wedding."

We both laugh as I shake my head. "Shouldn't that be Lucas's wedding? I'm not even in a relationship with Daniel."

"Bella, the way that man looks at you, he'd marry you tomorrow if you'd let him."

My heart races at this. "You think so?" I ask, my tone wistful.

"He dropped everything to be by your side. That man couldn't be more in love if he tried."

"And yet he let me go...I haven't heard from him."

She gives me a knowing look. "Yours isn't the only heart at stake here. I think it's time to book that flight home and fight for that man."

"And then what?"

"And then, you hope he fights for you back."

CHAPTER 26

Bella

I WATCH AS THE TARMAC comes closer and feel the jolt of the plane's wheels touching down. I'm home. With a yawn and a stretch, I wait impatiently for the seatbelt sign to turn off so I can stand and get out of here. I'm feeling tired, rumpled and exhilarated all at the same time; the journey here has been every bit as arduous as the first one, but this one is accompanied by a desperate need to get back to Daniel as soon as possible. To see if there is still something left to salvage.

After queueing for the toilet, waiting for my luggage at baggage claim and clearing immigration, I walk through the sliding doors to see Amy and Lilly waiting for me with matching grins on their faces. I'd told them I was coming home in a moment of weakness, because I had wanted it to be a surprise, making them promise not to tell Daniel. I want that first moment with him to be in person, so I can read his feelings.

"Welcome home," Amy says as she squeezes me tight. "We're so glad you decided to come back."

"I even brought you cookies," Lilly says, handing over a small bag containing her signature double chocolate chip cookies with extra M&M's. I know they're Oliver's favourite cookies, and they quickly became mine as well.

"You guys didn't need to come and get me," I tell them as I take a bite of the cookie. *So good.* "I could've taken a taxi."

"Don't be silly," Amy says as we wheel my suitcase towards the carpark. "We've been dying to see you."

"And we thought this way we could help you with the game plan for dealing with Daniel," Lilly adds.

I need a game plan?

"He's been...different since he got home," Lilly says with a frown.

"Bad different?"

Amy nods. "It started almost as soon as we left you and Lucas in Florence. I tried to get him to talk about it, to reassure him that things will be OK, but he withdrew into himself. Kept mumbling something about trusting his instincts and not opening up to people. It was a long journey home."

I feel my stomach clench at her words, knowing that Daniel had been reluctant to let me in for fear of being hurt again. And that's just what I did. Even though it wasn't intentional, or even my fault, the result was the same. Another person leaving him behind. Leaving him alone.

"What do you think he'll be like when I land on his doorstep again?"

They both look at each other, exchanging worried glances.

"I'm not sure," Amy says finally. "He's been pretty miserable. Grumpy, moody, angry. Even Lucas can't get through to him."

"But seeing you again may fix all of that," Lilly says, ever the hopeful one. "It may be as simple as you coming home to have him change back again."

I think of how long it took last time to break through to him, to get him to lower his walls, and I wonder whether I'd made a mistake. Both in not telling him I'm coming back, and in fact, in coming back at all. Maybe there's nothing here for me to come home to?

"Well, we're here," Amy says after five more anxiety-filled minutes. "You'll know soon enough."

"Are you guys coming in?" I ask as they both remain seated, looking at me expectantly. "*Maybe you can be my buffer?*"

They shake their heads in unison.

"You need to do this on your own," Lilly says. "And we'll be cheering you on from the sidelines."

"Good luck," Amy yells as I take my suitcase out of the trunk and wheel it to the front door, a sense of déjà vu falling over me. It's a lot like last time, but this feels so much more momentous. What happens now could change everything.

I take a deep breath and steel myself. With determined hands, I knock on the door and, just like last time, I question again whether turning up unannounced is a good idea. What if he's not home?

"Coming." His deep voice from somewhere inside has my heart racing.

As Daniel opens the door, I feel like the wind has been knocked out of me. It's been two weeks since I've seen him and the impact of having him in front of me again has me feeling weak in the knees.

I watch his expression turn from wonder to joy and then just as quickly to nothing. A blank space.

"Isabella." Oh no, I'm back to being 'Isabella'.

"Hi," I squeak out. Clearing my throat, I try again. "Surprise?"

"What are you doing here?" His voice is flat, and he's looking behind me.

Is he looking for a car to put me back in and take me straight back to the airport?

"Can I come in?"

He blinks at me, his eyes travelling up and then back down my body, before settling on that spot just beyond my shoulder. That damn spot; I can't believe we're here again.

"Sure," is his less-than-enthusiastic response.

"How are you?" I say after we stand in the hallway staring at each other in awkward silence, me shuffling my feet and wishing the floor would open up under me. This is not how I thought this reunion would go. Where's the man who flew around the world to be with me?

"Fine," he says, turning his back and walking towards the kitchen. "You look like you need a coffee."

Hmm, how bad do I look? I wonder as I follow behind him.

"You took down all the decorations," I state the obvious as he gets to work turning on the coffee machine.

"It was time," he mumbles.

"Sorry I left you with all the mess."

He turns to look at me with raised eyebrows and I'm desperate to know what he's thinking. Granted, when we parted it had seemed like a permanent break, but surely now that I'm here, he has to be happy to see me.

"Here, sit," he says, handing me my hot drink. "You look exhausted."

I take a sip of the perfectly made coffee and sigh. I needed that.

"It's a long journey to get here," I parrot back to him, his words from a few weeks ago echoing between us. "There's no easy way to do it."

"So, why are you here?"

It's a question I'm now asking myself. I came for him, but he didn't look pleased to find me on his doorstep. It's like we've entered a time machine.

"Well, it turns out perhaps I jumped the gun a bit with how much my Mamma needed me..."

He tilts his head like he's inspecting me.

"It seems that my parents had a plan in place should anything like this happen, and they didn't need my help after all."

I watch as he takes a deep breath in, his nostrils flaring slightly, the only outward display of any emotion.

"What does that mean?"

I give a small chuckle because this *really* isn't going to plan. "I guess it means that I can make decisions regarding my future not tied in with my parents. I can choose where I want to live, who I want to be with..."

I trail off again as I watch him shake his head. It's almost imperceptible, but my eyes are glued to him and I'm not missing much.

"Can I stay here again? For a bit while I sort things out?" I ask when the silence has stretched on so long that I want to scream.

"Sure," he says in a neutral tone. "Stay until you figure out what you want."

His words, said so casually, run straight into my heart. Is he trying to tell me that I need to figure myself out before getting involved with him again? So that I don't risk hurting him, even if it is accidental?

"T-thanks," I say. "I'll keep out of your way."

He gives me a pained look and then takes my hand in his. At last, his skin is touching mine.

"How's your Papa?"

I smile, a proper smile this time. "So much better. He's getting stronger every day."

"I'm happy for you. And Lucas and your whole family," he says as he gets up, letting go of my hand. It's like he's retreating both emotionally and physically from me. "I've got to go out. Do you still have your key?"

I nod and watch him leave, the banging of the front door signalling his departure.

What was that? I wonder as I take my suitcase up to my room. *Did I ruin everything when I let him go? Was his heart fragile enough that one crack had it closing to me forever?* Whatever the case, I know one thing to be true: if Daniel no longer wants me, if I no longer have a place here with him, then this isn't where I belong.

The combination of jetlag and utter emotional turmoil has me in bed before 8 p.m., after waiting for Daniel's return, which never came. During that time, I spoke with my Mamma and then with Amelia, who both counselled me to be patient, to understand that this is a man who had been through a lot and who may need some time. And while I agreed with them, understanding that Daniel's past makes him predisposed to want to retreat instead of stand up and fight, from his reception earlier today, I'm thinking that maybe I'm too late. That the damage had been done and that I'd lost my chance to be with him.

These are the thoughts swirling through my head when I hear the front door open. Daniel's home. I listen to his movements around the house, holding my breath when his footsteps seem to stop right outside my bedroom door. I count to five, willing him to open the door and talk to me, before he continues down the hall, leaving me in a puddle of tears in my bed. What was supposed to be a joyous reunion, or even a lukewarm reception, has become a whole lot of nothing. Daniel isn't coming to me anytime soon.

With this delightful thought in mind, I sink back against my pillow and let the tears that I'd been holding in all day take over. And once I'd let one escape, it's like a dam had burst. Suddenly I was crying for my papa who is right now working so hard just to walk again; for my mamma who is being so strong for everyone around her while nursing her own sore heart; for Lucas who has had to shoulder the burden of being the decision maker, while also watching his hero suffer; for Daniel who has experienced more hurt than any person ever deserves; and finally, for me. For everything I've had to endure over the past weeks, to get through it all, only to face the prospect that I may have lost the only man I've ever loved.

As I'm turning over, wiping the never-ending tears from my cheeks, I hear my door open and feel rather than see Daniel climbing into bed with me. A flood of relief fills my body as I feel his arms around me, pulling me against the warmth of his body.

"Shhh, Iz. Don't cry," he whispers into my ears, his own voice sounding broken.

"I-I'm sorry." I turn around and sob into his chest. "I-I can't seem to stop."

He pulls me closer so that we are pressed together from head to toe, his hands soothing as he rubs my back.

"You're OK," he says. "Everything will be OK."

I try to take in his words, to believe him, but the magnitude of everything that has gone wrong until this moment has me all out of optimism.

"It's not," I tell his chest. "I ruined everything."

"Shhh, you've ruined nothing. You're perfect."

His sweet words have the opposite effect from what he'd desired, causing me to cry harder.

"But I hurt you," I gasped out between sobs. "I'm so sorry."

There's a pause while I try to get myself together.

"Iz, you did nothing wrong," he says once I've calmed down a bit. "None of this is your fault."

"But you're so angry with me."

His arms tighten their hold around my back and I'm pulled closer to him—if that's even possible. "I'm not angry with you, Iz. I'm just confused, maybe a bit wary. But never angry."

My heart rate picks up at this admission, and a tiny sliver of hope appears. Maybe all is not lost.

"I should have called before coming," I say as I subtly try to sniff his neck. He smells so good. He smells like home. "It all happened so fast."

I feel him nod and then there's more silence. What I wouldn't give to read his mind right now.

"Iz," he starts after several minutes of neither of us saying anything. "When I left you in Florence, I wasn't sure how I was going to cope. Turns out, I didn't cope at all."

I pull back slightly to look into his face. His beautiful, tortured face.

"I'm sorry." It's all I can think to say.

He shakes his head. "You don't have to be sorry. You just need to understand. When I thought we were done, I felt like I couldn't breathe. It was like how I felt when Mum died. And I was angry at myself for being in that place again. For letting myself be vulnerable enough to get hurt like that again."

There's more silence as I digest what he's saying, wishing I hadn't been the one to make him feel that way.

"And after many self-lectures, I told myself that I had to let you go, that I had to move on and be OK alone…" He leaves the sentence unfinished.

"And then I showed up," I add, feeling more miserable by the minute.

He gives me that half smile, the one that makes all my stomach butterflies dance. "And then you showed up. I just don't know what to do with all of this."

"Are you happy to see me?" I ask in a small voice, desperate to hear even a crumb of validation that I did the right thing in coming back here.

There's another tension-filled pause before he sighs. A sad sound. "I'm both delighted and terrified to see you."

This admission has me wanting to hold on to him and forever beg for his forgiveness. For his trust. But I stop myself, knowing that I need to navigate this carefully.

"I understand," I say. "I've been giving a few mixed signals."

"And I'm not sure if I can trust that you're here for good." These are the words he says, but I can hear the subtext; he's wondering if I will stay for him.

"I came back to see if there was something here worth staying for," I tell him truthfully. "But I'm still filled with guilt at leaving my parents behind, with their future so unsettled."

He wipes away the tears I hadn't known I was shedding and then hugs me to him.

"I understand. Being away from your parents at this time must be hard. Maybe you should go back?"

With my head resting on his chest, I can hear his heart rate pick up, and I wonder what those words have cost him. And I know then that this man is so selfless that he'll let me go if it means that I'll be happier somewhere else.

"I don't know what to do," I admit, because even though I'd come back to him, my heart is still torn about what I left behind.

"What can I do to help?" he asks, evoking more tears with just this simple sentence.

I shrug because I know the answer, but I can't say it to him. I can't ask any more of this man who has already given me so much.

When no answers are forthcoming, he doesn't push me. He just settles on his back, tucking me into his side, and closes his eyes. A deep, satisfied sigh comes from him and I watch as his breathing becomes more regular. My gorgeous man had fallen asleep.

With a yawn I lean over a press a kiss on his stubbled jaw before whispering into the quiet room, "I need you to ask me to stay."

And then, cuddled up next to the man I love, I fall asleep

CHAPTER 27

Bella

T HE NEXT MORNING, I WAKE up alone, with no Daniel in sight. I get up to see if I can find him, so we can continue our conversation, and see that the house is empty. He's gone. As I take a moment to think about this, what it means that he just up and left without another word, I wonder if I've read more into our nighttime chat than was actually there. Sure, he was vulnerable with me, but he never outright admitted that he wanted to be with me. That he wanted me to stay. And the more I think about it, the more anxious I get. I flew all the way here to be with him, to see if we can be something, and he's received this by putting a wall between us. It's making me question everything I thought I knew.

"Hold on, Bella," Amelia says as I run her through what feels like every thought in my head. "You show up unannounced after telling him you're not coming back. And then he holds you while you cry, admitting to you that he's scared to trust you again and you're questioning him?"

When she puts it that way, I do sound a little emotionally unstable. But hey—if the crazy shoe fits…!

"I just don't know what to do with him," I say as I fill up our coffee cups and we sit at the small kitchen table. "He's been closed, then open, then closed, then open. He's effusive with his actions but not so much with his words. I mean, we've never even gone on an actual date and I'm what? Moving across the world to be with him?"

"OK, let's unravel all of that," she says with emphasis on the word *all*. Like there is a lot to unpack. "The man flew to Italy to be with you when you needed him the most. You know how he feels about you. I think you're both just scared. He's worried about risking his heart for someone who may be a flight risk."

I smile at this description.

"And you're wanting some sort of commitment from him to make leaving your parents seem like the right decision."

When she puts it that way, it does seem like a lot. And like we have many hurdles to overcome just to get to the starting line.

"Is it even worth it?" I hesitate to ask.

"Only you can answer that one. But I think you need to examine your own feelings first because he deserves to know you're all in."

I sigh. "I know I'm all in on him. I just need him to let me know he's the same."

"Hmmm, then you two need to have a conversation."

And so, I wait all day for Daniel to come home to have this conversation with me. To discuss our future. As I wait, I wander around the empty house, rueing the still blank white walls and become inspired to paint something meaningful for him to hang up. Perhaps if things don't work out for us, it can be something to remember me by.

I SET UP IN THE garage where the light is perfect and start painting. The scene pours out from my paintbrush like it's coming from within my soul. I begin by painting the front of our house with me on a ladder, Thor's hammer in one hand, attempting to hang the twinkling lights. The Christmas gnomes are all on the front porch, as too is Snickers, sitting and watching the chaos unfold. In the front yard, I paint the snow machine as it was on that Christmas morning, and off to the side I put the BBQ that Daniel bought for me. Through the front window, I paint the overgrown Christmas tree that he'd so graciously let me buy despite his misgivings about the festive holiday, and I even paint little mistletoe wherever I can find a spot for them. And last, I paint Daniel standing at the bottom of the ladder, looking up at me, waiting to catch me if I fall. It's such a painfully accurate depiction of everything he's done for me, everything that he means to me, that I find myself in tears when I'm finished. It's the best painting I've ever done, and I hope Daniel will find a spot for it so that one of his walls can get back the colour it deserves.

With this done, I move the canvas to a position in the kitchen where Daniel will see it if he ever returns home and decide that I've had enough of waiting for him. I pick up my phone and send an SOS text message to Amy and Lilly.

BELLA: I need a girl chat. Please.

AMY: Come over now. I have wine.

LILLY: I'll bring cake.

I love these two women so much that even though I'm considering leaving, I know I'll always have a home with them.

After I've showered off the paint and the ever-lingering effects of jetlag, I walk over to Amy's place, grateful that all my friends live so close, so that in my time of need, I don't have to worry about navigating the public transport system.

"Bella!" Amy says as she opens her front door to let me in. "Come in."

"Hey Ames, thanks for having me over," I say as I lean into the hug she's giving me.

"Bella, I baked a chocolate fudge cake, and it's straight out of the oven. Come have a taste."

I follow Lilly's voice and the delightful smell of baked goods into the small kitchen, where I see Lucas shoving a slice of cake into his mouth.

"Big bro," I say, giving him a long hug, loving the way he squeezes me back tightly. "Happy to see you."

"I'm actually on my way out," he says with a meaningful look at Lilly and Amy. "You girls have fun."

That was weird, I think as I watch him leave the room and the girls smile at each other. *What's going on?*

"Sit, sit," Amy says as she puts plates in front of us. "Tell us everything."

I slide my fork through the smooth, buttery goodness of the cake—*gosh, Lilly is a baking genius*—taking a huge mouthful and chewing for a moment, wondering what I'm going to tell them.

"Basically, it's a mess," I start as they watch me with thoughtful expressions on their faces. "At first, Daniel seemed very unhappy to see me, then he admitted he's scared that I may not stay…and then he fell asleep."

"Hmm, that's a lot," Lilly says while licking chocolate off her fingers. "How do you feel?"

"I feel confused," I admit. "I've waited for him all day today, hoping he'd make some time to figure this all out, but he's been MIA. I haven't seen or heard from him since we fell asleep together last night."

"And if you were to see him, what would you say?" Amy asks, getting to the heart of the matter.

"I'd ask if he wants me to stay."

Again, they both exchange a look, one that has my spidey senses tingling. *Seriously, what's up with these two?*

"It's that simple?" she asks while Lilly looks on seriously.

"I mean, what else could I need?"

I'm about to ask for another piece of cake before I continue my therapy session, when Lucas pops his head back into the kitchen.

"Ames, can I borrow you for a second?"

Another strange look passes between the three of them, before Amy excuses herself and I hear them murmuring in the hallway.

"What's that about?" I ask Lilly, who's doing her best to avoid my eyes.

"Hmm? Oh nothing, I'm sure."

Not convinced, but also too tired to delve into whatever mystery is happening in this house, I take another bite of my cake and sigh. Lilly's baked goods alone may be worth staying in Melbourne for, even if things with Daniel don't work out.

"You know you've got your job at the café waiting for you, if you decide to stay?" she says, almost like she's reading my mind.

"Really?" I ask, shocked that she's kept it open for me this whole time. "How have you managed without filling the position?"

Her face heats up a bit and I watch as she potters around the kitchen, like someone with something to hide.

"Lilly?" I prompt, my tone firm.

"Fine," she says, blowing her hair out of her eyes with a sigh. "Daniel may have helped out while you were gone."

"What?"

"He just volunteered. Said it was to keep his mind busy. But really, Bella, I think he just wanted you to have a job to come back to. You know, just in case."

I'm shocked into silence, unable to process what she's just shared with me. Daniel, even after everything I'd said and done, and everything he'd feared would happen, still wanted me to have something to come home to. Like just being with him wasn't enough.

"That man," I say in a shaky voice. "So good with the actions."

"But not the words?" Amy asks as she re-enters the conversation. "You need to hear him say that he wants you to stay?"

I say yes, although my resolve is weakening. *Why should he have to tell me? I should already know by everything he's ever done for me that that's how he feels.*

"Part of me knows he wants to be with me. But there's also a part that's scared. And that feels guilty for being here after everything we went through back at home."

They give me matching sympathetic looks. "Lucas feels the same," Amy says with a sad smile. "The guilt. But he knows that your parents just want you both to be happy. And he's happiest when he's here. You just need to figure out if you feel the same."

I sit back and think about the two months that I lived here, a catalogue of memories flying through my mind. The days at the bakery, the night out with the girls, the book club sessions. Snickers, Amy, Lilly, Lucas, Amelia, Oliver. All the people I've grown to love. And then there's Daniel. Every single moment I spent with him can be classified as the happiest of my life. I can't imagine being anywhere that he's not.

"I want to be here," I say finally. "With Daniel."

Amy grabs my hand while Lilly wipes her eyes, both of them looking at me with bright smiles that again have me wondering what's going on.

"Hang on a second," Amy says as her phone pings with a new message. She picks it up and flashes the screen at Lilly, who grins and gives her a thumbs up. Weird.

"I've got to go now," Lilly says suddenly and in a strangely loud voice. "Amy, can you drive me home?"

Amy nods. "Yes," she says, like she's reading from a script. "Come on, Bella. I'll drive you home too."

I look outside to see that the sun is only just setting and shake my head. "That's OK, I feel like walking. To clear my head."

Lilly gives Amy a panicked look and they both shake their heads. "Ah, no, that won't work," Lilly says.

"No, it won't," Amy agrees.

"It won't?"

"No, it's getting dark. I'll feel better if you aren't walking alone late at night."

I'm about to point out that 8.30 p.m. isn't exactly the dead of night, but the two of them are already hustling me out of the door. Too tired and emotionally drained to argue, I follow along behind them, kind of happy to not have to walk home after all.

The car ride home is quiet, broken only by Lilly and Amy's phone notifications going crazy.

"Do you guys need to get that?" I ask, pointing to where their phones are sitting in their laps. "Seems like someone is trying to get through to you."

Lilly glances at Amy, biting her lip before she shoots off a quick message. "All good, Bella. Just some spam messages that we need to block."

Strange, I think, not for the first time tonight. *These two are acting strange. And who gets spam messages at exactly the same time?* I'm pondering this when Amy pulls over to the side of the road, turning to look at me with a sheepish smile.

"Do you mind getting out here, Bella? It's easier for me to get to Lilly's if I drop you off at the end of your street."

I look to see that she has, in fact, stopped at the top of our street. I shrug. This is just the cherry on top of all the weirdness that has surrounded this night.

"Sure," I say as I lean forward to kiss both of them goodbye. "Thanks for the chat and the cake. I feel much better now."

"And we're sure you'll feel even better soon," Amy says cryptically while Lilly smiles an odd smile. "We'll see you soon."

I close the door and start walking the five hundred metres to Daniel's house, hoping he'll be there when I get back, while wondering why Amy hasn't yet driven away. As I round the bend and walk up the slight hill to get home, I notice the floodlights on over our front lawn. Quickening my pace, I pull up short in front of the house and am rooted in place, utterly shocked by what I see in front of me.

Because there by the garage is Daniel. And he's standing next to a white sheet that has been painted to look like a wall. And on top of that, there are the words, written in big red letters:
I want you to stay.

CHAPTER 28

Bella

I BLINK SEVERAL TIMES, TRYING to comprehend what I'm seeing in front of me. As I stand there, speechless and dazed, Daniel shifts on his feet, running a paint-spattered hand through his hair.

"What did you do?" I ask, finally finding some words.

He gives me his crooked grin and walks to where I'm standing.

"Did you know that buying a wall is actually very expensive?" he says, taking my hand. "I don't know how that Pacey could afford it on the money he made working at the video store."

I look at him and shake my head. *This is his grand gesture? This is him trying to win my heart?*

"You did this?" I can't seem to move past this.

He shows me his hands, which are covered in paint, along with his jeans, t-shirt and shoes. "I did," he says. "I'd do anything for you."

I release a shaky breath and walk into his waiting arms.

"Izzy, you mean everything to me. You turned up on my doorstep and brought me back to life. And when I thought I'd lost you, I wanted to crawl back into my hole and shut the world away."

He swallows hard, and I reach up to stroke his face, a sign that I'm here with him.

"But then you came back, and you asked me to trust you again. So, this is me doing the same."

I watch as he turns us both to the sign, with its big red letters dripping paint as gravity takes its course.

He takes a big breath and says, in that deep voice of his. "Stay here and be with me. Or if you have to go, please let me come with you."

As these words, these most perfect words, come out of his mouth, I can't hold myself back. I launch myself at him, crashing my lips to his, pouring what feels like a lifetime's worth of emotion into the kiss. And he kisses me back with equal passion, like he can't get enough of me, like I'm his reason for everything.

"I love you, Isabella," he says, his voice hoarse from the aftermath of our kiss. "I've loved you from the moment you landed at my front door."

My heart takes off at this declaration. "I love you too. I loved you when you were trying to be grumpy, but still making me hot chocolate with marshmallows. I loved you when you allowed Snickers to stay the weekend and he ended up in bed with you. I loved you when you let me decorate your house for Christmas, even when you didn't want to celebrate it. I love that you bought me a BBQ, and you organised a snow machine to give me a white Christmas. I love that you flew to the other side of the world to hold my hand in the worst days of my life and I love that you were willing to let me go when you thought it would make me happy—"

He cuts off the rest of my ode to him with another kiss and I melt into him, knowing that this is it. This is where I'm meant to be. In his arms, I am home.

"And I love," I continue when he lets my lips go for the briefest of moments, "that you are willing to be with me, even if it means that you have to be the one to move. Daniel, you've never taken me for granted. You've never expected me to do something you weren't willing to do yourself. And I think that makes me love you even more."

His eyes fill with tears as he listens to me and he cups my face, his thumbs tracing over my lips in the lightest of caresses. "I don't care where we are. I just want to be with you."

My face breaks out into what must be the happiest of smiles. "Then this is where I want to be, right here with you."

He picks me up, spinning me around while letting out a triumphant whooping sound.

"She's staying!" he yells into the darkness.

"She is?" the darkness yells back.

What?

I turn around to see four happy faces emerging from a nearby bush, all of them wearing matching grins.

"It worked?" Lucas asks. As he draws closer, I notice splotches of red paint on his hands and clothes. And there they are on Oliver as well. They'd all been a part of this!

"I told you it would," Daniel says smugly. "Your sister loves a grand gesture, and she loves *Dawson's Creek*. A sign like this was the perfect way to convince her to stay."

"Well, I'm glad it worked," Oliver chimes in as he pulls Lilly close to his side, pressing a gentle kiss on the top of her head. "Otherwise, that would have been a whole afternoon wasted."

"You guys spent *all afternoon* working on this?" I ask, looking at the men in wonder. They did that for me?

"I spent *almost* all day working on it," Daniel clarifies. "Over at Oliver's place. It wasn't until you made plans to go to Amy's place that I roped the boys in to get it done in time."

"Daniel tasked us with keeping you away until they were done," Lilly says in a proud tone. "And then we had to get you here on time. It wasn't easy."

Suddenly all the strange behaviour from earlier today starts to make sense. The strange looks, the random text messages, the offering to drive me home, only to leave me a few doors shy of the actual driveway. These guys are sneaky and I love them for it.

"Thank you all so much," I say as I look back at the giant declaration of Daniel's love for me, out for everyone to see. "This is too much."

"No, it's not. It's just enough," Daniel says with another small kiss, like he can't help himself. And hey, I'm not complaining.

"We're just glad it worked. And that you're going to stay," Amy says, her eyes looking misty. "We all love you so much, Bella."

I look between them all, my found family, and then back at Daniel who is watching me with adoration written all over his face, and I finally feel like I've found what I was searching for all those months ago when coming to Melbourne was just a dream. I'd found who I am, where I'm supposed to be and, most of all, who I'm meant to spend the rest of my life with.

"Come on, guys, let's go inside and celebrate with some champagne."

I watch as they all file into the house, chattering amongst themselves, happy with their successful mission, and I put a hand on Daniel's arm, stopping him in place.

"You say that I brought you back to life," I say to him, my voice wavering at the end. "But you have given me mine. Daniel, I'm so happy to have found you and I can't wait to spend this and every other life with you by my side."

He sighs and holds me closer. "Isabella Mancini, I never plan on saying goodbye to you again. You are stuck with me. Wherever we go, you will be my home."

Home. I've finally found my home.

The End

EPILOGUE

Daniel

12 months later

B ELLA RUSHES INTO THE ROOM, her cheeks the colour of the Ferrari team t-shirt she's proudly wearing.

"Come on, Dan. We're going to be late!"

I look at the clock on the wall and only just refrain from rolling my eyes. The gates for today's Formula One Grand Prix race don't open for another hour and yet she's already itching to get out the front door. She's been counting down for today's race and her excitement is next level.

"Iz," I say as I pull her to me, loving the way her body melts into mine. "We've got heaps of time."

"But I want to get there before anything happens."

Again, I bite my tongue to not point out the obvious; it's Formula One, nothing is likely to happen. But it's Bella's favourite sport and it's been her dream to attend a race one day, so I guess I'll be getting on the excitement train with her.

"OK, give me one second to grab my stuff and then we can go."

She gives me a look while bouncing on her toes, impatience written all over her.

"Hurry up!"

I do as I'm told, rushing to the bedroom we share and riffling through my bottom drawer, my hands shaking as I pull out the jewellery box that had been burning a hole through the timber ever since I bought it, almost six months ago. Today is the day. The perfect opportunity to turn Bella's dream of attending the Grand Prix into my dream as well. That of having her say yes to me, to wanting to be my wife.

The past twelve months with Bella have been nothing short of amazing. After that day in front of my homemade sign, which she made me keep up for a full week—much to my utter embarrassment—we've gone from strength to strength. As I knew would happen, once she'd given me her heart, Bella was all in. We immediately moved her stuff into my bedroom and have been inseparable ever since.

And I don't think I've ever been happier. Bella has settled into her life here in Melbourne with complete ease. She started working again with Lilly and just last month the two of them signed a lease for the small shop space next to the café, with plans to turn it into a gallery for local artists. Including Bella, who loves to spend her free time painting her impressions of Melbourne and the people in it. Now all the walls in my house are filled with the evidence of her amazing talent, and I know we're both so excited for the rest of the world to see what she has to offer.

In addition to settling into her new life here, the news Bella has received from Florence has also been positive. After a few months of rehab and physical therapy, Bella's dad moved home and has been making amazing progress. So much so that her parents could make the trip over to celebrate the wedding of Lucas and Amy. It made the magical day absolutely perfect and I don't think I've ever seen Bella happier. She, along with Lilly, were bridesmaids and I was honoured to play the part of groomsman for Lucas, a man I admire and respect so much. Upon seeing the woman I love float down the aisle in her blue gown, looking like a vision, I'd been tempted to ruin the whole ceremony by proposing to her on the spot. Luckily, I was able to control myself, but it was a close call. Because damn, do I want to marry Bella.

So that brings me here to today, finally. I plan to propose just before the race begins, so she can be in the moment without being distracted by that damn Ferrari team of hers (who have shown no signs of improving this year, much to her dismay). I've had it all planned in my head for months and I can't wait to see her face when I get down on one knee.

"Dan-iel," she yells from what sounds like the front yard. She's an eager beaver today. "Hurry up."

I put the ring in my pocket and race to the front door. When I get there, I'm left breathless as I so often am by the woman standing in front of me. She's on the front porch, like she was that very first day, and she's looking at me with that same expectant expression on her face. And now, just like back then, my heart stutters to a stop briefly before it starts racing again.

"Bella," I say, no longer in control of my actions.

She looks at me, her eyes widening as she sees me getting down on one knee, a ring in my hand.

"Daniel, what are you doing?" she asks, her voice breathless and squeaky.

"Bella, I've loved you since the minute I saw you on this very doorstep. And I know I will never stop loving you." I pause to gather my emotions as I see the tears running down her cheeks. "Will you marry me?"

Bella jumps up and down, squealing with excitement, before grabbing my cheeks in her hands and kissing me senseless.

"I will! I can't wait to be your wife."

And as I place my ring on her finger, I feel a sense of peace washing over me. After so many years of being alone, here with this woman I've made a family of my very own. Bella is the answer to every question I didn't even know to ask. And with her by my side, I am complete. With Bella, there are no more goodbyes. There is only forever.

If you loved Ciao, Bella, it would mean the world to me if you could leave a review or a rating on a site like, Amazon, Goodreads or wherever you review books.

Reviews mean so much to authors and could very well be the motivation needed to keep writing, and to publish that next novel.

If you'd like the latest news and information about my books and writing journey, please subscribe to my newsletter on my website at www.belindamary.com

ACKNOWLEDGEMENTS

To my husband and partner in crime, Philip. You know that I couldn't do this without you, we talk about it all the time! Thank you for every single thing—big and small—that you continue to do to make my dream a reality. I love you. Forever.

To Lorissa, the designer of my beautiful book covers. Thank you for bringing to life my vision each and every time and for being such a pleasure to work with. To my editor Sarah, thank you for your quick turnaround times and your attention to detail. With your help, we took this story to another level and I'm forever grateful for your guidance.

To my family and friends, thank you for your continued support and enthusiasm. And to my beautiful readers, thank you for every word of encouragement you've given me. I read all your Instagram posts, messages and reviews, and am always buoyed by your excitement for my characters. You make doing this so much fun!

And finally, to my gorgeous children, who are my everything. Hunter and Sienna, you two make everything worth while and I don't think you will ever know how much I love you. You both chose this book cover as your favourite, and so I'm dedicating this story, and the love I poured into it, to you.

Belinda Mary

ABOUT THE AUTHOR

Belinda Mary has dreamed of being a writer her whole life. And after many, many years of excuses and procrastination, she has taken the leap and is finally ready to share some stories. Belinda is a long-time lover of all the books, and when she is not reading or writing, she can be found spending time with her family she adores, watching all things Bravo, or listening to true crime podcasts. Belinda hopes to write the kind of stories that she loves to read; filled with laughter, longing and love.

You can find out more about Belinda and connect with her online and on social media.

g @belindamary   a @belindamary

@belindamary.author   f @belindamary.author

www.belindamary.com

HAVE YOU READ THE FIRST BOOK?

He's her best friend's brother and completely out of her league...

Twenty-three-year-old Lilly is the quirky girl, the one with the c-c-curly hair. She's always late, is rarely neat and does not have her life together. She will never be that girl, the one who gets the perfect guy. But hopefully, this is about to change. It is a new year and Lilly has made some resolutions to get her act together.

Her best friend's brother Oliver is the reliable guy, the one who rescues Lilly from all of her disasters. He's organised, makes lots of lists and has a strict five-year plan in place to get ahead in life. He never makes rash decisions, unless it relates to Lilly, and then he can't seem to help himself.

With this in mind, it would seem that these two friends have little in common. Except perhaps a secret pining for each other that has gone unspoken for too long.

Can a weekend of fake dating convince Lilly and Oliver that they are actually perfect for each other? And that opposites really do attract, after all?

AVAILABLE NOW ON AMAZON

www.ingramcontent.com/pod-product-compliance
Lightning Source LLC
Chambersburg PA
CBHW020911130726
47904CB00006BA/1836